Anna from Atlanta

By Catherine Team & Beverly Smirnis

MAPLE VALLEY BRANCH LIBRARY
1187 COPLEY ROAD
AKRON, OHIO 44320
330-864-5721

ANNA FROM ATLANTA

Published by Cat LeDeux Partners

Copyright © 2014 by Catherine Team and Beverly Smirnis

All rights reserved. This Book may not be reproduced in whole or in part, in any form (beyond copying permitted by Sections 107 and 108 of the United States Copyright Law, and except limited excerpts by reviewer for the public press), without written permission from Catherine Team and Beverly Smirnis.

Author services by Pedernales Publishing, LLC.
www.pedernalespublishing.com

Library of Congress Control Number: 2017937625

ISBN 978-0-9988296-1-6 Paperback Edition
ISBN 978-0-9988296-0-9 Digital Edition

Printed in the United States of America

"This tale is like good dessert. You find yourself scrapin' the plate for more …"

—Anna

Preface

We have tried to lovingly portray people who lived in Marshalltown, Iowa, as well as give the reader an understanding of what it was like to live in a small town during the Great Depression. Some of the people were real and some not, however, Anna and Fritzy were real people who lived in Marshalltown with their very real families. Catherine Team's father, Dan Bechtel, was one of the boys who would read to Fritzy in the afternoons after school. It made such an impact on her dad as a young boy that he never forgot the stories. He often spoke of hardships that came during the Depression and after the banks closed. Retelling these stories brought Catherine's father comfort and solace when he was a very old man, and they entertained her during daily visits with him. Of course, we have doctored-up their escapades and added characters similar to the ones who lived in the town. However, the real Anna was wise beyond her years and was loved by all in the town, very much like the woman portrayed in these pages.

We used regional dialect to reflect Anna's family and community, and slang from the era to reflect the times and the humor. But more importantly, we wanted to contrast how people acted then versus now. As you can tell, the Anna portrayed in this book had an innate understanding of life and was miles ahead of those around her. The real Anna was that way too, and just like in the book, she never backed down. The real Anna never let discrimination shortchange her outlook on the world, and the real Anna did not let hurtful words pierce her considerable armor. She was like a rock, and she never wavered from her faith in God or her love for those around her. She always thought the ultimate revenge for the naughty, the racist, or the sinful was enlightenment.

The real Fritzy was very much like the character portrayed in this book. We wanted to give him the same respect and understanding that the real Anna gave him. We also wanted the reader to see and feel the love and support Fritzy's family showed him, along with highlighting the difficulties of having a special needs child. Fritzy's real dad was also a doctor in Marshalltown, Iowa, and a really nice man who would often give young Dan tickets to the circus when it came to town.

The families were very straightlaced people who never gambled, never had extramarital affairs, and never murdered people. They lived the American dream with all the bumps along the way. We have changed their names to make sure no one would be angry about our fictional portrayals. Everything else is straight from our very active imaginations.

Here's to you, Anna and Fritzy—for lives well-lived! Life is hard, but you didn't back down, and you showed us the most important thing—never give up.

Dedication

This story is dedicated to caregivers everywhere. As we live our lives we never imagine what sorts of needs we will have for ourselves or those we love. To be cared for, respectfully and graciously by total strangers is hard to imagine, but it happens every day all over the world. We must give heartfelt thanks to them for caring-- day in and day out.

Bless you all for working at a sometimes difficult and thankless job. You are loved and respected so please don't stop.

Table of Contents

Preface v
Dedication vii

PART I: 7
Chapter 1: "I gave it my best. Nature didn't." —Dr. Donald Calloway 9
Chapter 2: Joyce Worrell: Facing Fritzy 14
Chapter 3: Elegant Edwina Forever Changes Joyce's World 21
Chapter 4: Smoking Tea and Other Delights 31
Chapter 5: Sneakin' Out of Atlanta 35
Chapter 6: Leopards Don't Change 40

PART II: 49
Chapter 7: Conscience Cleared and Chicago Bound 50
Chapter 8: Iowa and Other White Objects 58
Chapter 9: Edwina Makes an Offer 66
Chapter 10: "Fritzy knows more than he's letting on." 70
Chapter 11: Dogs Are Dirty 73

PART III: 77
Chapter 12: 1929 78
Chapter 13: The Thanksgiving 87
Chapter 14: Flowers Bloom 95
Chapter 15: Back for a Visit to Atlanta 101
Chapter 16: Christmas in Athens 108
Chapter 17: Extra Work and Somethin' Funny About That Phone 117
Chapter 18: School Days 122
Chapter 19: A Bad Thing at the Circus Brings Good Out of the Worst .. 126
Chapter 20: The Circus Being Here Was More Than Coincidence 136
Chapter 21: Suspicions and Shadows 142
Chapter 22: Secrets Uncovered 146

Chapter 23: Crime Doesn't Pay 153
Chapter 24: Money Isn't All It's Cracked Up to Be 163
Chapter 25: God's Gradin' Us...171
Chapter 26: An Uninvited Guest 178
Chapter 27: Not Time for Dyin' Yet 185
Chapter 28: Even Ruff Plays a Role in Fate 194
Chapter 29: We're All Good with a Little Bad Mixed In 200
Chapter 30: More Fate Brings Doc Phillips to Town 205
Chapter 31: Rings 'n Things 212
Chapter 32: A Flower Wilts 220
Chapter 33 Gettin' Closer to the Truth 227
Chapter 34: An Out-Of-Place Visitor at the Library 235
Chapter 35: Bone Lake: A Fittin' Place to Find Out About Some Bones .238
Chapter 36: The Nicest Place on Earth 251
Excerpted from the feature article, ...256
"A Mother's Day Tribute"..256
About the Authors 261
Acknowledgments...263

Anna from Atlanta
Introduction: 1974

As the country prepared for the upcoming Bicentennial celebration of the American Revolution in 1976, the reporting team at the Des Moines Register was charged with writing about Iowa history across various decades that had passed over the 200-year time period. Since I was a child during the Great Depression era, I was assigned to write about the 1920s and 30s. Almost immediately, I knew that the person I could gain a unique impression from was a lady simply known to me as "Anna."

"Young lady, are you sure you want to hear the whole story about Fritzy? It's long and funny and sad and a little mysterious, too."

At 51 years old, I was flattered to be referred to as a "young lady," but to Anna, I suppose I was.

"Yes, Anna, I do want to hear it."

I paused, placed the tape recorder on the table in front of her, and said, "I'm going to start the recorder now, OK?"

The dark, wrinkled woman with dancing eyes and bosoms the size of bread loaves looked at the recorder like it was a snake and started: "Well, my story is different from other folks and therein lies the best *part. It's a different kind of story about people being good and what happens to them when they are." She paused to look at me again, maybe just to see if I was really serious about interviewing her. I nodded my head for her to continue. Anna shifted in her seat and smiled.*

"Well, I wouldn't be here in Iowa at all if it weren't for Fritzy. Here's a sample of how I took care of him when other kids tried to take advantage of him. I'd tell those Bishop boys, "I don't give a whit what you think of me, 'cause I'm big and dark and scary, and I don't have to suffer your God-awful stupidness or you being mean to Fritzy. If you throw spit wads at him one more time, I'm gonna whack you two towheaded boys' heads together and make you idiots for the rest o' your days. Yah hear me?"

"I got another one for you, too. This one's a little sad." *Anna blinked and looked down as she said it.*

"There was this little girl, about eight, staring at Fritzy and me one day in Bishop's grocery store. She just stood there still as a statue. I could feel her stares. I knew it was 'cause she was curious about Fritzy and why he was in a wheelchair, and I looked down at Fritzy's little face. He was staring back and I could see a small tear runnin' down his cheek, real sad-like. It was a bad moment, and I knew I needed to tend to it. "Why, little girl, come here and meet Fritzy Worrell. He doesn't bite but he does laugh." Fritzy gave out with a strange sound she probably never heard before as she moved slow toward us. Fritzy tried to smile. I couldn't stop.

The girl said her name slow in case he couldn't understand. Fritzy nodded. She put her hand out and touched Fritzy on the arm. He moved and she jumped a little. They both smiled, and then she turned around real slow-like and waved bye as she went to find her mama. Mama was up ahead and never noticed she wasn't behind her. We never saw them again, but ever after that we always try to make friends. It cuts back on staring."

Anna drew in a deep, sad breath as she remembered.

"You see, Fritzy couldn't move on his own, so he's a prisoner to his chair, and he couldn't talk much neither. So I talk for him. The hard part is, I have to tell you his sad story to tell you my good story, 'cause they're linked together like Siamese twins.

As I said, this story is like good dessert, and the people in it are like a meal. O'course there's Fritzy, who is a cake that didn't rise jes' right. He's destined never to get out of the pan. And Miss Edwina who had a big hand in creating this whole story 'cause she possess jes' the right amount of spark, like a vinegar that makes a salad perfect. Then there's Mrs. Joyce Worrell who is the vegetable we all need to survive. She's good as vitamins."

Anna shook her head and rolled her eyes as she remembered all the people who played a key role in her life.

"I couldn't in good conscience leave out that sexy, saucy Mrs. Susan Calloway, who pours herself all over Dr. Joe Worrell—and Dr. Joe himself, 'cause he's got those puddin' feet that succumb to anythin' blonde," Anna continued. "And how could I have forgot saucy Miz Susan's husband—mashed potatoes Donny Doc Calloway? He's so stiff there isn't even butter or salt there—jes' starch. There's crusty-bread Bishop, too, who doesn't like people of color. And me? I'm the meat that slides right down—tender as butter and cooked jes' right, to satisfy your true, bitin' hunger.

The Depression and the war threatened to turn ever'thing we loved to ashes. I describe it so good you're gonna cry with me, but you're gonna laugh with me, too—and that's what makes a story good. It's a sad story anytime you got a kid that isn't jes' right, but I try to move you beyond that by makin' you aware of my world and how Fritzy and I deter bank robbers, solve a mystery, and all sorts of shenanigans. I make it look easy as snappin' my fingers, but it isn't, not by a long shot.

My story tells you how to be a real good person with real

living and excitin' examples, 'cause you need to be the best kind of soul you can, or else God won't take you when your time come. So you gotta get up every darn day and be kind to sruffy ol' dogs, retarded children, and them vagrants on the street. You ask me, 'Why so?' Well, after all, a scruffy ol' dog didn't ask to be born that way. That's why so. And we don't know their story, so who are we to judge them?

And, not to put too fine a point on it, there are some real bad people in my story, but we best them right along—which is a good and excitin' thing."

Anna smiled and gazed out the window as she remembered. She suddenly paused to look up at me again.

"Young lady, what did you say your name was?"

To which I replied, "My name is C.J. Renfro. I'm writing an article for the *Des Moines Register* about life in the 1920s and 30s. The lady at the front desk said you could help me. She said you are always describing what it was like to live back then."

The truth is, it wasn't the lady at the front desk that brought me there, but I didn't want Anna to know that I grew up in Marshalltown and had known her as a child. And to be honest, my mission here was a bit more than just my reporting assignment. I flashed what I hoped was a reassuring smile, and she continued.

"I'm old now and don't see much. I cain't walk without help, but at least I had my brain and my abilities for most of my life. And it's only in the last few years that I have lost considerable amounts of both, much to my consternation. I was stout and strong and could lift about anythin' before old age jumped up and bit me in the ass—and it was that strength that made me different and also made me able to take care of Fritzy." *She smiled and nodded to herself.* "Most of the time we tried to do the right thing, and that goodness came full circle to me and to the Worrells, makin' us feel certain happiness about life again. Some of the white-folk friends of the Worrells even described Fritzy as what you would call a muse for us. And I have to agree. He was.

I know I'm lucky to be alive, and I'm lucky to have been born able to do the things I do. You know, there are those people who cain't, 'cause they were born like a rag doll. Cain't move a thing. Fritzy had that kind of malady.

This all started in 1923 with Fritzy being born. He was one of those rag dolls. He couldn't move nothin' but his left knee and foot. If he thought somethin' was funny, he'd jiggle that leg, and if he was angry, he'd do the same. It was his way of talkin' to the world. Leg down—nothin' goin'. Leg up—somethin' on his mind. I talked to him every day like that for fourteen years, and don't think it wasn't interesting, 'cause it was.

It may be 1974 now, but I can remember it like it was last week. I can still smell the wonderful smells of my cookin' and remember what people were wearing. It's jes' that clear. I even remember the workers finding bodies in our backyard one day. I remember the looks on the people's faces and what Miss Joyce was wearing while she was lookin' down in the hole. I remember how interested Fritzy was in all the goin's on.

Lookin' back, it's hard to figure out why some people, like me for instance, have long lives and grow old—so old that on some days we find ourselves wishin' the Lord would jes' hurry up and take us. By the same token, we cain't understand the Lord's plan for taking some folks way before their time—like those people in that backyard for instance. The memory of that afternoon has never faded. Jes' like bright colors, they burn in your memory like a rainbow—each color different and important. All so dang different, but all goin' real well together jes' the same. But I'm getting a little ahead of myself.

The first part is that Fritzy was born, and that's a nice and also a sad place to start. O'course, I wasn't there with him yet, so

I'm gonna let old Dr. Calloway and Fritzy's mama, Joyce Worrell, tell this part, since they can tell it better than me. But first, you gonna have to go down the street to the white folks' nursin' home to find them, and they'll tell you the first part. Then, you come back to me, and I'll take you on in toward the finish—and it's some finish."

Anna turned her chin up at the end of her statement like she was reviewing what she had just said. She decided what she said was more than acceptable.

It seemed like we were just getting started when a nurse popped her head in and asked Anna if she was ready for her dinner. My watch read a quarter to five.

So as I prepared to leave, I said to Anna, "I'd like to come visit you over the next few weeks and hear the whole story that you've started telling me today … if it's OK with you?"

"Oh, sure it's OK. I can always use a little company," *she said, pausing to add,* "But if it's snowin,' don't come. You know, the roads can kill."

"Of course. I will do exactly as you say," *I said, smiling at her.*

PART I:

Fritzy, as told to me by Dr. Donald Calloway and Fritzy's mother, Joyce Worrell

Chapter 1

"I gave it my best. Nature didn't." —Dr. Donald Calloway

I took Anna's advice and found my way to what Anna referred to as the "white folks' nursing home."

When I arrived, the man known as Dr. Donald Calloway was having a conversation with one of the nursing home attendants about the picture quality of the television and the fact that the coffee was too weak and not ever hot. I understood why the nurses just refer to him as "the General." Though he hadn't practiced medicine for some years now, he was still as busy as ever practicing the routines that make up life as he now lives it. It seems the nurses now fill in for the role that his wife and children used to play—receiving his regular inspections and critical analysis when any little thing is altered from the way he thinks it should be.

"Why, what brings you out our way?" Dr. Calloway asked when he spotted me, giving his version of a smile and extending his hand.

I took his hand and gave him a quick hug. After the usual exchange of small talk, I got to the point. "I'm working on a story about Anna and Fritzy. She said you could tell me all about the first part of Fritzy's life."

He was visibly agitated and queried me about the purpose of such a story. But, thankfully, he was bored enough to be in a mood for talking and was willing to tell the story of the sad event with an imperfect outcome that had weighed on his mind for decades.

"Unfortunately," he said, "I will never forget it." *The old doctor sat down. I noticed that his whole body sagged at the mere thought of Fritzy.*

"Between Joe Worrell and me, we knew virtually everyone in town. It was the kind of place where neighbors were expected to help neighbors. Everyone has to wear many hats in a small town, and we all pitched in. So I not only delivered the babies, but I took care of all the children and young people while my partner, Joe, mostly took care of the adults. I knew everything about everybody; and the ones I didn't know, I heard all about secondhand. In short, our lives had purpose and went according to plan most of the time. But, that doesn't mean life is always sweet and kind."

Dr. Calloway frowned as he continued. It hurt me to see the pain in his eyes.

"It was the fall of 1923. The dark-haired crown of the baby eased out slowly, and I caught him squarely around his shoulders—head first. The damn cord was wrapped twice around his neck. I cut it off quickly. 'Hurry!' I yelled at the top of my lungs. Everyone in the delivery room moved as if I had just given them a jolt of electricity. You could see tears of fear in some of the nurses' eyes. I couldn't take time to do more than notice.

I knew we were doomed as soon as I saw that cord. My nurse rushed the oxygen tent over and a second nurse tried to clean out his gagging mouth and lungs. He was making a deep gurgling noise. We ignored the noise and worked on what was causing it. Just about that time, a helpless feeling began to roll over us like a low-hanging cloud. There wasn't a thing we could do. We peered through the window of the oxygen tent to see if he would start breathing on his own—and he did, but he still wasn't moving, and that was a very bad sign. The damage was already done. There was a dead silence in the delivery room. All I could think of was that I would have to tell Joe.

It's about that time when you start playing the what-if game. However, that game is fruitless and never ends, so pretty soon you have to move on from it. What if I had thought to do a Caesarian? There was nothing to merit it, but still you ask yourself—'What if?'

After so many deliveries, I could read my nurse's mind. Jillian had worked for the old doctor who had the practice before Joe and I moved here, and there was no better nurse around. We had delivered a lot of babies together, and most of those deliveries were joyous occasions. This was not going to be one of them.

When Jillian asked me what I thought, I remember telling her, 'I don't think anything; I can't predict the damn future; I'm not God,' and I walked away.

Of course, it wasn't going to be OK, because the baby had taken too long in the birth canal, and that damn umbilical cord was twisted around his neck as tight as a preacher's starched collar. I didn't need a medical degree to see the damage. He was blue from lack of air. Even though he was breathing now, he wasn't moving. I've seen a couple of precious minutes make all the difference between a healthy baby and a retarded baby. This looked like—and definitely was—a retarded baby. I felt numb as I slowly washed my hands. I would have to tell Joe Worrell that his baby was in peril—and not just in peril. If the baby lived, it would be a shame.

All this happened while Joyce Worrell slept peacefully through her anesthesia-induced coma. I considered her husband, Joe, my best friend. He was also, of course, my business colleague and a damn good surgeon, too. I wasn't looking forward to telling him what had transpired. It made me wish I hadn't delivered the baby.

In fact, it made me wish I lived in another little Iowa town, and not this one. There was a strong possibility that life as we knew it might change if the Worrells blamed me for the sorry fate of their baby.

Joe and Joyce were alone in the room when the nurse brought the baby in. The room was quiet and no one was smiling. I slipped in without a word. Joe and Joyce were already aware there was a problem. I was young then, but I already had experience delivering many healthy babies while I worked in Chicago—not to mention the ones here in Iowa. I had completed my medical internship at St. Luke's Hospital and delivered hundreds more babies there. I mainly delivered the babies of indigent mothers on Chicago's South Side, where the slums show the painful side of life, every minute of every day. The irony was that most of those babies were born healthy, and rarely was there a catch with a delivery. When the mother was on dope, the babies were usually born mentally retarded, but this sure wasn't the case with Fritzy. It was just pure bad luck. Here in Iowa, where life was better, kinder, and more relaxed, I had to face the fact that this horrible thing happened in such a wonderful place to two wonderful people. I had been unable to control the outcome.

We stood there, silently staring at the baby. Finally, Joyce said something that will remain with me forever. "Hell, I can't undo what's happened. However, I can make the best of it. This little baby had the good luck to be born to people who will always love him—no matter what. We can pray for things to be different, but they won't be."

Joe and I looked at each other as a tear ran down her cheek.

Joe took Joyce's hand and squeezed it. I put my hand on his shoulder as we all worked hard to stifle the tears. Then I quietly left the room and walked down the freshly scrubbed hallway out into the early morning air of an Iowa Indian summer. It was

September, and I thought about what they say about September babies being born nine months after Christmas celebrations. Could something good come of this birth? I didn't think so.

Over the years, I used to review Fritzy's birth in my mind at least once every few days. It was always with me. And always the same outcome faced me in the wee hours of any night. I always concluded there was nothing anyone could have done. However, what had happened that night was going to hurt for a lifetime, and it continued to haunt me. Things like that never go away, they just continue a little quieter on some days.

I had always liked being a doctor, but the pain of a patient's death, or something gone woefully wrong, would always sting worse than any bite. Sometimes it would stay with me for days, but eventually, I would get on top of those helpless feelings. Fritzy would prove to be different from the others. His birth remained an open wound that never healed. Whereas I had the luxury of being free to live my life with my healthy children, the Worrells' life would be different with a sick child weighing them down every single day."

I could see a tear glistening in the corner of the old doctor's right eye. I knew he still felt badly about it more than fifty years later. We said our goodbyes after that, and I quietly left him dozing in his chair.

Chapter 2

Joyce Worrell: Facing Fritzy

The next day I was back at the "white folk nursing home."

"Mrs. Worrell, my name is C.J. Renfro, and I would like to talk to you about Fritzy."

"Oh," *she said.* "That was so long ago. It seems like another life." *Her still beautiful eyes gazed at me and then darted away in the distance while her mouth quivered a little, eventually turning up into a sad smile.*

"Yes, it does seem long ago, doesn't it?" *I said.* "Can you describe the early time before Anna came to live with you?"

I gave her a polite, expectant look and explained, "I work for the *Des Moines Register* and want to describe life in the 20s and 30s for a story."

I knew this was hard for her, but her eyes lit up when I said the name of the newspaper.

"Of course, I used to work for the *Marshalltown Times-Republican*. I was a journalist, too, you know. I loved it. I loved interviewing people just the way you're doing it now.

And after all was said and done, I loved being Fritzy's mother, too. Though, it was very hard at first, and I was crazy from it the first five or so years."

The old lady looked at me as if to say I couldn't possibly understand.

"You see, I was educated at the University of Iowa, and that's where I met Joe. All my life, all I really wanted to be was a wife and mother. When I was young, I envisioned beautiful children in front of a Christmas tree on my holiday cards—hopefully, a boy and girl at the minimum, maybe more. I thought about happy family dinners, playing sports with the boys and shopping with the girls. The picture was perfect in my mind, but as I found out later, it would hold not an ounce of reality for me. Instead, I was given a bundle of helpless child with no hope for his future. I couldn't help loving him and feeling sorry for him at the same time.

The fates had given me a living anchor. After all, he would never run into my arms or have a conversation with me. At first, I couldn't come to grips with his condition and, even then, I could only face it some days. I had planned to give up my job as a reporter after the baby came, but hadn't envisioned my days being spent the way they were then. At first, I stayed in bed most of the day and only got up to change and feed the baby. After all, I never had to worry about him climbing out of his crib, did I?"

The once beautiful dark hair had long since lost its battle with age and was now a ghostlike white, and her dark blue eyes had faded into a light gray. Her smile was still the same as in an old photograph I had seen of the young Joyce Worrell.

Mrs. Worrell pursed her lips and said: "The looming questions were, 'Could he think? Was he working with a full deck?' I know people wanted to ask me those questions. But most didn't have the nerve—except Sidney, the filling station attendant. He was the only one that had the nerve to ask such things, because he was known to be a little slow himself. They said his mother was an alcoholic and that made him that way. Who knows? Those people who talked about Sidney's mother might have said I did something like that to cause Fritzy's problems. But that sure wasn't the case. Of course, even though I knew I did everything I was supposed to do during my pregnancy and didn't do anything I wasn't supposed to do, I still felt guilty like I had done something wrong.

One day Fritzy and I were sitting in the car, getting our gas tank filled up, when Sidney asked me, 'Mrs. Worrell is he workin' with a full deck? Or is that a problem too?'

I had to tell the truth, so I said, 'Sidney, I honestly don't know.'

Sidney looked embarrassed. Then he confided in me, 'I ain't working with a full deck neither, but at least I can move around and fill your tank with ethyl. I guess it wouldn't be so bad for him if he's not working with a full deck neither—might even be easier for him.'

'I don't know, Sidney,' I told him.

'Why, look at that! He knows I'm talking about him.' Sidney reached in and touched Fritzy's hand. 'Supposin' he does have a full deck up there … together he and I would add up to one whole human bein'.' He laughed at his own humor.

That was the big question. It was one that was solved on one crisp autumn day just after Fritzy's first birthday. As I held him in my arms I said, 'Now Fritzy, we are going to have lunch, and then you are going to take a nap while I clean out the pantry.' I tickled his little side and started to put him down. 'Nnnoo.' Here was my twelve-month-old baby talking to me and telling me what he thought. I was shocked. I put my face up close to his and repeated my statement about the pantry. He said it again, 'Nnnoo.' Then we both got quiet.

Of course time passes. Fritzy was soon getting bigger and harder to carry. He wasn't as big as the other babies his age, but at about eighteen months, he was still getting to be more than I could lift all the time. My back was going out from picking him up and down all the time.

Joe was almost afraid of Fritzy in a way. He said we needed to begin to get back to living our lives like before he was born. To that end, he felt we needed to have somebody come in and help.

You know, for a long time Joe never called Fritzy by name. He just called him, 'him.' Many of Fritzy's features were just like his father's—his dark hair and deep brown eyes. I couldn't help but think about how proud Joe would have been if Fritzy had been born normal. I always wondered if he would have been handsome and successful like his father. I always thought, because Joe was a doctor, he also knew death was imminent for Fritzy. Somehow, I could never feel or think like Joe did.

Fritzy was intelligent. You could look at him and see his mind was sharp and his little wheels were turning. His eyebrows would arch, that leg would jiggle and you could see him straining to talk to us, but the sound always came out like a drunken gurgle and words seemed just beyond his grasp. One day I heard him mouth, 'I love you.' Except it was, 'I wa ooo.' I went in my room, closed the door and cried. It was then that I learned a painful reality: A mother feels pain for her child because she can visualize the future, whereas the child cannot.

My back was getting worse and my emotions were getting frayed. I was stuck in the house day-in and day-out. I couldn't see my friends and was constantly working on keeping the house clean. I couldn't cope without some kind of help. So one day I told Joe that I really would love to go on a vacation. That signaled the end of my emotional and physical endurance."

In my impatience to move Mrs. Worrell along a little more quickly, I interrupted her and blurted out the part that I was dying to get to. "So, you hadn't started building the pool yet? Or found the bodies? Or run into the bank robbers?"

She looked a little stunned. I told her that I knew about the mystery at her old home back in Marshalltown as I had done some research on her life prior to our interview. I was kicking myself for taking this chance in losing her trust and apologized for the interruption and my jumping ahead.

I was relieved as she replied, "Oh, no, we hadn't found Anna yet or gone to Atlanta. None of that had happened yet. Joe, being the brilliant guy he was, called a doctor friend in Atlanta he'd interned with in Chicago." *She continued, apparently unscathed by my insensitive blurting-out episode.*

"That night Joe told me that he would like for us to plan a trip to go see his friend Troy in Atlanta. 'Troy thinks we should come for a visit,' he announced. 'He says Edwina is a great hostess and lots of fun, too.'

Troy was a good man, but a Southerner through and through. He didn't like the Chicago winters or the cold midwestern attitude toward strangers, so he moved back to Atlanta after medical training. I knew Joe missed his friend, Troy, terribly and really enjoyed his company. They had worked long hours at the hospital and talked at length about their futures. They were true friends, laughed at the same jokes, and were both avowed Republicans.

We had missed Troy and Edwina's wedding, being so far away and with my being pregnant. This way, we would have a chance to get to know Edwina. Joe told me that I also had something in common with her. 'She will never have children,' he said. I looked over at Fritzy and sighed.

Joe took to the idea immediately and started making plans. 'Do we have to take him?' he asked me, pointing at Fritzy.

Joe was thinking of a real vacation without Fritzy, but I insisted that he had to go with us. The only person who had ever kept Fritzy so Joe and I could go out of the house together was Dr. Calloway's nurse, Jillian. I guess she felt some link to him through having been in the delivery room. But she had three kids of her own and would be needed full time at Dr. Calloway's office, because they would be seeing Joe's patients while we were away.

Unfortunately, it would be another year before we were able to take that vacation. We would take Fritzy with us and make the best of traveling with our retarded child on a train. It was 1927, and trains were the best way to travel in comfort. Fritzy had never been on a train before, and he cried all the way. Joe and I were drinking as often as we could get away with. We bought bathtub gin from the porter since it was Prohibition. It was a lifesaver.

Fritzy was relentless. He shook his little foot and tried to wave his little arms, but his lungs worked better than fine. He used those lungs to the fullest trying to tell us what was bothering him. He said, 'Stoooop ooop ooop.' I could feel his fear and frustration and tried to tell him where we were going, but it just made him more scared. The only time he ever quieted down was when we held him up to the train window. He would take it all in and momentarily quiet down. His little eyes tried to keep up with the speeding picture before him. It was then that I knew he was really working with a 'full deck,' as Sidney the gas attendant had suggested a long time before. Being smart was actually the worst part, because he was going to figure out very soon that things weren't right with his body. And that time came sooner than I thought.

I was walking him up and down the train's hallway, trying to get him to doze off, when a little boy came up to me and said, 'Isn't he kind of big to be carrying like that? Make him walk. Then maybe he'll stop crying and I can get by.'

'I wish I could,' I snapped. 'Lord, don't you think I would if I could, you little twit? He can't walk. Of course I wish he could.'

The little boy turned and ran the other way without a word. It was then that Fritzy, who was about three-and-a-half years old at the time, figured out he wasn't ever going to walk or talk like other people. He cried the next 300 miles, and I cried right along with him. Joe and I took turns holding him up to the window, and he watched the scenery with intensity, and then he finally quieted down the last 150 miles. I was devastated."

I could see that Mrs. Worrell was ready to join her friends at the card table, so it was decided that we would continue our conversation the next day.

Chapter 3

Elegant Edwina Forever Changes Joyce's World

*T*he next morning, I returned to find Mrs. Worrell was right where I left her.

"Ah, you're back. Ready for the next leg of the journey?"

She started almost before I could get the recorder turned on. "Let's see. We were on the train and when we got off, the humid air of Atlanta hit me as if I was jumping into a pool—sudden and intense. I had never seen so many people of color all in one place. In Iowa there was one family of color, and they just lived among us like anyone else. But here in Atlanta, the white people were the exception. All I could see in the station was a sea of dark faces and shining eyes. I almost used a restroom labeled, Colored Only, until a young colored woman pointed me to the White Only restroom. That struck me as odd at the time, but in my momentary confusion it flew out of my head immediately. I felt like I was in this wonderful world of different accents and ways of talking. Everyone was more polite in Georgia and had a smoother way of talking. They were not in a hurry. There was something to be said for Southern hospitality, and the state of colored affairs could be easily ignored.

A big dark porter carried our luggage as if it weighed nothing to where the cabs were waiting, and a small dark taxi driver took us to Troy and Edwina's house in a grand area of Atlanta. The little taxi driver also picked our luggage up like it weighed nothing. I remember asking Joe if everyone in Atlanta was strong.

I'll never forget the first time I saw Troy and Edwina's house. It was a palatial Georgian design, with red brick and black trim. We stood and looked at it with dutiful reverence. It had a beautiful veranda wrapping around the rest of the house so people could sit out in the evenings. On the porches were slow fans that blew a constant cool, lazy breeze. The white wicker furniture looked very old and comfortable with green plant designs on the cushions. I envisioned those cushions greeting any tired rear end with a comfortable embrace.

It seemed like folks moved slower and smiled easier down there, and I began to relax after our frantic train trip. We looked at one another, and I could read Joe's mind—we were both wondering why we hadn't made the trip earlier. Joe rang the bell, and a large, ebony black woman opened the grand door and smiled. She was as tall as Joe, and her white teeth seemed as big as piano keys. She welcomed us in a grand way with her big arms. With the heat, her blouse had short sleeves, and you could see the loose fat on them hanging like drapery folds as she held out her arms to take Fritzy. I got the feeling she had done this before with many kids, because she had a confidence that made me feel content.

She said, 'Here, give him to me.' And I did.

After I relinquished Fritzy, I looked around. I was dog-tired because thirty pounds of child that couldn't toddle was a lot of weight, and anyone would gladly hand that off.

'My name's Isabelle, but you jes' call me Izzy,' she smiled back with those shiny piano keys.

When I introduced us as 'Joyce and Joe' Izzy looked surprised.

I realized later that you have to put a 'Miss' or 'Mister' in front of your name if you're white and they are Negro. We don't do that in Iowa.

Edwina and Troy came down one of those beautiful winding staircases that curved around one of the most beautiful crystal chandeliers I had ever seen. The stairs were carved in some intricate, scrolled ironwork design. It was blindingly beautiful.

I leaned on the end of the stair rail and drew in my breath, because their entryway seemed bigger than my whole house.

'Ah, you're here. The fun awaits you,' Edwina said and rushed in, hugging me like an old friend, and I hugged her back. I liked Southern hospitality right off, and being a reporter by education caused me to take note of every little, wonderful thing.

She had a drink in her hand, 'I hope you're not too tired. We have dinner and drinks planned for tonight, and it's cool enough to sit out afterward on the veranda.'

Edwina had this smile that turned up on the end of her sentences and made you wonder what else she had on her mind. My first reaction was that she had a little naughtiness about her that might prove to be interesting and fun.

A very dark man named George, who moved as quietly and smoothly as an ebony ghost, took our drink orders before he whisked our luggage away like it, too, was light as a feather. 'Dr. and Mrs. Worrell, what be you drinking tonight?' he asked us in a melodious voice that could sing like a deep-throated bird on any Sunday morning. For a second, we simply smiled before we realized he was real, and Joe said, 'Gin and tonic for the lady, and I'll have bourbon on the rocks.'

Edwina and Troy walked us to the back of the house where there was a beautiful den that reeked of quiet, expensive comfort. The pictures on the wall were of horses running with hounds.

Troy had a kind of regal air about him that made him look

like he belonged in one of those paintings, yet there was nothing pretentious about him at all. He was putting more ice in his drink. 'What do you think of Atlanta?' he asked Joe. Joe replied that he thought it was beautiful and a great place.

'Wouldn't you want to live here? It's an easy place, and there's an opening in my practice,' he said. It suddenly dawned on me that Troy wanted us to stay for an extended amount of time—somewhere around a decade would be to his liking. But Joe cleared that up immediately by saying, 'I am an Iowa farm boy with my heart forever a part of those corn fields.' I didn't say a word. Good wives didn't pipe up in those days, but I could tell he liked Atlanta just the same.

Edwina was close to six feet tall with the most exquisite way of moving. She was thin as a rail and graceful as a dancer. Her blonde hair was rather long, framing her face in a Mae West style with lots of curls that cascaded down the sides of her face. She wore the kind of square-shouldered, high-priced dresses and high heels that accentuated her striking figure. Large gold earrings shone like floodlights on her ears, and she never stopped smiling. It seemed like everyone in Atlanta smiled all the time, along with being very strong. But no one smiled as Edwina did. She was gorgeous.

'OK, Joyce, tell me everything; all about havin' Fritzy and living in your Iowa town. I want to know you like a sister before we're done here.' She put her arm around me in a comfortable embrace. I could tell Edwina sincerely meant what she said. And that's how our friendship started—easy and fun.

We spent the next two hours—and three drinks later—talking about our lives. Somehow, we got on the subject of our parents along with what kind of work they did. I said, 'My dad worked for the railroad. How about yours?' My summation was that our fathers were hard-working men, who taught us good, basic Christian family values.

Edwina said, 'My dad was a mechanic and chauffeur for a rich family here in Atlanta. However, he was smart and raised us to be more. He put both my brothers through medical school; luckily, I met Troy through them. Dad was always spending his money on us—never on himself. He was a wonderful man.'

I nodded and shared with Edwina that I had a similar background. My dad was a carpenter for the railroad company that made the railcars. All the beautiful woodwork on those Missouri-Pacific trains you see these days was made by his carpentry group.

Edwina giggled and said, 'So I married up. And you did too.' That sounded good to us both, and we sipped our drinks in tipsy unison. I momentarily wondered where they got the liquor.

We both laughed and were glad our husbands weren't around to hear us. They had moved into the billiard room.

'I'm good lookin' and you're good lookin'. It's nice we're both good lookin',' Edwina slurred her words a little as she said that. I was sure she'd had more than just our three drinks together before we arrived.

She leaned her head in a drunken tilt and continued, 'We are both beautiful, me in a blonde way and you in a brunette way, and we are both loved dearly.' She grinned.

I grinned back and held up my drink. 'You've got that right. Yep, I feel an immediate bond with you, Edwina, because you can't have children.' I'd had just enough to drink that I got right to the heart of the matter and continued on, 'I understand your pain because I could have children, however, I would never do that again for fear of having another child like Fritzy.'

'So we are bound together by what we both perceive as our mutual failure. Now, take that failure and mix it in with our naturally happy outlook on life, and you have a very confused person,' Edwina replied.

I nodded. I couldn't help frowning. Thinking about Fritzy devastated me.

'Yeah, we want to make the best of the cards we were dealt, and being good wives is a big part of it,' Edwina said as she got up from the beautiful loveseat and walked outside. I dutifully followed, however, I was a little shaky on my feet. The alcohol was taking its effect on me, too.

Edwina knitted her brow and twisted her lip up in a pained expression. She had asked this question because she was very direct and looked at the world in a practical way. She genuinely cared about us, which was pleasing to me, because most people just turned away from Fritzy and simply pretended he wasn't there. Edwina didn't. She had been a teacher before she met Troy, and she cared about children. Moreover, she was kind to everyone and never seemed to flaunt her great beauty or wealth. She was who she was and nothing more. Edwina whispered, 'What will you do about Fritzy?'

I almost couldn't reply, but said, 'I am just not sure.' This was the most honest answer I could muster. 'I hate the thought of putting him away in a sanitarium. He's got all his mental faculties, but he just can't move or talk so that people can understand.' I couldn't look her in the eye. 'It makes me so sad. I feel guilty every time I look at him. I ask myself, 'What did I do? Was it my fault?'

'No, hell no, you just did what any young mother would have done. You had a baby. Everyone takes a chance when they have a baby. The odds are with you that everything will turn out all right, but sometimes things happen beyond your control. Your guilt and your love are all mixed up together, and you need to get over that.' She sat down on one of those comfortable wicker chairs with the nifty cushions, and I sat down with her. My rear end did, indeed, feel embraced. We were quiet for a moment because I didn't really have an answer to her question. That bothered me.

I looked out across an impossibly green lawn running down to a small lake, where there was a gaggle line of white geese and ducks waddling quickly toward the water. The geese abruptly stopped at the water's edge, but the ducks jumped right in and swam away. I found myself wishing Fritzy could swim like those ducks. And that's how my mind would work. It would always turn back to Fritzy. I'd be OK, and then I'd see something that would remind me of him, and this time was no different. Fritzy was everything. Sure enough, my first thought was to go check on him. It had been a good hour since he'd gone with the big Negro woman. I fidgeted and said, 'I had better check on Fritzy.'

Edwina put her hand over mine and said, 'Don't worry, he's doing quite well right now; I feel sure. You know how I know?' She smiled and continued, 'Camellia and Izzy have five children between them and there is nobody sweeter and kinder. Take a load off and think about something else.'

I noticed Silent George standing by the door, waiting until we finished our conversation before he announced, 'Ladies, dinner is served.' Then, he ever so quietly returned ghostlike through the door—and closed it without a sound.

'Say, I've never seen anyone move that smooth before? Is he always that way?'

Edwina nodded solemnly. 'Always.'

Somehow, that made us both giggle.

I was hungry as we walked quickly toward the dining room with our drinks in hand. The men were already at the table when we arrived, appearing just moments before we did. They were quietly handsome as they stood in the palatial dining room. It was good for Joe to be with his friend, Troy, again. Like Edwina, he had such a kindness about him that he brought out the gentle side of Joe and rekindled his spirit. It had been awhile since I had seen that handsome smile of his that I fell in love with in those days before our lives became so complicated.

I looked around and saw a beautiful table set with Waterford crystal goblets filled perfectly with the smoothest red wine I ever had the joyous pleasure to drink. The Haviland china plates featured a simple embossed band of 18-karat gold. I knew that beautiful pattern because I had seen the same one at Marshall Field's last Christmas. The Marshall Field's table didn't compare to Edwina's glorious table decorations. There was a sizable stalk of magnolia in each big, round glass fishbowl, with real goldfish swimming in and around the stems.

While I was impressed, the very best was yet to come. The same rather large ebony-colored woman, whom I figured to be Camellia, appeared with a rack of lamb standing upright on a huge silver platter with crab apples topping each delicious bone. The scene was almost magical—and it tasted that way, too. The rack was sitting on an array of bay leaves that radiated out from the center in a sunburst design—flat on the platter. I couldn't figure out how they got the leaves to stay down flat, but it was a work of art. With a flourish, Camellia placed the platter in the center of a side table to be carved and quietly disappeared. I racked it up to being one of the best meals, ever.

The mashed potatoes were swimming in butter and cream, with a wave of freshly cut parsley across the top. There was some other wonderful flavor in them that I couldn't place, but I was just loopy enough from the alcohol that I didn't care. Last of all, the vegetables were lovingly cooked in a casserole that even the most finicky person would have downed with pleasure. They were nestled in cheeses and herbs, thereby hiding any of those potentially unkind vegetable flavors. I had no room for the pecan pie, which looked wonderful too. My last thought, before I squelched a ladylike burp, was that this food beat the heck out of anything they had in Iowa.

The same large woman brought the coffee out to the side table, and Edwina quietly asked under her breath how Fritzy was doing. 'Oh, he good. He playin' patty-cake with the other kids.'

I had to see this, so I rose and followed her into the large black-and-white kitchen, and there, around a big table, sat more Negroes than I could count. Young kids to old men. They were all laughing and eating pie and my little, white Fritzy was waving and kicking his good leg and trying to play patty-cake back with a little girl of about eight. I hadn't seen him so happy, ever. And his giggles were the loudest, happiest noise in the room. An old man was holding him on his knee and bouncing him up and down. We smiled, Fritzy gave me a sort of wave, and we went back to our coffee on the white side of the door. Somehow, I knew the most interesting part was on the Negro side of that door, and I was glad Fritzy was there with them.

Edwina said, 'See, I told you he was doin' good. He's learning there is life outside of you all, and that's a good thing.' She sat back and lit a cigarette, exhaling slowly."

Mrs. Worrell's crepe-like face twitched a little as she continued: "Edwina showed me I could relax and accept things. This had been hard for me, because I kept fighting with myself over what had happened when he was born. I couldn't accept the way things were going to be, but that particular evening in Atlanta signaled a small twinge of healing.

We continued to laugh and talk and eventually moved outside. By then, night had gently settled in, and the lightning bugs were everywhere. The velvet darkness was alive with their slowly moving neon show. I stood motionless, taking it all in. The crickets and the cicadas contributed their own gentle background hum, and those gentle noises were the perfect undercurrent to our idle chatter.

After a little while George silently appeared and took the

coffee cups away. He leaned down and said in my ear, 'We changed and bathed your little man, and then we put him down for the night. He was tired as a coonhound after a hunt.' George whispered this in his rich voice, almost song-like, and gave me a gentle smile. I loved Atlanta and all the gentle people of color. I now understood why they loved Edwina and Troy so much. They had a lot of reasons, but then Troy and Edwina had a lot of reasons to love them. Love and respect is a two-way street as Joe and I were to find out.

The next morning came early with a gentle knock on our door. In waltzed a Negro woman no bigger than myself, with a serious look on her face and a huge breakfast tray. 'My name is Silvy, and I'm your mornin' maid. And iffen you need anythin', jes' pull this thing right here, and it rings a bell for me downstairs. It takes me a few long minutes to get up those three flights of stairs, so have a little patience. I be there after a little while.'

Then she reported, 'Fritzy done risen early and already had breakfast.' She went over to the window and pointed to the back lawn. Joe and I both walked over and looked out on that perfectly mown lawn. There, on a blanket, were two young Negro women holding Fritzy and laughing. Fritzy was laughing, too. We opened the window to listen. Fritzy's laugh was slow and out of sync with the girls' voices, but the girls didn't seem to care, nor did his presence seem to stop them from talking about whatever it was they thought was so funny.

Silvy turned to leave and said, 'I be back. Jes' ring the donger.' Joe and I ate like starved idiots and kept looking out the window at Fritzy between bites. Then we dressed and ran down the grand stairs like little kids. This was truly a wonderful place. We had forgotten to ring the donger because we were so excited about just being there. I guessed Silvy would get the tray when she made the bed."

Chapter 4

Smoking Tea and Other Delights

I took a brief break while Mrs. Worrell went to have her lunch. She told me that she ordinarily would have taken a nap afterward, but on that day, she would forego it as we were right in the middle of a part of the conversation that made her happy to remember. Sure enough, when she returned she was full of energy and ready to continue.

"You know, I smoked tea once with Edwina." Mrs. Worrell gave me a sly smile as she said this, and I just looked blankly back at her. Then she asked, "You know tea, don't you?"

"Well, no, I don't—I've never heard of it. Is it like—oolong or Earl Grey?"

"No. Heck no. It's like silly stuff. It makes you think everything is funny and makes you hungry like you've been in the desert starving for days. Edwina's doctor prescribed it when she found out she couldn't have children. Just like me, she was hit with depression so deep she couldn't get out of bed. She said that she just lay there 'like a muffin waiting to be buttered.' It was terrible. So her doctor, who had a rather big backdoor clientele, gave her some cigarettes he had collected from a patient who couldn't pay.

Edwina said the doctor was one of Troy's friends, and he gave her some of these funny little cigarettes.

That old doctor told Edwina to smoke one every Friday night before Troy got home from work. 'Get dressed up like you're going out and smoke one right then—but don't go out. Just make the whole evening a happy night. Don't think of your troubles that whole evening. Have yourself a good time and just don't try to do anything the doctor had told her. So, she followed his instructions. Edwina said that when Troy came home, they laughed and had a private, formal dinner—just the two of them, and Edwina acted silly. Troy loved it.

So, on one of the evenings during that first time I met Edwina, she got out one of those cigarettes and shared just a couple of puffs with me, and then she told me, 'It's a long road back, but it's one you gotta take.' She shrugged and leaned toward me, 'I just woke up one day, got outta bed, and decided my life wasn't over just because I couldn't have children. Besides, the cigarettes made me lose focus on my troubles somehow—even if it was for a short few hours.'"

Mrs. Worrell looked down, imagining the moment. "Edwina continued, 'And you know what? After that, I decided I would help all the little children that weren't lucky enough to be mine. So I started the Children's Benevolence Fund here in Atlanta. My fund helps kids get their shoes and clothes and school supplies, so they can look like all the other children at school. I started it because ever since I was a kid, maybe around the third grade, I noticed kids who weren't dressed as nicely as I was. It bothered me, so I decided to do something about it.' Edwina gave me a superior smile. 'I now have a reason to get up every day. And the best part is, now, everyone thinks I'm a better person than I really am—which is great, because I have a real naughty streak.'

'Oh, you are naughty,' I said to her. Meeting her and having these conversations was exactly what I needed after the last several years of heartbreak with Fritzy. Then I asked, 'Edwina, can I get some of those funny cigarettes?'

Edwina looked taken back. 'Oh, Joyce, don't you see? You don't need them. I've quit them now, except for every once in a great while. I gained ten pounds after that silly stuff. You just need to wake up one morning and make a plan for your life. Once you have a plan, you need all the energy you can get, and those cigarettes will only make you lazy and unable to get all the things done that you'll feel the need to do. You have what it takes to do great things—so get out there and do them.'

Edwina tossed an after-dinner mint in her mouth, signaling the end of our funny-cigarette smoking conversation. I never again saw her smoke any of that tea or speak about it; I never did again either. I just think Edwina was trying to doctor me in the same way that the doctor had done for her. Those little cigarettes were just a crutch to be used as a last resort to get people to see something they couldn't see before—when their normal state of mind put them at a breaking point. Some people just keep using crutches like that because they like an excuse to be lazy. Edwina and I knew we didn't want to be somebody like that.

Yes, Edwina was truly a wonderful person, and I would have been lucky to have her as a sister, if I'd had a sister. And that's how she became my best friend. There are some people you are just drawn to when you need an ear to listen and crave a piece of advice. Edwina was one of those people. It seemed like she was always in a conversation—listening and advising whoever was in need at that moment.

The next day, when we walked into the sunroom, we found Troy and Edwina deep in a serious conversation. It was fairly obvious that we had walked in on a private commiseration, because they jumped and turned toward us like kids caught talking in school. I said, 'I hope we didn't catch you in the middle of something?'

'Oh, no, we were just addressing a little problem that seems to be escalating. One of Camellia's sisters was just beaten within an inch of her life by her husband. It's been getting worse over the years, but his drinking has gotten so bad of late. The sister, Anna, is afraid for her life. Her husband, his name is Martin, gets crazy drunk and takes his troubles out on her. Now Anna's whole family fears him, not only for her, but for the children.'

What a bad situation. We couldn't imagine what her life must have been like. We really couldn't. We didn't know anything about Anna then.

Edwina went on to tell us the story of Martin, who had always been good to his family, but had finally let his drinking get the best of him. He was out of work now and had become just an angry sort over his loss. Camellia had convinced her sister to move her girls over to Athens with their grandmother for their safety, and they were doing fine. Anna had three girls who were just about ready to graduate from high school and hoping to go to secretarial school.

But Anna, she was a different story: she stayed. She loved Martin. All that was a sad thing she couldn't face. She just couldn't let him go; she loved him and he loved her. She was going to stay with him and die, I guess."

Mrs. Worrell sat silently for a while, reflecting on what had happened so long ago. I figured it was time to leave. That signaled the end of our conversations. But I had one more question, so I asked, "If Anna hadn't come to Marshalltown, would the mystery have been solved?"

"Oh, you're talking about the mystery of the dead bodies they dug up? No. We would still be wondering about their identities, and where their families were, and if they were looking for them—without a doubt."

Chapter 5

Sneakin' Out of Atlanta

"*Why hello young lady,*" *Anna said the next day when she saw me. We exchanged some banter back and forth, and I told her what I had learned from Dr. Calloway and Mrs. Worrell—before the small click of the tape recorder signaled the beginning of the real story I was yearning to hear. Anna smiled and jumped right in.*

"Well, here I am back in the story again. What had happened here next was that Martin *was* getting a sort of undeserved reputation with my relatives. Yes, he *drank* too much; yes, he *got* violent; but he did not beat me up. I did that myself. You ask how?"

I nodded my head, yes, back to her, because I didn't know what else to say.

"When he ran at me with the knife, threatening to filet me, I turned and ran out the back door into the night. I couldn't see a thing, and I was runnin' from a fear so deep, I couldn't think straight. It was darker than a wolf's mouth and the wind was blowing so hard I was listing like a big boat. So I ran smack-dab into a large tree. I bounced off that tree like a spring and fell on my very ample rear end. My face was bleeding, and I could taste the trickle-down, but otherwise I was in one piece. I didn't hear him coming, so I jes' lay there, and then I finally fell asleep. When the dawn came, I walked to Camellia's house, and she took it on herself to think Martin smacked me. He didn't, but he did scare me within an inch of my life."

"What year would that have been?"

Anna replied, "Don't ask me about years. I got so many of them I cain't remember." *She smiled at me like I could really figure that out myself.*

"Camellia already took the children to stay with our mama in Athens, so I jes' needed to worry about me. I know I am safe at her house, 'cause Martin and Camellia's husband, Abe, had a falling out a year ealier. It was over a barbeque pit that Abe wanted to sell. Martin wanted to buy it, but didn't want to pay full price, and Abe wasn't gonna part with it for less. One thing led to another, and all their hostility of being married to sisters for years jes' oozed right out into a fight. Martin is bigger and meaner than Abe, so he smacked him on the nose and all hell broke out, along with a lot of nose blood. They wrestled like mad dogs on the front lawn until my cryin' broke them up. The upshot is that Martin wouldn't show up around Camellia's house ever again. Especially since Abe threatened him with his gun. If Martin did show up there again, he knew he'd be dead meat, 'cause Abe meant it and he jes' cleaned his huntin' gun.

I slept like a baby that next night at Camellia's, but I knew I needed to make some decisions. I couldn't go on living in fear whenever night came. It wasn't fair to me. I had to move away where Martin couldn't see me for a while. I was hoping he might appreciate me when I wasn't around.

Hope does spring eternal. I was thinking that he would get a job and come back to his senses, and we could be together again like it used to be. It took a lot of gut strength to decide to make a change like this, since my odds of finding a new husband were nil. I understood if I kicked him out, it would be good-bye to all the good things about a man, too. Men are so good at some things, from emptying garbage to scratching your back—and a few other things I don't choose to mention here among mixed company. There jes' isn't an acceptable substitute." *Anna smiled again.*

"Martin had been a good man for many years—he hadn't always been bad. Oh, he always liked his liquor, but he always liked us better. But drink is a mysterious thing, 'cause it works its devil magic so slow, jes' a little every day. They say the road to hell is paved an inch at a time, and that's so true. A person starts out a little bad one way and then ends up so far gone down the road to hell they cain't ever crawl back. It's that way with alcohol; a person starts out drinkin' here and there, and then they start drinkin' here, there, and ever'where. Liquor becomes their main woman. Pretty soon, they cain't get up the next mornin'. Or when they do get up then they have to have a drink to start their battery. It starts a vicious circle and the *alcohol woman* always wins.

Now, we owned our house free and clear from our hard work and our true devotion to our children, so I needed to figure out what if I sold it. I knew I could probably move to Athens and be with my girls, 'cause I loved them so much, and I'd be happy there. I had also been thinking that if I did sell my house, it would give me enough money to send the girls to The Draughon Secretarial College on the proceeds. I felt very strong about this 'cause an education is somethin' no one can ever take away from you once you got it. Bad folks can take your house, or your horse, or your car, or your purse, or your money, but they cain't take your education away. Once you get it, you take it with you to your grave. Nothin' but your name lasts longer than that. Why, they even put your education information in your obituary when you die. Now, that's a long time to have somethin'—plus, that education helps you every day of your life. What a great gift to give to my girls. They never would have to clean toilets for a living or live with a husband that beats them, 'cause they couldn't afford to get away. They'd be their own person and make their own money. They'd be in control and feel good and confident. What a gift to give to my three daughters. Thank goodness they took after my thin Martin, but, they got my good brain—and that's the best of us both.

I'd been stayin' with Camellia for a couple of days, so I felt like I should do somethin' good for her, so I said, 'Why, Camellia, can I make you a couple of fruit pies for your Parker people? They're good people, and I feel like I ought to do somethin' to earn my keep here. That way, you wouldn't have to work so hard makin' their dinner tonight. I'll bring the pies after lunch and maybe somethin' else that tickles my fancy.'

'Oh, Anna, don't worry about that,' she said. 'We good here. You been so good to me over the years, it's a treat jes' to be with you now. But if you want to keep busy, I won't say, no. I know how good your apple and cherry pies are—better than mine for sure.'"

Anna recounted the conversation like it was yesterday.

"So I hurried around at the market and got together the pies. By the time they came outta the oven, there was a smell through the house that would make even the surliest person smile. I made four pies and kept two for us. It's good to give, but also good to keep, too.

I was jes' leaving the Parkers' mansion, when I saw Martin sitting on a curb down the street. He was layin' in wait for me. How stupid could I have been? There he was; couldn't go to Abe's house 'cause of angry Abe, and the only other place he could find me was at the Parkers'. So he jes' took his chances under a large oak, waiting. No telling how long he had been waiting. He stood up and put his arms out. I hung back.

I made a good living bakin' pies, cookies, and cakes and delivering them to the rich, hungry people of Atlanta. I have to say, my baked goods rivaled any and all around there. I had a certain route that I would take on my deliveries. I usually had a big bunch of hungry people that expected their pies, so there was a huge bunch more than I could take care of. But, that day, the only delivery I was gonna make was to the Parkers'.

Martin didn't love me for my cookin'. He loved me for the money it brought in. Sometimes he would snatch a day's wages right outta my apron and take it off to the racetrack for a day of drinkin' and gamblin'. He wasn't even sorry for what he did; he'd jes' do it and come back around midnight, drunk as a skunk and jes' as proud. When you're down low, there's always someone lower, and those *down lows* try to take it away from down lowers. Martin did that to me all the time.

'Anna, I'm powerful sorry for the other night,' he said. 'You know I didn't mean it. I *will* quit the awful drinkin' and carousin' and get a job. I promise.' He reached out for my hand, and I let him take it. I wanted us to be a family again. About that time, his good-for-nothin' friend Altus Andrews stepped outta the tree shadows and said, 'Martin, get the money and let's get goin'. We losin' daylight.'

'Daylight about what?' I asked Martin. He told me they were jes' goin' into town to get some supplies. But I knew better."

Chapter 6

Leopards Don't Change

"Now, I'm stupid in love with Martin, but I knew right then and there he wasn't changing his spots. A leopard stay the same with the same spots, forever. Martin had jes' shown his leopard-ness, and I knew he wasn't gonna change one little bit.

I took my hand back and walked away. There wasn't anythin' to be gained from this talking. And he and I both knew it, but that didn't stop him. He ran after me and grabbed my shoulders. He was a skinny man but very strong, and there was no getting loose from his grasp.

'Jes' stop and give me some money for today. I swear I won't bother you again,' he said.

'No, you'll jes' be back tomorrow for more and the next day after. Get lost.' I finally managed to shake his hands away and kept walking down the street, but he wouldn't let me move forward, so I pushed him away as best I could. We were havin' this tug-of-war when I gave him a big push. Then he gave me one big push back. I fell sideways to miss him. He fell forward. It all happened so fast. The brakes on a livery truck screeched tryin' to swerve around him, but there was nothin' the driver could do. I heard this awful crunch and knew instantly that was Martin's bones I was hearing. He was spun around and back toward me from the force and took me down with him. His bloody body covered me, and poor Martin was dead before we hit the ground. I was screaming at the top of my lungs as the truck driver and Altus lifted Martin's crushed body off me.

Altus was yelling back at me that I had done this on purpose. 'I saw you push him right into the oncomin' traffic. You lousy woman. All he ever did was love you, and this is how you treat him.' Altus gave me that 'hurrumph' look that people do when they catch you doin' somethin' wrong.

I was so upset. I was ready to get after Altus and knock out what teeth he still had left in his snaggle-toothed mouth. He had caused this whole problem when he talked Martin into coming after me for some more money. The cops came and got ready to take me down to the station, and the ambulance came and picked up Martin's crumpled body. It was a sad, sad day. And I was in hot, hot water. In the meantime, Camellia and Miss Edwina ran out to stop the cop from taking me down to the station, but he was having none of that.

'Don't you touch my chef.' Miss Edwina said this with as much force as she could muster-up on short notice. We both knew I wasn't a chef, but the cop didn't know that. He looked like he'd heard it all before.

"Look, Ma'am, I have to take this woman downtown, and you are welcome to follow along behind, but Mr. Altus Andrews here says she done it on purpose. So you're gonna have to tell it to the judge. I am sure he will take care of the matter." He just kept repeatin', "Tell it to the judge." You could tell things were done as far as he was concerned.

We were cryin' and Miss Edwina was pulling me firmly in

one direction, toward her big beautiful house. But the cop wasn't letting go. So I was stuck between the angel and the devil, with Altus Andrews in between, pointing an angry finger right in my face. My tears weren't dryin' up one bit, and there were two strangers standing on the other side of the street, covering their mouths in utter shock. I didn't know it at the time, but it was the Worrells, and they were horrified by the violence, not to mention being scared to death of me. The police put me in the paddy wagon, and there I sat with my hands folded in my lap, like I was taught when I was a little child. This was my deepest, darkest moment, and I didn't see a way out. I noticed the Parkers' big, long seven-passenger Hudson following close behind, and it gave me confidence that maybe I could get outta this. I couldn't see where Altus was gone to, but I hoped to never see him again.

When we got to the police station, I got out and they led me to a cell, where I sat with my hands folded neatly in my lap again, like some perfect lady. After a while, a woman came and said, 'You're free to go.'

'Really? That easy?' I waited to hear a *but*, but one didn't come.

'Yep, your accuser changed his story.'

'Oh, Lord, have mercy,' I recall saying. I wanted to jump for joy, but knew it might be a bit premature. I stood up and waivered a little before I walked out. I saw Miss Edwina, the Worrells, and Camellia standing there lookin' like they were afraid to touch anythin'. I hugged them all.

'Oh, Anna!' Camellia said and hugged me. 'You look all shook up, but you be needin' to plan the buryin'. You gotta lot of things to think about, and they will be wantin' to know what to do with Martin right away.'

But, Miss Edwina just wanted us to get outta there, so she pushed us along like we were carts on wheels. We all obeyed Miss

Edwina, 'cause a jail is a stinky, not-nice place, where low-life people come when there isn't any other place for them.

After I got back to Camellia's house, we cried and said a lot of prayers. Not ever'one had started to show up for the wake and the vigil, so we had some precious time with ourselves. Word travels fast in the Negro community, and Camellia was a born planner. Her hotline for such things worked smoother than normal 'cause of the extenuatin' circumstances. The next day people started showin' up around noon.

The old folks sat on the comfortable furniture, and the young folks stood and wished there was a seat for them, too. It was gonna be a long day into night with all my relatives. I was a little surprised that Martin's family didn't show up. After a couple of hours and some hushed conversations in the corners, I figured that there was a school of thought that felt I had pushed him in front of the truck on purpose. I was glad I made the pies, though. People brought all manner of food, and their kindness made me feel a comfort, but I had a distinctly cool reception from certain people who I normally wouldn't have thought for such things. I might have been innocent in the eyes of the law, but I was guilty as sin accordin' to Martin's relatives, certain people, and even some of my own kin.

Living here was sure gonna be hard for a while. People would look at me and whisper. I knew what they were saying, but I couldn't run over and answer their whispers. Life doesn't work that way. I finally went to the kitchen and hung my head. I was tore up about Martin, but nobody said to me they felt bad about his passin' or that they were real sorry. He already had run off many of our kinfolk. Most people had seen how he went after the booze and gamblin' over the last few years, and many said the girls and me would be better off without him. My mother didn't bring the girls from Athens 'cause of all the bad stories goin' around, so the next day I went to Athens, and we cried ourselves a good one. He had been a lovin' daddy to them and, o' course, they knew I didn't mean him any harm.

I paid to have him shipped to Athens, and we buried him there, where the girls could have a visit with their daddy when they needed. I came up in Athens, and sometimes I felt like Atlanta was jes' too big for our simple ways. I never felt at home in big cities, so I passed a few comfortable months with Mama and the girls while I tried to get my pie-bakin' business goin' there. The problem was, ever'body seemed to be a good cook in Athens and didn't need my pies. Plus, there jes' wasn't that layer of hungry, *rich* people like in Atlanta.

After a while, I gave up and took on a job cleaning a white lady's house down the road. She lived alone and was almost blind, and she really didn't do too much messin' up of her house. I think she hired me mostly 'cause she jes' needed a friend to listen. I was that friend for her. So Miss Helen and I talked ever'day. I told her the truth about me and Martin's accident, 'cause I didn't want her hearing it secondhand from some nosey person. I finally told her, 'I accidentally killed my husband on a busy street.' Then I told her all the little details. She somehow seemed happy in the telling and wasn't horrified like I thought she would be. I hadn't revisited the Martin story in a while, and it helped me lots to get it all out and in the open again.

I was shocked when she told me that she, too, had somethin' bad happen to her when she was young. She told me she became pregnant by a very handsome young man. He said that he wanted her to love him so badly, and she'd never felt like that about a man before or since. 'Just being in the same room with him made me light-headed,' she said. 'I can still remember his smile, although his face faded from my blind memory long ago. I took that giant leap of faith that people, particularly young women, do when infatuation weighs heavy on a girl. I trusted that he liked me, or maybe even loved me, enough to have my best interest at heart. However, the only throbbing heart he felt was down there.' She motioned to her lower parts and gave a heavy sigh.

'He invited me to go swimming one Saturday afternoon over on Tybee Island. I was so naïve. I didn't understand why men like to take women swimming. They're already halfway undressed, and it doesn't take far to go after that—especially if they are a little forceful as men sometimes are. I wouldn't call it a rape, but it was a lot of talking and a lot of friendly forcing till I gave in. I just knew we would get married and told myself the whole thing was OK. That's what naïve young girls can do.' I saw a little tear sneak out on her cheek from a pain still raw even after so many years.

'When my family found out I was pregnant, I was sent to live with an old woman who owned a furniture store here in Athens. She wasn't even a relative, just someone who had business with my father. I was never allowed to come back to my home in Savannah. The reason, I found out later, was because the young man was already married and had a family. He was a husband who chose to stay with his wife and small children. He was well known and well respected. He got what he wanted from me and moved on. No one ever found out, and it wouldn't have been good if they did. You have to understand, when you have a situation like that, it would have been worse for his family. His wife and children would have been forced into hardship if they divorced, and we would have been "labeled" if he married me. I would always have been the other woman. But I don't think he ever thought for a second about a divorce or making me a wife anyway. So … it had to happen the way it did. But I never could get over the fact that he had told me such a lie. And what's worse, I never got over the fact that I believed that lie.

'Now, looking back, if women would understand they own

one hundred percent of their you-know-what, they would look at men in a different way and know they got something that's really worth something. They sure wouldn't go drinking or swimming with the opposite sex, and they sure wouldn't leave the house without a chaperone. Kind of like they do down in Mexico.'

I thought to myself that I was sure glad my mama was watchin' over the girls. Nobody was gonna get near them!

Poor Miss Helen was broken from her encounter decades ago. I could also look at her and tell she once had a certain style that would have appealed to men; I decided it was that style that had got her into trouble.

She went on. 'So, I moved to Athens, I had the baby, and I met a new man not long after. We married and settled here. Oh, the man I married was not educated or handsome. He worked at the furniture store. But he was kind and provided for us, and he never questioned the story I told him about being a widow. I never had another child because having Andrea almost killed me. I was only seventeen when I had her. I sure gave up a lot to that man on Tybee Island.'

She went on to tell me that the man that got her pregnant still lived in Savannah. He lived in a big house, his children went to college, and he played golf at the country club. He never tried to contact poor Miss Helen. I wonder if he ever thinks about what he did.

There was a certain sad condolence knowin' someone else had a bad time of it, too. It didn't help my hurtin' heart any. 'Miss Helen,' I said, 'you've helped me see that a man generally does what is best for a man. He doesn't necessarily do what's best for family or others around him.'

Then I asked her, 'Did your life turn out OK?' I looked around and the house was pretty nice. What did I know?

'Well, I worked up until the time my sweet husband died

at work, right there on the furniture showroom floor.' Her lip quivered a little. She sat up a little straighter and continued, 'After a little while, time passes and you look back at something like it was a dream. Finally, you just wake up and forget it. Doesn't even seem real to you anymore. Life goes on.'

'What became of Andrea?' I saw no evidence of a daughter in the house, but then she would have been grown and gone by that point. I also knew I might be treading on thin ice.

Miss Helen told me, 'Well, when Andrea started growing up, I guess I was just so intent on not letting her make the same mistakes in life that I had, that I drove her off. After the only daddy she ever knew passed away, I broke down one day and confessed to her the story of how she came to be. She had a hard time accepting that, as you would expect. I guess she just lost respect for me and didn't know how to handle this news. Sometimes people just want to run off and hide from the truth, and that's what she did. I got a letter from her saying that she had joined the circus. She always loved animals, and she said the circus would give her the opportunity to work with all kinds of animals. I worry about her safety doing all those tricks that the circus people do with the animals, but it's the human kind of animals that I still worry about doing the most harm to her. And I worry about that each and every day, but she's grown up now and there's nothing at all I can do to keep her from making life's mistakes. I only wish now that I hadn't expressed my disapproval about the circus to her, because she hasn't written to me since, and she hasn't ever been back here.'

Then Miss Helen turned to me and said, 'Women, too, make choices to leave men behind all the time, when they get too rough or they start running around too much. Doesn't matter what color they are. But worst of all, most of us put up with their actions long before we do anything about it.'

Miss Helen smiled a sad smile at me then. I was beginning to understand completely. 'Oh Anna, a person does what's best for the person—not anybody else—goes for women, too,' she told me."

Anna stopped talking and suddenly turned to me and said, "I feel a sense that I know you somehow. There's somethin' familiar."

I resolved that I would reveal to her that we had met before, but this wasn't the time yet. The meat of the story was about to unfold, so I just brushed it off.

"You may be right; our paths may have crossed somewhere, Anna."

PART II:

Goodbye Georgia—Hello Iowa: In Anna's Words

Although many of the characters that Anna speaks of are no longer with us, her words truly make the characters come alive again. So, I invite you to sit back with me to relive life long ago. Anna is going to take over the story now, and I wouldn't want to change one thing in the way she tells it. —C.J. Renfro

Chapter 7

Conscience Cleared and Chicago Bound

Camellia wrote a letter to me in Athens and said that Altus Andrews had been caught stealin' some nitwit's billfold in a bar and a fight broke out. He had seven stab wounds in various places including a nasty one on his face. Camellia said he had a slash that started at his mouth and went almost to his ear. He wasn't expected to make it, and if he did, he was gonna be one ugly son of a gun. But the good lowdown was that he told ever'one standing around his deathbed that I didn't push Martin.

"Why no, she such a big woman, he bounce off her when he push," he told them. I was annoyed that he talked about my size that way, but at least I was set free from his accusin'. Word spread through the Negro part of Atlanta that I was innocent, and Camellia said it was OK to come back—but I couldn't. I was sad that ever'one believed Altus in the first place, and it made me embarrassed and angry. I decided I needed to get far away and start a new life with folks that didn't think I murdered my husband. I wrote Camellia that I wasn't coming back to Atlanta. And the rich, hungry white folk of Atlanta breathed a sad sigh, 'cause my pies would be gone forever from their fair city. Pie makin' is an art, and I am the only person I know who can do it right ever' time out. O' course, that's the case with ever'thing—you can be real good at somethin' some of the time, but the true mark of success is being consistently good. I was consistently good at pie makin'.

So I went back to Atlanta to empty out the house and put it up for sale. It had been about six months since Martin had passed, and it took me a few weeks of goin' through all those things that meant somethin' to me. I relived my life with Martin by goin' through all those things, and I packed away what little I couldn't part with. Surprisin'ly, it wasn't the stuff that would bring money, but the stuff that brings tears that I held on to. I had to dry my emotions and put so many things behind me. There was my life sitting there in a huge pile. But I knew if I sold the house, it would pay for the girls' schooling. One day, while I was cleaning the last bit out in the kitchen, Miss Edwina arrived with that sly smile she had. I was glad to see her, 'cause I hadn't seen her since that awful day. I felt I owed her an apology and a thank-you for her help.

So Miss Edwina put her arm around me and said, "Anna, you were just an unfortunate part of that problem, and there was not a thing you could do. You were plumb stuck in the middle. That awful Altus Andrews caused it all. Why, we had to give him fifty dollars to make him go away."

"You what?" My voice rose a little when I said that.

"Oh, yes, Troy paid him off that afternoon, and then we were able to spring you from jail since there was no complaint filed. It all worked out for the best—see?"

"I wondered why the problem went away so fast. Thank you." I closed my eyes and felt I had the full story now. I was hoppin' mad they paid that roach off, but so be it.

"Well, Anna what do you think you are going to be doing now? The girls are with your mama in Athens and going to school. What about you?" Miss Edwina asked me.

"Well, Miss Edwina, I don't rightly know. I'm jes' glad I'm not in jail."

"Me too. Have you thought about a full-time job with a family?"

"That would be nice, but I don't know anyone right now that's lookin'."

Miss Edwina gave that naughty smile and said, "I do."

"You don't need anybody. You have a full fleet of people at your beck and call."

"Well, it's not for me; it's for my friends, the Worrells. They live in Iowa, and they have a little boy that needs caring for, because he can't walk or move around. You were in the kitchen that day last spring when a bunch of you were holding the little boy. Remember, Fritzy?"

"Oh yeah, he's cute but not jes' right?"

"Yes, that's the one," she said. "I'm going to Iowa in a week to visit them and help Joyce and Joe get their house organized. I want you to go with me."

Miss Edwina went on to say that Miss Joyce couldn't get hold of the situation with Fritzy very well and was overwhelmed. Plus, she admitted to being a lousy cook, and her husband agreed with her. So she must be pretty bad. Miss Edwina said we'd likely be up there a couple of weeks. We'd ride the train on into Chicago and then get a driver to take us to Marshalltown—it was jes' 200 miles west of Chicago.

"I've never been to Chicago. Sounds like an adventure," I said, thinking in the back of my mind that Iowa couldn't be an adventure like Chicago, but I didn't want to offend her.

"Oh Anna, life is an adventure if you treat it right." Edwina grinned and turned to go, adding that we'd have fun on the train and asking me if I played cards.

"Well, I play cards almost as well as I bake pies. I bet I can whip you at gin rummy."

Miss Edwina laughed at my reply and said, "We'll see about that. Then it's settled. We'll leave next week. Be at our house at 9 a.m. on Thursday—packed and ready to go."

And jes' like that she was gone, and my life would be forever different.

I went back to Athens to say goodbye to Mama and the girls and to Miss Helen. We found another lady to go do the cleaning and the listening that Miss Helen needed.

Thursday came quicker than expected, but I was back in Atlanta with my things in some kind of order. Orleans, the chauffeur, ushered us into the seven-passenger Hudson, and it was then that I saw how the rich travel. The Hudson was huge on the inside and had two rows of seating behind the chauffeur. All the pieces of Miss Edwina's luggage matched each other, and she was wearing high heels and a smart gray suit and this hat that reminded me of Robin Hood. It had a long pheasant feather pointed out the back and a pointy part on the front. Ever'where we went in the train station, people turned their heads 'cause she looked so rich and important. Miss Edwina didn't seem to notice; she was used to it, I suppose. She was intent on getting settled on the train, and I didn't notice much 'cause I was busy trying to keep up with her.

Miss Edwina took her gloves off and stared at me intently. I sat across from her and stared intently back. "Are you hungry?" she asked me.

"Now, why even ask that question of a 300-pound Negro woman? I am always hungry," I said.

Then Miss Edwina whipped out some crackers and Coca-Cola from one of her great, big, expensive lookin' bags, and we gobbled it right up. The train pulled away from the station, and I took a nap. It had been a very long bunch of months, and I was jes' glad to be sitting still on a fast moving train. We travelled across land bathed in the reds and golds of that autumn.

Around noon we went to the club car, and Miss Edwina bought me a sandwich and a Nehi grape soda. Since people of color were not permitted to sit in the club car, we went back to her sitting room. Miss Edwina dealt the cards, and I proceeded to win most of the hands. Pretty soon I was betting more and winning more. Miss Edwina pulled out a bottle of gin and some mixer and proceeded to drink faster than I could drink a Nehi. The more gin she drank, the more I won, 'cause ever'one knows a tipsy person cain't remember which card's been played, what the other guy is collecting, or what groups of cards you can collect the fastest. My mind snaps to those cards like flies to potato salad, so I won almost every hand except the ones I wanted to lose. That way Miss Edwina wouldn't lose interest and want to stop.

After I won a whole month's pay off Miss Edwina, she had an early dinner brought to us. I had a club sandwich and Miss Edwina slept. She eats like a bird—jes' a little bit here and there. We passed the rest of the trip sleeping, eating, joking, and playing cards. Miss Edwina drank every chance she got, which bothered me a little after my experience with Martin and his drinking alcohol. Alcohol is a bad thing when it makes you its partner in ever'thing you do. I could see that familiar inch by inchin' move toward alcoholism happenin' to her, and it bothered me. It seemed to me that if she had a child, that child would have scratched that itch she had for drinkin'. A child is a challenge in life, and that challenge fills every corner of your soul. A child makes you forget about whatever else is goin' on 'cause you have to focus on what the child needs. Yeah, a child is a void that gets filled with love. Poor Miss Edwina didn't have anythin' to fill her void with—so a drink was the convenient, closest thing to fill it.

Now the fickle finger of fate figures into our lives on a daily basis. As I was sitting there on the train, I realized that fate had stepped in to take me away from Atlanta. Sometimes fate changes our lives all by itself, and sometimes fate is caused by a person or a thing—either way, fate happens. And fate caused Miss Edwina not to be able to bear children, and since she couldn't do that, she was out there helpin' ever'one around her, includin' Miss Joyce and me. She changed all our fates jes' 'cause her inside plumbing was no good.

Good deeds or bad deeds affect other folks and ourselves in most fate-full-ishous ways while we are busy living our lives and not realizing we could cause such far-ranging effects. Ever'thing can change by jes' makin' a simple choice about somethin'. As it turned out, fate was on my side.

I also figured out that Dr. Troy monitored Miss Edwina's alcohol intake on a day-to-day basis. As a result, she felt a freedom she didn't usually have living in Atlanta with Dr. Troy lookin' over her shoulder. She took advantage of it on the train.

As the evenin' wore on, Miss Edwina's eyes began to roll around in her head like two marbles in a bowl. And her words began to run together like she was talking with peanut butter in her mouth. I knew it was jes' the gin talking, and then she got sick and wretched like a jackal. I had to hold her over the tiny train toilet, which wasn't easy in the small space. "Oh, Miss Edwina, what you gone and done?" I said this as I was holdin' her over the toilet with one hand and holdin' a wet washcloth to her face in the other. Half of me was standing outside of the train toilet.

"Oh, Anna, I gone and got drunk is what I gone and done. And it feels just awful," she said, mimicking me. She was sitting on the floor propped up against the bathroom wall with her legs stretched out into the sitting room.

She wretched so much, there was nothin' but green stuff left in her and, oh, what a mess. "Miss Edwina, you need a keeper to keep you from getting in this situation." I tried to say this like I wasn't judging her, but Lord knows—I was.

"Anna, I've got one in Troy. He always watches me and keeps me safe, but he's in Atlanta wondering what the hell I'm doing right now." Miss Edwina paused and I wiped her mouth. "And, we're not gonna tell him what we is doin' right now. Are we?" She said, makin' fun of how I talked again.

"Why no, Miss Edwina, we most certainly ain't," I mimicked back. "And I want you to know that I'm watching you like a Troy-hawk after this. So don't get any ideas you can do this again."

That beautiful gray suit looked like she'd wadded it up. It was gonna take some serious washin' and blockin' to get it right again, and I knew I'd be the one on the washin' and blockin' end of that job. I sadly put it in my bag folded as flat as I could get it. I hoped they had good washin' mechanisms in Iowa.

We got off the train in Chicago and went direct to the Palmer House Hotel. I'd never seen so many tall buildings in my forty years, and the downtown was bustlin' with people, horses, and cars. I walked into that Palmer House Hotel and had to stand frozen-like for a while. I never saw anythin' like it. It was so grand.

The bellboy left our bags in our rooms and said, "Is that all I can do for you?" He held his hand out like he was speaking some kind of silent language, and Miss Edwina acted like she understood. She put some money in his open palm. They both nodded like the other had said somethin', but they hadn't.

Now I was thinking that it sure felt good to be where I could walk around. Being cooped up on a train is hard on a body, especially one as big as mine. Miss Edwina had bounced back as good as a bouncing ball. She had on her perfect makeup and clothes. You couldn't tell that she had been sick as a dog twelve hours ago.

Chapter 8

Iowa and Other White Objects

The next day we climbed into a limousine that drove us past rolling hills and farmland toward the Worrells' home in Marshalltown, Iowa. I was feeling a little more disappointed every mile closer to Marshalltown 'cause the state of Iowa sure didn't look like it was gonna hold any interest for me. There were no cities, no shops, no restaurants, and no manufacturin', jes' miles of farmland and gentle rolling hills.

But Marshalltown was different, 'cause it had manufacturin', a nearby university, and it was a little more citified, as I was to find out later. I would even come to realize that if you lived in a town this interesting, you'd never want to leave.

We arrived and drove through Main Street on our way to the Worrells' house. Main Street was wide and had shops lining both sides of it. I saw a bakery, grocery market, and millenery shop right off. I knew I could stand it here with those sorta things. Miss Edwina said I was only supposed to stay for a couple of weeks, but I think she had designs on the situation as becoming somethin' more than two weeks. Heck, I knew I could stand it here if the money was right. I could almost stand it anywhere—if the money right.

We drove on through the town, and toward the end of town, there were some houses and a couple of doctors' offices. Dr. Joe Worrell's office was at the end of the street, and his house was next door. It wasn't grand like the Parkers' Atlanta mansion, but it was nice and had a big backyard. I figured they bought this house hoping for a bunch of kids. O' course, we both know what happened to that idea. At the time, I didn't realize how important a role that backyard was gonna play in our lives, 'cause that's where they found the bodies.

I was ready to stretch my bones and so was Miss Edwina. Somehow, she looked fresh after all this traveling, but I felt tired as a ninety-year-old. When we walked through the door, Miss Joyce was there with the little boy. She was a pretty woman with dark hair. She had the most beautiful pair of blue eyes I'd ever seen; these eyes were sweet and sad at the same time. The boy was sitting in a stroller, even though he was now much too old and big for one. Yeah, he was about four years old when I first arrived there. Miss Joyce was reading a Horatio Alger book to him. I could tell he was taking in the story very intent-like. He smiled at me, and I think he remembered me from his visit to Atlanta. I held out my arms, forgetting he couldn't do the same, but he tried, and that was enough for me. I picked him up and patted his dark wavy hair, and my tiredness jes' drifted away like smoke. Dr. Joe Worrell showed up when he saw the limousine. He was tall, dark, and handsome. He didn't say much, but when he did, we all jumped. We all sat for a visit, and I sat by Fritzy and started tending to him. His mama saw this and right away moved to the center of the conversation in a different chair. It was like a weight had been lifted off her shoulders.

Miss Edwina told them all about our traveling adventures,

but she neglected to mention the drinkin' part. Then the Worrells talked about dinner, which is always a good topic to my way of thinking. So, it was decided that we would eat at the house and then go for a drive around the town to look at what they got in Marshalltown.

But first, Miss Edwina had to go and start talking about Martin, and how all that had simmered out. They stared a hole through me, and I felt terribly embarrassed. I guess it was good to get it outta the way, so they wouldn't be wonderin' about Martin and me anymore. After a while, that topic died out and we started dinner. Now, I had heard what a lousy cook Miss Joyce was, which made me wonder what dinner would be like. Miss Joyce was gonna cook an Iowa dinner for us that would mean fried pork cutlets, mashed potatoes, Iowa corn, and bread from the nearby Amish colonies. She was so proud of that dinner, but all I could see was gray pork, gray potatoes, gray corn, and white bread. It was some light-colored plate, and it looked like all the color in that dinner jes' got up and ran away. I looked over at Miss Edwina, who was drinkin' some kind of wine that I could tell didn't agree with her palate. But Miss Edwina, being Miss Edwina, got up and walked over to the liquor cabinet and poured herself a little gin. She glared at me, thinking that I might object, but I kept quiet. It was funny to me, 'cause I figured she stoved herself up with the gin so she could eat that pale-face pale food. She dug right in. I laughed at them from my seat in the kitchen, and ever'one figured out why I was laughin'. And then, after that, they laughed with me. Miss Joyce had made an apple pie that was quite passable and the coffee was delicious. Fritzy loved our laughter. The dinner wasn't a total loss, and Miss Joyce was pretty thick-skinned about her cookin'. We complimented her on the pie, which proved to be enough. I promised to cook us a Southern meal for tomorrow.

That night, I put Fritzy down for the first time. He was a sweet boy. He looked up at me with those big brown eyes and smiled at me. He knew I was good, but what he didn't know was that we were gonna be best friends. The next morning I told ever'body I need to go to the grocery market. He and I needed our time. It would prove the first of many adventures. Miss Joyce offered to drive me, but I told her I was gonna put Fritzy in the stroller, and we were gonna walk to the store. I hoped that Miss Joyce didn't get the idea that I was tryin' to separate her from Fritzy, but I wanted Fritzy to know that we could do different things when he was with me.

Now, Fritzy and I were a sight walking down Marshalltown. The fall weather was so beautiful and the store had ever'thing. I walked right in and sashayed through the wide aisles like I was meant to be there. We bought all my important things. My list had lard, prime beef, fruit, potatoes, green beans, flour, sugar, salt, vanilla, and almond extract, as well as red food coloring; ever'thing to make our dinner that night a fancy one. What I didn't expect to get was the what-for from the owner of the store, Mr. Bishop. He was surly to ever'one but extra surly to me, 'cause I wouldn't back down to him. All the other women took whatever he cut off the cow for them. Not me. My sister Camellia taught me what a cut of meat should look like, and it sure didn't look like what he tried to call prime rib. "Ahem, Mr. Bishop, I would like prime rib and not roast beef. This is roast beef." I pointed at it like it was yesterday's trash. He was trying to pass it off, but I was too smart for him.

"Now, whoever you are, that's prime and you can just take it and go on with you. Take the kid, too," he said. Why, my eyes got big as moons. No one dared speak to me that way in Atlanta and this nitwit with shaved hair wasn't about to neither.

"I am Anna Washington, and you can call me by my name. I

work for the Worrells, and I came for prime rib. Now give it to me and I'll be on my way. I not leaving unless I get the prime rib, and I will call Dr. Joe Worrell to come on over here." There was an awkward silence. "If you don't give me what I came for," I said and squinted my eyes, evil-like for extra effect, drawing myself up to my full, considerable height. "He will be angry and make you wait in his waiting room for an extra hour when you're sick, if you don't do right by us." That Mr. Bishop never smiled. He frowned at me and didn't say anythin'.

Miss Joyce said his wife ran off with another man and never showed up again. I now had an idea of why she ran off. He was sneery and surly. Seemed like the type that would yell at anyone and maybe even beat up on them if he got a chance to. Later, when I found out about those bodies, I always thought one of them might have been his wife and he might be responsible. There was somethin' he was hidin' behind that stone face of his, and his eyes were jes' full of hate. But I could never figure out how he would have gotten her into the Worrells' backyard. It was perplexin'.

After we walked out with the prime rib and all the other things, I began to sing to Fritzy and he hummed a little back. I sang, *Give My Regards to Broadway!* I asked Fritzy if he ever heard that song, and his leg jiggled. I realized Fritzy talked with his leg, so I said, "Fritzy, when you mean, yes, jiggle your leg up and hold it for a bit, when you mean, *no*, wiggle it a bunch—down. That way I know what you're thinking." He held his leg up a bit, and I clapped my hands. He was on the road to livin' and I was gonna help him with it.

When I got all the things from Bishop's put away, Miss Joyce came into the kitchen. "Did you meet Mr. Bishop?"

"Yes, if you could call it a meetin'. He isn't a nice man."

"I know. Everyone says he's that way because his wife ran off a few years ago and left him, but I think he was that way before she left." Miss Joyce shook her head.

"I don't know about that, but he sure is prickly."

Miss Joyce added, "His sons are also a handful. They're always roaming around town in search of trouble. That could be from not having their mother with them. It's a shame."

I wasn't feelin' sympathetic.

With the things put away, we started the pies for dinner. Lard is the best thing about cookin'. You jes' start out with a little dab and swirl it around in the pan and it melts up real good. Then, you jes' add whatever else to it and you're on the road to some delishishness. Now, I have to say that cookin' is somethin' that has to be mastered. Camellia mastered it first and taught me. I expect she's the best cook in Atlanta. I hadn't seen any competition at all up in Marshalltown yet. So, I reckoned I'd be the undisputed queen here. After dinner, I thought I'd take a vote jes' to build my ego up a little.

Miss Joyce had beautiful settings for the table and a real nice tablecloth. There weren't any goldfish up here to put in the huge flower bowls, but there were things bloomin' in the garden. I put together a bouquet that was nice, and Fritzy watched my every move.

He began to jiggle his leg a bunch. "Why, little man, what do you want?" I asked. After a while I figured out what he wanted. "Oh, my little friend, you want to smell the flowers?" He jiggled again. "Here take a whiff." I held them up to his nose. "Aren't flowers wonderful?" He gave another jiggle. After that, we always made arrangements for the dinner table, and I let him smell the flowers. He always jiggled that leg, and we always talked about Miss Edwina's goldfish.

I said, "Fritzy, do you remember Miss Edwina's house and the goldfish in the flower bowls?" He jiggled, yes.

"I promise you we'll have big bowls with goldfish someday, even if we have to go all the way to Chicago to get them." He jiggled, yes.

I finished the dinner and put it out formal-style for Miss Edwina and the Worrells, but I asked if Fritzy could take his dinner with me in the kitchen. I knew they needed adult talk. Fritzy and I listened to Miss Edwina's stories through the door, along with that silly laugh that made her so much fun. I knew Fritzy understood ever'thing. After a while, I served my special cherry pie for dessert and then put Fritzy down for the night. I settled him in and said, "Fritzy, now we're gonna say our prayers." And we said our prayers, but I was a little shocked that he didn't know any. Fritzy was best on the last part. He said, "Aaaah-meeee." I think he needed to be close to God. It would make it easier for him when the time came, but I didn't tell him that. I jes' closed the door and went out to clear the table.

And by the by, that prime rib won me the vote. But it was my dark red cherry pie, along with my secret ingredient (almond extract) that pushed things over the top. Did I tell you I put a dollop of whipped cream on it, too? Yum.

And jes' like that, it was easy as that pie, I began to read and teach Fritzy about the world. He caught on and jiggled a lot. Even that first week we were together, I read to Fritzy for hours, and I was cross-eyed from all those words. I had to take us out-and-about to get somethin' cool to drink and go to the market to annoy old Bishop, jes' to recover from allthat reading.

Toward the end of the first weeks, Miss Edwina took me aside and said, "Anna, do you want to stay here?"

"Well, it is real nice here, and they're real nice to me."

Miss Edwina nodded her head back, "Yes, you're doing quite well."

"Besides, they really need me. Don't they?" I knew they did need me.

"More than you will ever know. Joyce has been relieved since you came."

"And they understand about Martin, I guess?"

Miss Edwina grinned and said, "Actually, they do. In fact, they wondered why you put up with him for so long." She kept talking, "They will pay you what you ask, within reason, and give you time off to go to Atlanta and Athens to see your girls and Camellia."

"That makes me happy jes' knowin' I can go home when I like."

So it was settled. I would stay in Iowa.

Chapter 9

Edwina Makes an Offer

"Anna, Troy and I want to do some traveling with Joyce and Joe this spring. I would love to go someplace with a beautiful beach. Someplace that has quaint little tables with umbrellas, great food, and very cold drinks."

Miss Edwina leaned back and rolled her eyes. I knew she was thinking about the cold drinks more than the rest of the trip. "Of course, that will give Joyce the rest she needs. You'll need to take care of Fritzy while we're gone, but I bet you're up to the challenge."

"You bet." I grinned back.

"It will just be taking care of Fritzy and cooking. They already have a cleaning lady for the house, so that won't be part of your job. Oh, by the way, you're as good as Camellia in the kitchen. I never thought anyone could rival her, but it must run in the family." Edwina smiled.

"Why, thank you," I said, and I really meant it.

I thought to myself, "Hallelujah. No toilets." And for the first time in my life, I wasn't the queen of the porcelain. The

Worrells only have two bathrooms, but it was still a big deal to me.

Our business was done, and I was not goin' back to Georgia. Somehow, I wasn't surprised; I had unpacked my things in a more permanent manner when I first arrived and thought in the back of my mind this might be my new home. I would be banking almost all my money, which was good, 'cause the girls could sure use it back in Athens. It jes' felt right to stay here in Iowa. Miss Edwina had been right when she said they needed me—Miss Joyce was a lousy cook.

I cooked a special dinner for us all on Miss Edwina's last night in Marshalltown. But, jes' as they sat down, the doctor got called away to fix a broken arm next door at his office.

"OK, I'll meet you there," said Dr. Joe as he hung up the phone. He turned toward Miss Joyce and said, "Do you think you can give me some assistance on this one? Nurse Franny is out of town for the weekend."

"Sure. I'll kiss Fritzy good night and be right there." Dr. Joe was already out the door and Miss Joyce soon followed after givin' us a few instructions. The dinner went from dining room to kitchen table in an instant.

Miss Edwina and I sat down at the kitchen table with Fritzy as we ate my special dinner. "Anna," she said, "they are so fragile right now, and your being here is such a good thing. It gives them a normal life, or as normal as a life can be, with a child that's been hurt like that."

Miss Edwina was doin' what most folks do when talking around Fritzy; they jes' forget he's there. I nodded my head in Fritzy's direction to remind her he was in the room. She got the picture and change the subject. "I'll be going back tomorrow. Is there anyone you want me to see or talk to for you?"

I thought about it for a minute and said, "Yes, I need you to give somethin' to Martin's mother. It's a letter I'll write tonight. If you will deliver it, I can close that part away from my life."

Miss Edwina nodded. "I know that's been hard, and sometimes a letter brings closure—but don't think it will end her pain. She's always going to think you killed her son. It's just human nature, because people need someone to blame for things that go awry in their lives. I'm convinced Martin's mother will give Altus your address, too." Miss Edwina looked me down. "Be careful because you really don't want to hear from that horrible Altus Andrews again."

"I know, but I need to get it behind me, and this is the best way I know. So, I'll write the letter."

And I did. It was a simple letter. It just said I was sorry and that I didn't do it on purpose.

It snowed in the night, and when we woke up the next mornin', it was ever'where. I hadn't seen snow like that since I was a child. But more important, Fritzy had never played in it.

I grabbed Fritzy and we hurried outside in our pajamas. He wanted to touch some of the trees, so I pushed him over to them. He tried so hard to open his hand for a touch. He couldn't do it, so I leaned him real close, and he felt snow for the first time. "Ssssooooww."

It had begun to get a little cloudy and cold the night before, so I had an inklin' it might do that. I told Fritzy before we went to bed, "It might be snowy when we wake up. You'll like it, and it'll be real beautiful too. We'll go outside in it and make tire tracks with your little chair."

"Eeeeeee."

"Then, we'll go to the market and see what Bishop is tryin' to pawn off on us today."

Jiggle, yes.

That mornin' ever'one was up and about, and Miss Edwina

had her bags by the door. Dr. Joe said in a very doctorly tone: "Now Anna, Joyce and I are going to drive Edwina to the train in Chicago, and we'll be staying after for a few days at the Palmer House. It will just be you and Fritzy here, and you'll be alone for the first time. I hope that's OK."

"Oh, Dr. Joe, it will be jes' fine. I'll cook and we'll enjoy the snow. I'm gonna show Fritzy some new books. We'll bundle up and go to the library. Now you drive careful. The road's icy."

He turned to pick up a bag and was out the door before I could say another word. He worked hard and was a good man, but sometimes he was a little abrupt. They all waved out the windows as their simple, black Chevy made its way down the street. I thought it didn't hold a candle to the Parkers' seven-passenger Hudson.

Chapter 10

"Fritzy knows more than he's letting on."

I realized that Fritzy needed "reading to" in a powerful way. He needed love and he needed a way to express himself—and Miss Joyce was a loss on all those counts. She couldn't do anythin' but sit and look out the window. Taking her to Chicago was the right thing to do. It left Fritzy and me to do as we pleased without dampenin' our spirits and bringin' us down like she was wont to do.

    I dressed Fritzy for the cold, carefully tucking his dark wavy hair into a cap and being sure that his ears were well covered. We went outside to make figure-eight designs with his little chair in the snow. One day, instead of goin' straight to old Bishop's to harass him, we went to the library. Now the library in Marshalltown was a real nice place. Some rich farmer died and willed all his books to the library, along with a wagonload of money, and then there was a library. It had a bunch of children's books and a real nice reading area.

    There, on one of our first of what would be many visits to that library, I wrote up a sign language for Fritzy. It was simple, and it all had to do with movin' his feet. We ate leftovers for lunch, 'cause we didn't want to go to Bishop's, and neither one of us cared. By that afternoon, we had five or so signals he could give me. We had our own private language that would come in handy in some most-important times ahead. Now, I don't mean to leave you with the impression that Fritzy couldn't talk, he could, but it was slowed like a Victrola before it gets up to speed.

We were ready to try things. We continued goin' to that library all the time. I checked out a book to bring home with us and then I read it over and over to him until he almost had it memorized. One time I asked him, "Fritzy, can you tell what these words mean?"

"Daaaw."

"Yep, Dog."

Darned if he couldn't already read. I figured it was jes' by accident, 'cause when you read to a child a lot they begin to see the words and know what they mean. They call it sight reading, and Fritzy took to it right away. A white girl in the family my parents worked for taught me ever'thing I know in a kind of similar way. She would come home from school and tell me what she learned that day. My parents stopped workin' for them when she would have been in the ninth grade. So, I don't know much more than that. But I have that girl to thank for my ability to read and think critical.

One afternoon after our visit to the library, we showed up at Bishop's. Bishop was in his regular surly mood. I asked him, "What've you got on sale this day for us, Mr. Bishop?"

"Why, nothing you're going to like, Anna."

"Well, that's jes' fine with me. I'll let ever'one in the store know that." And then I walked Fritzy and me away with a "Harrumph!" Fritzy could make that sound pretty good too.

Bishop had to watch me tell ever'one he had no meat on sale today. Ever'one laughed, and he got red in the face like a drunken

Santa Claus. Ha-ha, Mr. Bishop. We jes' walked out of the store with nothin'. I broke my rule about talkin' too much to strangers; I couldn't help myself. We had to do without new food another day, but I had a few things left in the larder at home. We made the best of it.

After that, we had a few frosty conversations with Mr. Bishop. Then one day he warmed up over the stupidest thing, but that's for another time.

The Worrells returned from Chicago and were pleased that Fritzy and I had done so good. O' course! Cookin', eatin', and reading is fun.

Chapter 11

Dogs Are Dirty

Fritzy and I were well on our way to becoming the best of friends. We spent the next spring and summer enjoyin' our routine, which included lots of reading adventures. Life seemed to have taken a real turn for the better for the Worrell family. Why Miss Joyce and Dr. Joe even seemed to start enjoyin' their time with Fritzy rather than lookin' at it as a burden. Dr. Joe was finally callin' him by his name now instead of jes' "him."

One day a hot summer wind had jes' about blown us to pieces when we got in from Bishop's grocery. Fritzy and I had done some shoppin', and as I unloaded ever'thing, I noticed a can of dog food in Fritzy's chair. "Now, Fritzy, how in the heck did you get that can? Did you grab it?" I couldn't say that I was exactly proud of him for havin' enough strength to grab a can, but it did my heart good to know he was makin' that kind of progress.

"Auuugh." Jiggle. That was a yes on the foot position.

His eyes twinkled, and I almost gave him a little slap on the wrist, but I jes' tried to look serious. I was standing there with the can of dog food in my hand when it dawned on me that was his way of letting me know he wanted a dog. "Does this mean you want a dog?"

"Auugh, auurgh." Jiggle. I couldn't stop him; his whole body was in motion.

"Are you gonna take care of this dog?"

"Noooo."

"I didn't think so. You know, that's somethin' that your daddy will have to take care of and make the decision to get. Look, I much prefer a cat. They don't get in the way and they don't bark and they don't stink." I had to think of reasons not to get a dog real fast. "Dogs are stinky, and besides that, they also drool. I never saw a dog that didn't drool. Not to mention, they jump up on a lady and run her stockings."

"Aruugh." No position on the foot.

"No cat?" I let the question end with a long pause. "Cats stealth around and hunt mice, and out here in corn land, you gotta bunch of rats."

"Noooo."

"Cats purr."

"Nooooo."

That night, when Dr. Joe came in from work, I cooked them an especially good dinner. And while he and Miss Joyce were sitting with their after-dinner coffee, I let them know what was goin' on. "Why, Fritzy wants a dog. He wants it bad enough he grabbed a can of dog food off old Bishop's shelf and made off with it while I wasn't lookin'. That's when I figured out what he wanted. He is very unapologetic about this." We all looked over at Fritzy, and his foot was held in the yes position. He was smilin.'

Miss Joyce and Dr. Joe were smilin', too, so I knew I was gonna lose the cat battle. I still think a cat is a superior being. They're quiet and smart and don't bite except when they're hungry, and then it's jes' a nibble. They purr instead of pant, and they clean themselves up every chance they get—even if they show you their private parts while they're doin' it.

The next day Fritzy and I made the trek over to Bishop's once again, where I returned the can of dog food to him. I said, "Mr. Bishop, Fritzy and I accidentally got this can of dog food in our things. We're returnin' it."

"Why Anna, it doesn't matter who took it. I will gladly take it back." He gave me one of those 'I'm the lord over you' looks. I knew he was probably thinking I took it, 'cause he thinks I'm a foreigner.

My anger began to brew, so I put the can on the shelf and walked out. We went another day without groceries, and I wanted never to go back or ever see him again. Luckily, I am very good at thinking up dinner menus from outta the considerable pantry, so it was a few days before I had to show back up there again.

It was jes' a couple of weeks later, and I was makin' a special cake and planning on whippin' up some macaroni and cheese, 'cause there was a most special day coming up. There was gonna be a party like never before for Fritzy's fifth birthday. Every person deserves to be honored on birthdays, and I suspected that the Worrells hadn't properly celebrated any of Fritzy's birthdays before. Oh, they always gave some kind of present, but the hoopla is what a kid really cares about, and I was determined to be sure there was plenty of that this year.

On the afternoon of Fritzy's fifth birthday, Dr. Joe appeared with a little dog that looked like he shoulda been rejected from the pound. He was a little thing then, but one look at his feet told me he wasn't gonna be little for long. And like anyone that ever unloaded a dog on some nitwits like us, they said he wasn't gonna be big at all. I knew he was gonna be huge. People who need to get rid of a dog always say, "Oh, you don't have to worry, he's going to be a medium-to-small size dog." I say this in my whitest way of talkin', 'cause that's jes' the way they said it to Dr. Joe, who I figured hasn't ever had a dog. He bit for that like a snappin' turtle. Why, the first thing I noticed was that dog's feet were the size of saucers—and you can always tell a pup's grown size by their feet. So, we had ourselves a soon-to-be huge dog.

When I saw that ruffian I knew he was gonna be the size of a small pony. I told Dr. Joe, "You got taken." Dr. Joe walked away without replyin'. And I fed the dog the first of many meals, 'cause I knew I was the one that was on the losin' end of that stick.

I used the word ruffian so much that's what we started callin' him: Ruff. And Ruff was sure rough. He took every light cord in the house, every shoe that wasn't corralled, and every purse that wasn't up high, and branded it with those huge teeth of his. I drew the line when he started gnawin' on chair legs, so I rolled up a newspaper and got after him with it ever' time he gnawed. Nobody in that house knew how to discipline a dog, much less a little boy. I was not popular for a month. Miss Joyce started wearing pants all the time to protect her legs, 'cause wearing stockings was jes' not possible.

In no time, he sure enough became the huge, scruffy ruffian I had predicted. I would give Ruff my evil eye, and he knew not to bother with me after that. But Fritzy loved him better than anythin'. We had to walk Ruff twice a day. It was the best part of the day for those two. I made the best of it, though, and pushed Fritzy faster than I ever had before. I lost a precious few pounds hurryin' to keep up with Ruff. Ruff was always kissin' Fritzy, and the first hundred times I washed Fritzy off. After that, I didn't bother.

Ruff slept at the foot of the stairs, and he snored like a car engine with an exhaust problem. However, we all slept better knowin' we had our canine security. O' course, I didn't admit that to the family.

PART III:

The Mystery

Chapter 12

1929, "Dang, look what crashed and look what came outta the ground."

Even starting with those early days when Fritzy and I first began frequenting the library, I noticed there was somethin' real good goin' on in the reading part of his brain, 'cause he could read anythin'. First I read and read the story until he let me know he wanted to read it. Then I held the pages up for him to read and he read a page to himself. He'd wiggle his leg to turn each page until we were done. It was a shame he couldn't talk good, 'cause he could read like anythin', and he took to it like dust to furniture. He was reading books meant for ten-year-olds. We always made small talk with Miss Schultz during our visits to the library. She was nice and she loved waggin' her tongue about all sorts of things.

One day we sat in the corner of the children's section. It was decorated with bright pictures of characters from some of the famous books. Miss Schultz brought us some books she thought Fritzy might like to read. She didn't do that often, but she had some she thought were perfect for him. We loved reading, and Miss Schultz loved talking. That day she was askin' me about the house. "Oh, you live in a lovely house. The doctor who was here in Marshalltown before the Worrells used to live there. His name was Dr. Phillips, and he and his wife worked so hard in his practice that they didn't have much time for housekeeping or makin' the house look good. The house looks a whole lot better since the Worrells bought it. Those green shutters really make it look so much better." Miss Schultz looked over at us to see if she was borin' us. She was, but she continued anyway. "Mrs. Phillips never did much to the outside or the inside. She mainly helped the doctor in his practice and doted on her son. They never struck me as particularly happy people, possibly that's why they moved away. I heard he banked almost every penny he made and that they bought a very nice home on a lake in Wisconsin." We got bored and left. Miss Schultz was still talking when we waved good-bye.

By the time Fritzy had his sixth birthday, he was beginning to show signs of his malady. His little body was not growin' very straight; in fact it wasn't growin' much at all. His skin had always been white like milk, but he was developin' some blotches. The areas were faint, but if you looked real close you could see them—subtle-like. Dr. Joe had noticed it, too.

Now in those days, there were a lot of people contractin' polio, includin' the soon-to-be president, Franklin Roosevelt. People were talking about the healin' powers of water. While it wasn't polio that made Fritzy unable to walk, he was in the same boat as some of the other children whose only opportunity to exercise was splashin' around in water. So Dr. Joe decided to build a swimmin' hole right there in the backyard. It was gonna be a mini-version of the public pools being built at that time and thankfully not too deep. The water was gonna be run through heaters, he said. And he even talked about buildin' a structure around it so Fritzy could get his exercise for more months of the year. I thought this was a pretty extravagant idea, but I think Dr. Joe really wanted to do somethin' special for Fritzy on account of some guilt he might have felt for jes' treatin' him like a rag doll during his first few years and not even callin' him by his name.

He walked us out to the backyard and stood in an area near the patio. "We are going to build a small swimming pool about right here." He pointed to the spot. "And we're going to make it just big enough for two or three people." He held out both arms to show about how big it was gonna be, as he walked from side to side. "Now, it's going to have some wide steps so someone can sit on them and hold Fritzy."

Somehow I knew I was gonna be that someone.

"We're going to have a cement man come and do the digging for the pool in the next week or so. That is, if there isn't any bad weather to slow things down. Then he can lay the cement all at once," Dr. Joe shook his head with enthusiasm. "That early snow was just a fluke—I hope." Then Dr. Joe hurried off to work and left me thinking about how to cover my considerable body in a swimmin' pool and if they made swimsuits that big. I was also thinking that summer would never come, 'cause we had to get through what looked like it would be a hard winter that year.

The leaves had fallen from the trees well before the middle of October, which ever'one said was the sign of a big winter. Fritzy and I were sitting by the fireplace with Miss Joyce when Dr. Joe rushed in from next door and said, "Joyce, the stock market crashed. Turn on the radio." Well, I didn't own any stocks, however, I could see Miss Joyce's face drop when he told her, so I figured they did. I had my money safe in the bank, and what I didn't have in the bank, I had sent to the girls by Western Union. They had spent it on food and school and tucked the rest away in their genuine leather billfolds I bought for them the Christmas before. I was feelin' a little smug.

We all sat down around the radio and listened to Walter Winchell tell us the bad news. He had a bad Yankee sound, but Dr. Joe and Miss Joyce liked him jes' fine. I didn't like that he was breakin' in on one of my favorite radio shows, but I didn't say anythin'. Dr. Joe said, "One of my patients came in and told me this occurred, but I didn't believe him, and then another one told me right after that. This means some bad times for everyone. People will lose their jobs and then people won't be able to pay us. Of course, people still get sick, no matter what's going on in the world. Life does go on."

Miss Joyce couldn't believe what they said. "You mean our stocks are gone? Just like that?" Her expression looked like she smelled somethin' bad as she snapped her fingers.

Dr. Joe looked like somethin' hurt him bad and he was in considerable pain, too. I guess money means different things to different people, but it means certain pain if you don't have any.

Fritzy and Ruff jes' looked blank. Neither one knew what stocks were, but even Ruff knew somethin' bad was up, 'cause he could feel the angst goin' around the room. Ruff kept movin' from spot to spot and wouldn't be still, and Fritzy was makin' more 'oo' and 'aa' sounds than usual. I told Fritzy, "Heck, I'm not even too sure what a stock is, but I do have a firm understanding of havin' money and not havin' money. And one is a whole lot better than the other."

"I need to go back to the office, but I had to come here to tell you." Dr. Joe nodded as he kissed Miss Joyce.

She said, "I'm glad you did. I was going shopping this afternoon for things I didn't really need. I'm just going to stay here and finish up a costume for Fritzy and Anna, so they can go trick-or-treating."

"You're makin' a costume for Fritzy and me?" I asked this tentative-like.

"Yes, Anna, it was going to be a surprise for you two, but now I have to see if it fits. So, let me show it to you."

Fritzy's expression was a little off, and he grabbed at me with the no look and his foot in the no position. I ignored this and whispered, "Come on Fritzy, don't dampen her spirits." And then I started laughin'. "Spirits—get it?"

Fritzy wasn't laughin'.

I could tell Miss Joyce was very proud of her sewin' skills, but those had to be the ugliest costumes ever—and uncomfortable—oooeee.

Did Fritzy and I say an unkind word? No. We jes' smiled and ever' time I saw Fritzy's foot in the no position, I move it to the yes. He may have been in a wheelchair, but he could sure sneer like Simon Legree when he wanted. We stood there lookin' in the mirror—a scrutiny I don't particularly like. And I had to admit, I was the biggest orange punkin' I ever saw. I looked over at Fritzy, who was the most misshapen punkin' I ever saw, 'cause he listed to one side then.

Halloween night came, and we started walking from house to house. Pretty soon, I saw some junior hoodlums walking along behind us. They were goin' along behind us as slow as we were, which I considered a bad sign. We were infirmed and slow; they were young and brash. This didn't add up to my way of thinking, so about that time I noticed spit wads rainin' down on us, and I turned around to face them, and then I stared them right down and I said: "I don't give a whit what you think of me. I'm big and dark and scary, and I don't have to suffer your God-awful stupidness or you being mean to Fritzy. If you throw spit wads at him one more time, I'm gonna whack you two towheaded boys' heads together and make you idiots for the rest o' your days. Yah hear me?" I felt real stupid in that costume while I was saying that.

They ran like roaches when you turn on the lights in a kitchen. I'd seen them little turdlets before and knew who they were.

They were crusty Bishop's boys, and the kind of people that were never gonna amount to anythin'. Those are the kind of people that always gotta show their power over the little and less fortunate, 'cause they're less fortunate themselves. They just have to make it look like there's a bigger separation between them and us. They are those down lows tryin' to crush the down lowers. Nitwits.

I looked down at Fritzy, and he was laughin' hard. He loved it when I got after someone. I loved it, too. "Fritzy, what say we go back and eat some of this candy?"

Jiggle, yes.

When we got back Dr. Joe and Miss Joyce were listenin' to that awful soundin' Yankee again. "The markets are continuing the downward slide from October 29th—Black Tuesday. Wall Street lost some of their best and brightest this week. Fortunes were lost in an afternoon and some investors that lost everything simply jumped out windows to their deaths. The market is in a free fall."

Dr. Joe chuckled, "These folks took a financial nose dive and then a physical one, too." But we weren't laughin' at his joke.

We went back to Fritzy's room, and I ate candy corn for the first time in my life. Miss Joyce said it had been around for a very long time in Iowa, but it sure hadn't made the rounds to Georgia. It was new on the market to Fritzy and me. We thought it was real tasty. I loved the stripes; Fritzy loved the color. We ate a little, but then I decided we needed to get out of those awful punkin' costumes as fast as I could get us out.

I looked over at Fritzy. "Fritzy, thank me for getting us outta these costumes so fast."

Jiggle, yes.

We settled in for the night and heard people laughin' up and down Main Street after we were in bed. It was good to hear people laugh after all that serious talking by that Walter Winchell. It reminded me of past Halloweens with my children, and for the first time in a long while, I cried for my children. Once I started cryin' I couldn't stop. I cried for Fritzy and Miss Joyce and Dr. Joe. Then I dried my tears, but I woke up in the night again, and I cried for all the people that jumped out the windows on Wall Street two days ago. That, in turn, made me think of all the families that were left behind without a daddy 'cause of that. O' course, I started worryin' about the folks left behind that lost money in the stock market and didn't choose to jump out a window but jes' had to grin and bear it. Then I cried for those nitwit boys that were no-counts and had nothin' to live for, whose mama ran off and left them. Then I cried for Martin, who was gone forever and didn't deserve to die. I jes' knew he would have found the right way of being and come back a changed man to me, but he never got the chance. Why, I even cried for Walter Winchell with that horrible Yankee voice he had. Did he know how bad he sounded?

I woke up the next mornin' a wreck. I'd cried for ever'one and gotten so upset. I had developed what my mother used to call the mollygotwabbles. That's what happens when a person cain't calm down and go to sleep. Somethin' jes' bother them and makes them fidget all night long. I decided that night Fritzy and I would have a very long list of people to pray for—and maybe that would help us go to bed with a clean and tired soul, ready for sleep. But, in the meantime, I had an awful furrow in my brow from all this. I walked around all that day tryin' to smooth that furrow back to its original position.

I figured we needed good, good food that night and then, maybe, we could all sleep. Dr. Joe walked in after work, and he said the Depression was already upon us. "Fewer patients showed up today, and some folks canceled their appointments altogether. I don't want people to stay away just because they can't pay. Hell, I'd even take a live chicken if Anna has the gumption to ring its neck." He looked over at me like I might be afraid of some live chicken.

"Now, Dr. Joe, do you think a little ole live chicken is a problem for me? The only problem is if I should fry it, fricassee it, or bake it, and I'll let you decide that part."

Winter had begun to set in real good, and we were makin' the best of it. But even so, construction on that pool had begun. The people came and started diggin' and dug real fast. I figured they thought Dr. Joe might ask for his money back, so they wanted to finish before he got any ideas. There was dirt ever'where and that Ruff was in the middle of it. I had to hose him off almost hourly. He was a muddy mess.

It's true that the pool would have never been built if Dr. Joe hadn't decided to pay for it the week before the stock market crashed. That's one of those fickle finger of fate things I mentioned earlier. One week later and the pool wouldn't have been built at all. It also was a fickle finger thing about where the pool got built. The reason Dr. Joe chose the spot he did was 'cause Ruff was always diggin' there and it made a constant mess. Dr. Joe decided that Ruff would move his diggin' to a farther place in the yard.

Late in the afternoon, right after they started diggin', we heard a frantic knock at the door, and the workmen were standing there lookin' real scared and upset. They didn't speak English, so they motioned to the hole and made foreign sounds. Dr. Joe was home, so he and Miss Joyce came runnin' out to see what was up. There was a ring in the mud, and Miss Joyce bent down and tried to grab it. The problem was there was an old, overcooked-chicken lookin' dried-up hand attached to it. She almost fell down when she realize it was attached to a dead body. Dr. Joe grabbed Fritzy and took him in the house. I stayed on lookin', 'cause I had never seen anythin' so interesting or so ugly in my life. I was plum mesmor-eyed. I watched ever'thing and assisted the doctor.

Dr. Joe joined us and took the ring in the house, handin' it, as muddy as it was, to Miss Joyce. She carefully washed it. I stayed out and sat on a bench and watched ever'thing. The cops came and dug the bones up and took them away for the coroner in Ames to look at.

Afterward, I asked Dr. Joe about it, since people won't tell Negro people anythin' usually, and that was the only way I was gonna find out somethin'. "Dr. Joe, who do you think they are?"

"I have absolutely no idea."

"Were they murdered do you think?"

"I have absolutely no idea."

I could tell this conversation was goin' nowhere. "Do you think they've been there long?"

"I have absolutely no idea. However, I think Ruff knew what was buried there. That's why he always chose that place to dig."

"I guess you have absolutely no idea when the pool guys are coming back?"

"Actually, they are coming tomorrow to finish the digging. Now the hole is a lot bigger, thanks to the police." Then, he just walked away.

I couldn't tell if he meant to be such a prickly person over that, or if he was just in a prickly mood. Either way, I had absolutely no idea what was goin' on with the investigation into the bodies. Oh yeah, it was the talk of the town for a few days, but 'cause it just so happened at the same time as the stock market crash, people were more concerned about themselves than some dead people, who it was too late to worry about anyway. But I sure didn't like the idea of dead people laying around the house I was living in and kept thinking about it all the time, especially after it got dark.

Chapter 13

The Thanksgiving

Sure enough, life went on, and we began to get as payment all manner of interesting things in Dr. Joe's office, as predicted. One lady gave Dr. Joe gold earrings to take her appendix out. Dr. Joe wouldn't take them, though. He said that was too rich a deal. So, they jes' agreed on several bushels of corn from her big farm. There was so much corn, more than we knew what to do with. Miss Joyce and I made corn relish, and we took the rest of the corn to the miller outside of town and traded it for cornmeal. I made corn bread until I couldn't stand it anymore. After that, we canned the corn in every way we could think of, and one time we even tried to pop it—didn't work. But, we had sweet corn with every meal for quite a while, and it was good, too. And yes, those live chickens came through the door, under people's arms just like Dr. Joe said, and he would call me over to pick them up and 'minister' to them. I found out he prefered fricassee. But, I always thought he should've taken the gold earrings.

During all this, Fritzy was getting bigger and smarter. He had jes' turned six years old, and the Depression was in full swing. The mood was sad by most people's count, but Christmas was coming and ever'one tried to forget about the hard economic times. I couldn't be sad. I was goin' back home again.

Usually at Christmastime, I would go to Atlanta to spend Christmas with my people. I could tell Miss Joyce wasn't ever too keen on the idea. This year, I couldn't wait. In fact, I was countin' the days and had started a pile of things I was taking with me on the train. But, before I left, the Worrells were gonna have a grand Thanksgiving with Dr. Donald Calloway, all his spoilt little children, and his nitpicky wife, Miss Susan. They even invited the Mayor, since he was widowed and didn't cook. He was sure big for a man that didn't cook. I wondered if he drank a little beer. That always gives a man a wide girth, and he sure had one. We would be about ten people, altogether, and I wanted to make it a Thanksgiving like they never had before. And it was, but in a way I will never forget.

Now, I had found sweet potatoes at Bishop's market, but they were puny. I realized after I first moved to Iowa that these farmers don't grow them, and Iowa people don't eat them. I also found out that people in Iowa feed the black-eyed peas to the pigs, not the people. And they haven't ever heard of okra. And to my chagrin, I noticed they treated somethin' that looked like okra as a weed, and it grew ever'where along the roads. So when Miss Joyce suggested they needed rice with the turkey, I wasn't too surprised. Who ever heard of rice with a darn turkey? I figured it had somethin' to do with their idea of white-colored food on a plate again.

I figured these Yankees need somethin' Southern and sweet to put them in a happy place and chose to ignore her suggestion for rice.

"Whatever you think, Anna. We just want a Happy Thanksgiving," she said. I rolled my eyes. I didn't think of this as a happy place all the time. I was sitting in frozen Iowa away from my beloved Georgia. And those bodies they found out there in the backyard must not have found this to be a happy place neither. But Miss Joyce was so fragile I always gave her the benefit of the doubt. She was stuck in her own world. I was stuck in her world, too. I finally talked her into the sweet potatoes.

So, it was decided I would make my sherried sweet potatoes with marshmallows on top, in place of that rice with gravy that Midwesterners like. I reasoned that I could make the sweet potatoes blend in to look more Iowa-like with their white marshmallow tops.

Thanksgiving Day came and I got up early, stuffed the bird, and popped him in the oven. He was a big, fresh bird from a farm close-by, and he would have to cook all day. Then I set my sights on getting ever'thing organized. I began to breathe easy after a while, 'cause things were coming together. I had cooked many a grand meal and learned the good ways to getting things done.

I set out a cheese dip, along with a tray of corn relish, pickles, olives, and the cutest, tiny pickled corns. The tray was beautiful and ever'one, upon arrivin', would get a little snack from it, along with a cracker or two. Dr. Joe greeted the kids with soda pop, and the adults got out the gin. I put the kids in the playroom with Fritzy, and yelled at Ruff for good measure, before I started to work my magic with the vegetables.

The adults were drinkin' and wouldn't notice a freight train, so I popped in once in a while, but wasn't too worried about them. Dr. Donald Calloway had a way of lookin' down that crooked nose of his that he broke playing football at the University of Iowa. He was an average lookin' guy, but rigid as a statue on Main Street and had just about as much personality. The only time he opened his mouth was to correct somethin' his wife said. She was very beautiful but equally dizzy, and he seemed to enjoy puttin' her in her place any chance he got. And the Mayor had too much personality if you know what I mean; it seemed like he never stopped talking for one second. His gabberin' and Miss Susan Calloway's gigglin' were the main sounds coming from the room. The Mayor was goin' on and on about some new company that was movin' to town. It just so happened the new company was buyin' a buildin' the Mayor owned. I ask you: Who was gonna make the money on that deal?

I was happy to be back in the kitchen and remember saying, "Good riddance to you Ruff. You stink like old garbage and sweat socks," as I kicked him out into the backyard. He was not only big, he was bigger than I even thought he was gonna be. I jes' know he was part horse. Now, Ruff had fur like a Fuller brush. It was gray like all the food in Iowa and about as ugly too. He had a long nose and legs like a horse, so he didn't have to reach very hard to grab somethin' off my kitchen counter. He would drive me crazy sometimes, 'cause I would look over and see that nose crusin' along the counter edge. That was the main reason I kept a keen eye on him, and I threw him outside every chance I got.

Ever' time I opened that back door to shoo Ruff out, I wondered about who might have been buried out there. On that day, I wondered if there was a family eatin' Thanksgiving dinner somewhere who was missin' whoever died and wonderin' where they were and what happened to them. But life keeps you so busy that, while somethin' like that is always in your mind, your brain cain't ponder on it too long, 'cause there is always somethin' else that needs attendin' to right at the same moment. On Thanksgiving Day, my brain had to be workin' jes' right, so I could coordinate having ever'thing ready at the right time so one thing wouldn't get cold waiting on somethin' else to finish cookin'.

I made green beans in a light butter sauce with mushrooms and onions. Now, color-wise, the green in those beans stuck outta the gray Iowa plate, so I had to make a plan. I put the onions and mushrooms on top to hide the green beans, and it looked real good. The crownin' glory was gonna be my vanilla bean cream cake with white fudge icin'. I think it's my best cake ever, 'cause it's made without butter, and instead of butter, you add heavy cream and eggs into the cake. Yum.

I was even gonna put some beautiful sugar-dipped red and green grapes around the cake's edge with some fresh ivy leaves as an accent. It was gonna be my own work of art. I was so excited about the cake. I visualized myself prancin' out with it on a platter at the end of our feast. But, things began to get goin' fast around me in the kitchen, and Ruff slipped in with some hungry kids that had been outside. "Anna, can we have something to tide us over until dinner?" Pete looked real pitiful. "Yeah, we're awfully hungry." Mick looked pitiful too. The two Calloway boys could be very convincin'. They always looked pitiful when they were workin' me for more food, 'cause their mother was a lousy cook, but no one knew it 'cause she never cooked. So, I gave Pete and Mick some rolls.

"OK. Grab a roll and be off." I relented about the roll and yelled them out of the kitchen. However, I didn't notice naughty Ruff, jes' watching and waiting for his chance to ruin my best meal of the year. He must have been part cat burglar, 'cause he snuck in stealth-like without me knowin' it.

About that time, Miss Joyce came in to see how things were goin'. We were talking about the second round of appetizers—which was my special ham in little biscuits with a sweet mustard-carrot sauce. I had them ready to put on a silver tray, and Miss Joyce was gonna pass them around. I turned my back on my perfect cake, jes' as the devil was sneakin' around my kitchen.

Miss Joyce looked over my shoulder and screamed. "Oh, Ruff. Dammit! Get off the cake." She jumped at Ruff and pushed him out the back door, and I turned around to see my beautiful cake had been licked almost clean by that wicked Ruffian.

Miss Joyce looked horrified. "What are we going to do, Anna?" I could see the whites of her eyes more than usual. She loved dessert.

"Oh, hell done settled its big ass on us today." I sat down on the kitchen stool. Then, I got right up close to the cake and looked it up and down; so did Miss Joyce. I could tell she didn't understand what I was thinking.

Miss Joyce and I scrutinized the cake for holes and whatnot, but it had been a clean lick. No bites. I straightened up my considerable body.

"Why, Miss Joyce, we are gonna do what all people do when they face somethin' bad." I paused to see if I would get any reluctance from my new partner in crime. None noted, I continued, "We are gonna pray and ask for forgiveness for the sin we are about to commit. We are gonna re-ice my creation and eat it right along with ever'one else—like we have good sense."

"Oh, Anna, we can't do that …" Miss Joyce still had that funny-sick look on her face.

I continued, "After all, how many times has Ruff kissed Fritzy with that long tongue of his? Is Fritzy dead from it? No. No ma'am. He isn't dead." I rested my case on that one.

"Oooo, we are bad, bad people, Anna." Then she started laughin' so hard she couldn't stop. Then I started laughin', and I couldn't stop. "Now shhhh. They're gonna hear us," I said.

We both laughed so hard we cried. That was the first time I'd ever done that. I always heard a body could succumb to laughin' and cryin', however, I'd never seen it until then. Pretty soon we were sitting on the floor of the kitchen, behind the counter, laughin' and cryin' so hard we couldn't stand up. I laughed so hard I could barely wield my knife or hold my considerable body up.

I got serious. "Now, Miss Joyce, let this be a lesson to you. That Ruff is Captain Hook reincarnated—and he is always lookin' for some of my good cookin'—and in a pinch he's gonna eat yours. While I am gone to Atlanta, you make him spend extra time outside." We both peered out the back door into the yard, and there was Ruff, with Mrs. Calloway's muffler, lookin' as innocent as original sin.

I thought Miss Joyce was gonna pull his whiskers out and make his carcass the next thing that was gonna get buried out there in the yard, 'cause she ran outside cussin' like I never heard her before. She ran all over the backyard after him, but Ruff thought it was a great game and just kept smilin' that naughty grin he had. He dodged her like a paper in the wind when you run up to it and try to catch it—it just keeps movin' outta your grasp. Miss Joyce got so flustered she came back inside and let Ruff have the muffler.

"That dog has ruined my dinner."

I thought to myself, 'Who did all the work for your dinner?' Me. And here's you callin' it your dinner? However, I held my tongue, 'cause she buttered my bread. I guess she could call it her bread, too.

I re-iced that cake like my knife had greased lightnin' on it, and Miss Joyce slipped out to the table and was real quiet. The other dinner preparations progressed without a hitch.

Then it was time to serve the dinner. Miss Joyce looked a little rattled, but they all sat there at the table drinkin' and didn't notice Miss Joyce actin' funny. However, I noticed she was doin' more drinkin' than normal. The adults all got tipsy and the children dug in like they hadn't eaten for days. The Calloway kids looked funny at the sweet potatoes, but they loved the marshmallows. So, they ended up eatin' the sweet potatoes, too. That's how you tempt kids. Cover somethin' they like over somethin' they haven't ever had before. They'll be suckers for it.

Then, it was time for the cake. I brought my beautiful cake out on a special stand—and it did taste and look perfect. Miss Joyce ate her piece of cake—real ladylike—and only looked up at me once with a silly grin while I was clearin' the plates. I noticed that she chewed like she had an obligation to do it. She didn't chew with the zeal a person usually has for my cream cake.

After I got ever'thing from dinner cleared away, I sat down on the kitchen stool. I was thinking how to kill that Ruffian, or else make him suffer a dog-disaster 'cause of his dog shenanigans. I was so deep in the thought of evil dog-tricks to play on Ruff that I didn't notice when Miss Susan came in to ask her own sneaky favor of me. She asked, "Anna, have you seen my muffler? I thought I came with it."

She reached into her purse and pulled out a compact and that real bright red lipstick that she wore and began touchin' herself up, pausin' to look over at me between glances in the mirror to check the lipstick and be sure there wasn't a single piece of dizzy blonde hair out of place.

"Why, no, Miss Susan. I haven't seen your muffler." I said this as I gazed over Miss Susan's shoulder to see Ruff givin' the muffler what-for. He was shakin' the hell out of it while he was runnin' around the yard holdin' his head up high so it wouldn't drag on the ground and get stepped on as he ran along.

Oh, Lord, once again I had the sin of omission sitting on my soul. I turned around to the counter so I wouldn't have to view my sin too closely.

Then Miss Susan asked what she really came in the kitchen to find out.

Chapter 14

Flowers Bloom

"Anna, could you start reading to Claudia, Pete, and Mick after school? I know you are the best at that, and you put so much into it," Miss Susan continued. "I could pay you a dollar a week for each child, and I promise you can send them home at 5 p.m."

I did like to read to the little ones every chance I got, plus I was excited, 'cause that meant I could send extra money to my kids in Atlanta. They'd been tellin' me about poor folks standin' in bread lines in Atlanta. President Herbert Hoover was tryin' to do things to get the country back in one piece again, but times were real tough.

So I told Miss Susan I would like that and Fritzy would, too. He gets so lonely for kids. Even though he was old enough at that point, he wasn't goin' to school, and I thought that was such a shame, 'cause he was sure smart enough. But the Worrells said the schools weren't set up for that sort of thing. I aimed to lay some pressure on them about that, but figured that in the meantime, Fritzy and I were doin' OK. Both of us were learnin' things together every day.

When I suggested to Miss Susan that we wait and start after Christmas, she said, "Well, I was thinking you could start right away until you leave for Atlanta. Then after you get back, too."

I didn't think too much about it at the time, but it made me wonder what she was up to. What was so hell-fire important she needed her kids taken care of in the afternoons so immediate? I hadn't heard any rumblin's from any folks in the town, but it still made me wonder. My first thought was that she must be helpin' her husband out at the office. Whatever the reason, I dismissed it from my mind.

Now, Miss Susan was beautiful in a Jean Harlow sort of way, with long blonde hair that fell over one eye and a slim body and no bosoms to speak of. But nothin' was ever jes' right with her, and she tended to whine with that little girl voice of hers about the smallest things. At our Thanksgiving dinner she sent the water back for more ice and said the gravy needed warmin' more. If I were Doc Calloway, I would've gotten a good bunch of sealin' wax for my ears, or else jes' learned to ignore her like she ignored her kids.

The kids were another story. All three of them were cute seven-, eight-, and nine-year-olds. They were so cute they almost looked like little cherubs, but they had too much energy and were way too loud. I figured I knew what to do with that type of kid. I would make sure the boys ran Ruff 'til he was ragged, 'cause I still could not bring myself to forgive Ruff for the cake disaster. I swear he knew exactly what he was committin' when he did that. And I couldn't think of anythin' naughty enough for his punishment, so I jes' let it ride.

One of the many things that bothered me about the Calloway kids was those two boys were always being so mean to that little girl. They would get their sister down on the floor and push her stomach just to make her break wind, and then they'd laugh their fool heads off. I'd yell at them to stop—and they would, but they would always start up again after my back was turned. Or, if the weather was bad, they would push her down in the snow to make her cry and wave her arms—jes' to see her make a snow angel. It was always those two big ones on the little one. It was frustratin' to see. She didn't stand a chance against them, and it was beginnin' to make her mean and snitchy like her mama. Her mama was always tryin' to grab at whatever would make her life better or easier. And we all know that when a woman feels threatened, she has to grab at the first thing that comes along. Miss Susan was that way, and I didn't want little Miss Claudia to turn out that way, too, but it was beginnin' to look bad for the little girl. She was beginnin' to get that look.

So, I did what any intelligent person would do. I gave the little girl her own time and space. I sent the boys in the backyard with Ruff and a ball every day. They did run that dog ragged, which he deserved, and the little girl got to sit with Fritzy and me and lick the bowl from my fudge cake, or whatever I was cookin' that particular day.

One day Miss Claudia asked me a simple question that proved to be anythin' but simple. "Tell me about Fritzy. How come he's that way?" Miss Claudia pointed her chocolate-covered finger in his direction and gave me that expectant look, which young white kids do, 'cause they're used to gettin' answers.

This caused Fritzy to give me his most annoyed look back, 'cause he didn't like it when people talked about him like he wasn't in the room. That's a pet peeve he had—and he had it for good reason—if you ask me.

I could tell we were startin' off all wrong with her pointy finger, but ignored the slight she made on Fritzy when she asked me. "Well, little thing," I told her, "first off, we don't point at other people and things—that shows our lack of breedin'."

Miss Claudia gave me an upside-down look and stuck the offendin' finger back in the bowl. I continued like she hadn't done that.

I went on, "Fritzy was born that way, but he's smart, so address him like he's a person and let him tell you what he wants."

Miss Claudia came over and got up close, eyeball-to-eyeball with Fritzy, and said, "Can you add two plus two?"

"Aruugh." He jiggled his foot four times.

"See, he knows." I pointed to his foot. "He's your age, so of course he already knows his numbers and alphabet. I bet he can read better than you can," I said that with a little tone to it, 'cause she needed to hear some tone.

Fritzy laughed, "Aruugh." I could tell he felt superior. It was what one would call a rare and beautiful moment for him, and it would stick in my mind for a long time to come.

Little Miss Claudia laughed again. "I bet you're gonna teach me more 'bout readin' and all sorts of things." She said this like it was my borne duty to do so.

"You can bet one of your nitwit brothers I'm gonna teach you more than you ever dreamed," I told her.

After that, we settled into our routine, and I read all kinds of books to the kids. The boys liked Mark Twain books and Miss Claudia liked princess stories, and Fritzy was jes' thrilled to be with us and didn't care what we read. I read every afternoon 'til my tongue jes' about fell outta my head.

One day, we had been readin' books while the boys were out runnin' Ruff ragged again, and little Miss Claudia asked me a question. "Will Fritzy ever get well?"

"Oh, you mean, walk and talk?" I looked over at Fritzy, 'cause he and I had talked about this recently. He knew his situation—even for a little kid—and we had decided that he should be aware of things from the get-go.

"Yes. Like that."

"No, not unless a miracle commences." I looked over at Fritzy, again, with my best apologetic face.

"Is he gonna die?"

I paused. The little twit had me there. So I told her, "Look. We all die. But, you won't have to think about that 'til you're shriveled up like a prune and go ever'where on a cane, and have grandchildren who ask you the same ninny questions."

She frowned, 'cause I had answered the question a little sideways. Little Miss Know-it-All asked again, "Is he gonna die?" and she nodded at Fritzy. I can't stand it when a kid won't give up with them why, why, why questions.

Fritzy had an angry look on his face. He was jigglin' that good foot and makin' his "Aruugh" sound. He hated not being addressed properly, and she did it again.

While she was pressin' me for an answer, I crossed the room, picked up a bunch of flowers and was standin' at the sink workin' on makin' them pretty for our Sunday dinner centerpiece. I was strippin' and clippin' the ends so they would fit in the vase. I sucked in my juices for this explanation: "See these flowers? They're all different types and colors—and they're all beautiful in their own way." I carefully pointed to all the different ones. "Some are actually more beautiful than others, and some people would argue which ones are the most beautiful, 'cause we all have a different opinion." I emphasized those words, so it would sink into her little, hard head.

"So?" She said this like I owed her an answer. They're like that, you know—thought 'cause I was the helper I was duty-bound to answer.

I knew this was gonna be a hard one to explain. She was used to readin' princess stories that always ended jes' right, but this wasn't gonna be one of her stories, and it would never end jes' right.

I started out like a preacher, lookin' to the heavens. "Well, over the next few days, some of these flowers will wilt and die—and some will continue on, as new lookin' as when I first made the bouquet." I pointed to the different flowers for effect. "Little girl, we are like those flowers." I looked over at the two kids to see what they were thinkin' and pressed on. "Some of us wilt faster than others and some jes' seem to go on forever—and we cain't know which is which."

There was a quietness in the room while the two kids eyeballed one another. I could tell they were wonderin' what kind of flower each was. That seemed to satisfy things, and we continued talkin' about flowers until the boys came in—cold and tired. Thank goodness they left rascal Ruff in the backyard.

I read to the kids for almost an hour, and afterward, the Calloway kids put on their coats to walk to their house on 4th Street.

Jes' as Miss Claudia was about to file out the door behind her hellion brothers, she leaned up to me and whispered, "I hope he don't wilt too soon."

I held her close and I whispered back in her ear, "I hope he doesn't, neither."

As the sun was goin' down that evenin' I stood at the window and looked out at the backyard and thought about that day's conversation havin' to do with dyin'. Of course, that got me back to thinkin' about those bodies again. Yeah, it came up in conversation. Ever'body that came over to visit the Worrells would ask questions, but since nobody knew any answers, it became one of those topics that made people's eyes dart around, and whoever brought it up would soon be clearin' their throat and start talkin' about the weather or one of the neighbor's ailments—anythin' to change the subject.

Chapter 15

Back for a Visit to Atlanta

The train rides back to Atlanta were never as much fun as that time when Miss Edwina and I were together ridin' up to Chicago. When I was with Miss Edwina, she bought us food, we laughed, and I clipped her for a month's wages playin' gin rummy. All the other trips I made back and forth were lonely, and I had to wear my maid uniform so people wouldn't be fearful of me. That way, they would think I was attached to someone white and that made it safer for me, but I still had to stay in my compartment almost the whole way, 'cause people of color weren't allowed in the dining car. I could only order food and take it back to my little sleepin' car. I had to order the big sleepin' car 'cause I was too big for the small berth. I was always glad when we finally got to Atlanta.

This was my third time back. Since I had jes' arrived in Iowa that first Christmas of 1927, I stayed in Iowa. That next year, I went to Atlanta twice. The only time I ever went back in the summer was that first year that I lived in Iowa, 'cause it was for Amelia's weddin' to Ceril. Then Hope and Gordon surprised me by plannin' their weddin' later that same year when I was home for Christmas. Faith turned around and surprised us all, runnin' off to elope with Newman the next summer. So, all of my babies were now married women.

I can recall the trip on that certain Christmas of 1929 so well. I lugged the things off the train and there was Camellia. All my down-at-the-mouth mood melted away 'cause my wonderful sister met me at the train station and hugged me with all her might. She started cryin' too. It had been a year since my last trip and she had aged during that time. I lied (forgive me, Lord), and said, "Don't you look good? I miss you so, so much." Take note, that wasn't a total lie 'cause of the way I said it.

Camellia asked me all about my life in Iowa, and I told her all about it but decided to leave out the part about bodies in the backyard. I didn't tell nobody back in Georgia about that, 'cause I didn't want people questionin' me about it. Hell, they'd probably find a way to think I had somethin' to do with it, since half the town already thought I might be a murderer on account of what happened to Martin.

As we walked off the gangway and into a taxi I said, "What's goin' on in Atlanta—did I miss anythin' being gone?"

"Well, as a matter of fact, you did miss a whole bunch. You remember Altus Andrews? He's in the pen." Now, Camellia said this with a delight I seldom see on her, and I jes' had to know why. She even giggled.

I had heard he got laid up in the hospital over that fight in the bar, but I didn't know they sent him to the pen. But Camellia explained to me it wasn't over that. It was over a house break-in. He tried to get inside some white folks' house and they caught him red-handed. She said he screamed like a stuck pig all the way to the jail. He was still real ugly and scary with that scar, so I am sure those white people were quakin' in their boots. Camillia said she heard the white folks shivered in fear for their lives when they caught him, and they had to hold a gun on him 'til the coppers got there.

I felt a twinge of sadness at that moment, 'cause Altus was jes' a pitiful person. He was manhandled by a mean mama and daddy that beat him every chance they got and told him he would grow up to be no-count. When that happens to a child, they usually oblige the parent and grow up jes' that a way. Altus was that way, and he ruined ever'one he came in contact with. If he jes' hadn't believed his parents, he might have been jes' fine. Which is the reason I always tell my children how good they are, and I make certain to tell them when they do a good job on somethin'. That way a person keeps strivin' for their all-time best to get praise on ever'thing they try—even after they grow up, they still hear that little voice in their head. I shudder to think how things might have turned out for Fritzy if the fickle finger of fate hadn't put us together. Lots of mamas and daddies of kids afflicted like that jes' send them away.

I hoped Altus would find reform in prison, and I made myself promise I would make some prayers for him, since he really, really needed them—and it didn't look like anyone else was gonna perform the service.

I changed the subject by askin' about the Parkers and ever'one on Mule Alley.

"Oh, Miss Edwina's workin' her fool head off with the children of the less fortunate, and some of her friends are even helpin', too. It's becomin' a big deal and they even havin' a bazaar to raise money. It gonna be happenin' this Saturday." Camellia looked expectant at me and continued. "She says we can set up a booth and sell pies. She said she'd buy the ingredients and we can cook in her kitchen." Camellia twinkled. "Then, we take a little profit and give the rest to her charity. I made a full month's pay last year, even after I gave some to the Children's Benevolence Fund. What do you think?"

I settled back in the taxi to think. I had to decide if I wanted to stick around Atlanta that long, 'cause I would have to see some of the folks that made me feel so bad after the Martin fiasco. On my last couple of trips back home, I usually made a quick round to say hello to Miss Edwina and then headed almost immediately off to Athens. This time, I decided that it was time for me to turn the other cheek toward those critical people, and realized I would see a bunch of people that had been good to me, too. I would ignore the ones that weren't, and it would be fairly obvious after this much time had passed—who was who.

So, we set off to make pies, and I made kitchen chitchat while we were workin'. "Camellia, guess what about pies in Yankee-land?" I said.

"Why Anna, I don't think about Yankee-land, much less about pies they eat," Camellia said, actin' like this was the most borin' topic in the world.

"Well, they don't know what the hell a pecan is up there," I told her. "Can you imagine life without pecans, much less life without a pecan pie?"

Camellia gave me a sad look and cookin' banter continued before she said that she could imagine life without a lot of things.

I ignored the statement and said, "Why, they even pronounce it pee-can, which sounds a bit odd. Since pecans are so hard to find up there, I do what I always do, I substitute and it turns out pretty good. I jes' make it with walnuts."

Camellia sniffed. "So, that's one more reason to come back here—for a pie rechargin'."

Wasn't that the truth! I bet we made about sixty pies in all. Yeah, a good bunch of kinds, too.

"Last year, I could only do about thirty, but I sold them for sixty cents each." Camellia fretted. "I know this is a whole bunch more and it's taking a chance, 'cause it's higher than my usual price, but Miss Edwina says the price can be higher 'cause it's for charity. I jes' hope people will buy pies again this year and help the charity even though their money seems to be gettin' tighter with this depression on."

We decided to keep them stored in Miss Edwina's kitchen overnight and set them up in the mornin'. Then, we'd be ready, and we could put some pretty tablecloths under them and maybe some greenery 'round, too. Well, we got the pies to the bazaar, and I saw a lot of friends, and those not-friends I was tellin' you about. The first person I saw there was Bee Bee Bennett. Bee Bee is very straightlaced and formal and she'd never been on my side. The reason was, I think she was sweet on Martin before we married.

"Why, Bee Bee, it is so good to see you." I gave her my best, teethy smile.

Bee Bee jes' looked me in the eyes and said, "Don't think I haven't forgotten the goin's-on with Martin. After all, he was such a nice man, and you jes' threw him away like the trash."

"Good to see you too, Bee Bee." I kept on walkin'. I knew what side of the fence that one was chewin' her cud on.

Then, I saw tall George's wife, who did most of the cleanin' and servin' at the Parkers'. "Hi, Miss Emily," I said. "Tell me how things are in your world?"

Emily smiled and said, "Pretty fine. We got new grandbabies and our son works with the railroad—it's a real good job. We all OK and thankful to have our jobs." But Emily looked pained as she went on, "Things look happy 'round here today, but you haven't seen the part that's hurtin' my heart. People are outta work. Children are being sent off to orphanages 'cause the parents cain't feed them. There are bread lines jes' to keep things goin'. It's horrible. Even white people with nice homes are being kicked outta of 'em. It's hurtin' us all."

Iowa had farmlands, which were savin' it. It wasn't as bad off as it was there where ever'one was sufferin'. But, it was still bad for all of us. "Thank goodness the girls graduated and got husbands. None have children yet, but I expect some soon. I guess they're waitin' until this depression gives itself up," I said to her.

"I know that Martin would have loved to see them all grown," Emily said. The sentence lingered in the air between us. I was a little uneasy about the Martin comment. I knew she was on my side, that wasn't what upset me, it was the fact that the whole thing was still in people's memories.

I asked God to give me strength. "Lord, help me to make the right decisions about Atlanta."

George was there helpin' with a booth, too, sellin' pinecone ornaments. They were beautiful and I had to have some, so I said, "How about I trade you two pies for six of those ornaments?"

Sure enough, we agreed that was an even trade. So, I took three ornaments for my daughters, one for Mother, and one for Fritzy. I'd hold it up when we did the shadow stories. Then, I'd give one to Dr. Joe and Miss Joyce so they could put it on their Christmas tree next year.

I have to say that bazaar was showin' all our best. So many people, all so happy to have a break from the misery of their worries about money, and Miss Edwina was in her element of happiness makin' money for her group. Folks were all about buyin' simple things like pies and pinecone ornaments that year, so Miss Edwina's charity came out OK. The department stores would be the ones sufferin'.

Sure enough we sold all our pies. I knew the icin' on the cake would be gin rummy night with Miss Edwina. She jes' hated to lose and I jes' loved to win.

So that night we played. Miss Edwina was down seven dollars. When I asked if she was sure she wanted to continue, she said, "Of course, I'm sure. I want to win it all. Why, I feel so good about the bazaar, I feel I can beat you, too!"

Well, after about three hours and more than a couple of drinks, Miss Edwina had lost about ten dollars all told. I felt positively rich with my extra money made from the pies plus ten dollars from Miss Edwina. I would put that away for a rainy day, but, I started thinkin' that if the darn depression was indicatin' anythin', the rainy day was already here and the clouds were set in for the long haul.

I noticed that Miss Edwina looked tired while we were playin' cards, and she wasn't her normal perky self after the bazaar. She'd looked a little thinner, too. So I asked her, "Miss Edwina, what's up with you? You look a little tired. You feelin' OK?"

"Oh, I'm just fine," she said. "I thought I was coming down with something, but the doctor says I'm fine."

She changed the subject, and I never gave it another thought.

Chapter 16

Christmas in Athens

I rode the train from Atlanta to Athens the next mornin', and it had been a full year since I'd seen my girls. My oldest, Amelia, drove over to the train station to pick me up. Hope and Faith, the twins, were back at the house cookin' and cleanin' to get ready for my arrival.

Atlanta is the capital of Georgia and a beautiful place. My mother had chosen with her heart when she settled in Athens. And it had been a good place for the girls when I needed them to have a safe place from the angst and energy of their father. Things always have a way of turnin' out and that sure did. The girls all had jobs with the same company, 'cause it hired Negroes, and particularly women, for the chain of hardware stores. They used them in the front office—somethin' that was very different from most companies. This hardware store was in the Negro section of town and had many people of color as customers. They hired the girls probably 'cause of that. It's good to have people that reflect your customers. For whatever reason, I was happy.

I saw Amelia standin' on the platform all bundled up, since it was breezy and cold—typical for a Georgia December day. I was coming down the train steps with a porter carryin' my satchel and made a run to put my arms around sweet Amelia.

I told her she was so beautiful and how lucky she was to be thin as a rail like Martin. "Now take care that you don't get like me after you have children. By the way, has anybody got any on the way?" I asked.

"Why no, Mama!" she said. "Not with this Depression and people not sure where their next meal is coming from. Are you crazy?"

I wasn't crazy, but I jes' love babies and had to ask that question. I tipped the porter and started walkin' toward the cars with my satchel. Amelia followed to catch up, 'sayin' I always walked like I was in a hurry. So we made it to the car, threw ever'thing in the boot, and drove to her house.

I asked her how she was doin' with her work and being a wife, and about her husband, Ceril. She told me Ceril worked very hard at his new job and had been promoted to line foreman in his area, and that the hardware store was doin' OK in spite of the Depression. The girls all did different things at that store—Amelia did accounts receivable, Hope did accounts payable, and Faith did payroll. They took turns preparin' lunch that they would bring with them to work and share when they ate together at lunchtime. Faith's husband, Newman, was a bricklayer. While he kept his job, it had gotten slow and he had to take a pay cut. Gordon was a school janitor. It was a miracle they were still doin' OK when so many others were less fortunate.

When we walked in the house ever'one was there—Ceril, Faith and Newman, Hope and Gordon.

Gordon grabbed me first and said, "Mama Anna take a load off right here and let us love on you a lot."

Ever'one got their turn huggin'. Then there was a brief silence while we all took ever'thing in before Hope said we'd best be gettin' over to see Grandma Gerdie.

My mama, Gerdie, was old but spry and could do about anythin' in the kitchen, which is why she was so loved by so many. We knocked on her door, and she answered with a big smile. I hugged her with all my heart and gently sat her back down. It felt good to sit with her and jes' let my heart flow out to her. I said, "Oh Mama, it's been hard without Martin, and without you and the girls, but it's been so good with the Iowa people. And so I know I'm doin' the right thing. I feel so good when I get in bed at night to say my prayers. I pray for you every night and for the girls and for their husbands. I pray that ever'thing will turn out all right for us all. That's a pretty big prayer."

My mother sniffed at the mention of Martin. "That Martin was a bad number; I told you not to marry him."

I told her old Martin was good for eighteen years, and that I knew cars that didn't even last that long. But that wasn't enough, she had to go in for the kill by askin' me what I thought was gonna happen in the next eighteen years.

"Heck, Mama, I have no idea," I told her. "All I know is that I have a good job with people that love me. The girls have good jobs and their husbands are doin' OK too—and these are supposed to be the bad times!" I thought about changin' the subject, but couldn't decide what subject I would change it to. She was gonna get me, no matter the subject.

Sure enough Mama started in again. "You don't know nothin' 'bout bad times. You don't know nothin' 'bout good people or bad people. You married Martin and look where you at. You had to sell your house and now you livin' with people that want you around—as long as they need you."

I felt like hangin' my head, and then I realized how angry my mama really was at the world, even down to the little things in it. I begged her not to be that way, 'cause ever'thing has a way of workin' out. Take Martin for instance, he was good and then he wasn't, but when he wasn't the good Lord took his tail to wherever—I'm hopin' heaven. I breathed in to get ready for the next sermon from Mama.

But then I said, "Sometimes the good outweighs the bad. We all have a little bad in us. Like when this dog named Ruff ate the icin' off the cake, and so we had to ice that cake again and eat it. We all got some bad."

Mama paused and said, "You really did that?"

"Yep, the devil is my witness and compatriot in it," I said. "We did jes' that. We ate that cake and that dog knew exactly what he had done. He sneered at me from the backyard. I'm sure he was thinkin', 'You idiot people—I got you again!'"

See it's good to get them off subject. That way they can't ream you out the whole time you're talkin' to them.

It was soon time to go over to Amelia's house and eat enough to feed a truckload of farm workers. Mama got her pocketbook under her arm and decided we should walk the two blocks to Amelia's house. As we walked along, I noticed the houses were beginnin' to look a little shoddy. They used to be all pretty on that street.

"Anna, people are without money these days, so the money they got goes to food, not paint or lawnmowers. Ain't you noticed how irritable peoples is? When you got no money it makes you angry as a red ant hill being stomped on," she said, and she was right.

On the way over to Amelia's Mama also told me, "You know, I don't like the one Hope is married to. He shifty. He got a wicked look in his eyes when he talks to the other sisters. I don't trust him. He's too light, too. He could be a spy."

"Now Mama, there aren't any spies among us. You're jes' gettin' strange on me," I said, and made a mental note never to set those two together at the dinner table; opposite ends of the table might be the best place for them.

Thankfully, we arrived at Amelia's. Ever'one was there and the table was set with new pretty dishes. We were all happy. I was sittin' at the table and I looked over at Gordon. He was the type that people noticed for his good looks, and I suppose his being so handsome might have swayed me away from lookin' at him with more scrutiny before. I had never looked at Gordon the way my mama did, but when I saw him through her eyes, it made me nervous. He was chewin' with his mouth open. He looked bored like he couldn't wait to be away, too. I began to fear he was a shifty fella after all, and I noticed he pinched Hope on her arm, one time hard, when she said somethin' he didn't like. I didn't take my eyes off him after that. He looked around to see what people were doin', as if he was taking mental notes on ever'one. And Hope seemed a little on edge, now that I was taking note of such.

Amelia said, "What do you think of dinner? I cooked it on my new stove that Ceril bought me for Christmas!" Ceril had gotten a bargain on that stove, 'cause the stores were practically givin' things away jes' to get any business. Mama smiled a big grin showin' some teeth gaps and said, "It's the best pork roast I ever had, and I've had a lot." We all laughed, 'cause Mama looked sure enough like she'd had a lot of pork.

Amelia suggested we all have some coffee and dessert in the living room while she cleared things away. So we got up and filed in the Christmas-decorated room with laughter and kind words to one another. We were standin' there gettin' ourselves together to leave after some polite conversation, when Gordon leaned over and said, "I heard that Altus is in the pen again."

I really wanted to change the subject, but he had me there.

"I also heard that he real angry at you 'cause he convinced that you cursed him over Martin."

"I did no such thing!" I said, and the room suddenly drew quiet and all the eyes were on me. I looked away.

Then I said, "I haven't heard from him since the day Martin died. He's been incarcerated almost the whole time for things he chose to do."

Gordon gave me a leery smile and I shuddered. He continued, "I hear he's comin' for you when he gets out."

"Pshaw!" My eyes rolled, nothin' seemed real, and I didn't believe him. It was a plain, bald-faced lie. He would sure have to come a long way to get me. Heck, most people can hardly find Iowa—he'd have to do some real good huntin'. I laughed, but you could tell it was a nervous one. I didn't want anybody sneakin' up on me in the middle of the night. I cursed Gordon for tellin' me somethin' so horrible and makin' me uneasy for the rest of my visit.

After a while, ever'one got their coats and left with a bunch of hugs and kisses. Gordon leaned over and hugged me. As he did, he said, "Don't fear Altus, he ain't that bad. I've known him for years."

Well, with that my heart stopped. Ain't that bad? Even though I had felt some sorrow for him on account of his upbringin', I still feared him more than any livin', breathin' thing. No wonder Mama didn't like Gordon. I was now seein' him in the right light.

We walked back to Mama's house, and I was quiet, thinkin' about what Gordon had said. It really bothered me that he chewed with his mouth open, too. How come I'd never noticed that before? Where was my head when we had Hope's wedding jes' a year ago? I was blinded by the wedding wonderfulnesses. I was like every mother of the bride; I was focusin' on the bride and not the groom. I notice at most weddings, the groom jes' looks like a deer in the headlights—'cause they are! And that wedding was no different. Gordon smiled a lot and that's why I thought he was so nice. All that smilin' makes a mother happy, and then the reception and the cake and what-not jes' takes a mother to new heights of happiness. It's like the groom is this mannequin standin' there getting' photographed. They jes' are there to take up space and say, "I do."

I stayed at my mama's house and not another word was spoken about Gordon. He didn't say another thing to me about Altus when we had several family get-togethers that week, and Mama didn't mention Gordon again, neither. I was careful to make sure they weren't seated together at any function, and I made double sure I didn't sit by him neither.

The happy holiday was drawin' to a close when I realized that I would be goin' home the day after Christmas. I felt glad and also sad all at once 'cause I wouldn't be back for a long while, but I was glad to go back to Iowa jes' the same. I liked the routine there, and the Worrells paid me so well. I had made a good start at gettin' the Calloway kids whipped into shape; I even thought they would turn out to be OK. Both docs liked me. My own kids were able to have all the little extras from the money, and I sometimes felt it replaced me in a good way—not that I thought I could be replaced.

On Christmas Eve mornin' Mama and I were makin' some sugar cookies with little decorations on them, and I was cuttin' red and green jelly beans up and makin' little holly designs with the pieces. Mama was poppin' the cookies in the oven, and I was decoratin' them while they were still hot, so the jelly bean pieces would stick. Last, I sprinkled raw sugar on them.

Hope knocked at the door and after we ushered her in, she said, "I wanted you to know that Gordon said not to worry 'bout Altus."

The hairs on the back of my neck stood up when she said that, 'cause that meant they had talked about it and it was weighin' on Hope, too.

I asked her how long she had known that Altus and Gordon were friends, and she said that she never really knew Altus, but Gordon used to see him around.

"I don't know what around means, but he's not a good person, and you and Gordon steer clear of him. You hear?" I told her.

"OK, Mama. He's where he's at for quite a while," she said and she started gettin' ready to leave, but not before she plucked a warm cookie from the wax paper it was sitting on. We all hugged and she said she would see us that night at church.

Christmas Eve we all gathered at the church. The plan was to listen to Reverend Franks and then go to Amelia's house again for dinner afterward. But when we got there, Hope and Gordon weren't at the church, and we waited around in the anteroom until we had to get in to the service so as to get a seat. I kept lookin' around during the first song to see if they were jes' late, but they never showed.

"Faith, Amelia, where's your sister?" I asked, and they replied, "We don't know, Mama. She said she was gonna be here." But Amelia looked over at Faith, and I could tell there was somethin' they weren't tellin'. They had that look of conspiracy. I let the topic drop and we went on to Amelia's house afterward.

I knew the only way I was gonna get the truth was to divide them like the cops do when they have suspects. What else could I do? But in all the bustlin' around I never got a good chance to corner either one of them.

That night at dinner Newman gave me the feelin' that he wanted to tell me somethin'. He was a decent hardworkin' man, and I knew he loved my daughter with all his heart. Thinkin' that Newman might tell me somethin', I purposely sat by him at the dinner. At first we made small talk, and then we talked about Altus being in jail.

"Did you know Altus at all?" I asked him.

"Why no, Miss Anna," he said. "My friend J. Frank told me to steer clear of him and not ever waste my time gettin' to know him." Newman said he was very glad that he paid attention to J. Frank, and I was, too.

"Altus was bad and he tempted those around him to be bad right along with him. I don't think Martin would have done the things he did if he hadn't been influenced by Altus," I said before changin' the subject. "What do you think about Hope and Gordon not being here?"

At about that very moment Hope came bristlin' in with her hair a bit mussed up from the wind and light mist outside.

"Mama, Gordon's not feelin' well; he's got a bug, so I stayed with him awhile until I thought I could leave." Hope said this with genuine feelin' as she looked around the table.

Ever'one nodded in understanding approval, except me. I knew somethin' was not right.

"Well, we're jes' glad you didn't catch that bug," I said.

Hope nodded.

I didn't see Hope again after Christmas Eve festivities. She said that she had the crud from Gordon and didn't want to give it to us. So, the day after Christmas rolled around and I kissed ever'one good-bye and went back to Iowa. I kept worrin' so much about Hope that I forgot about angry Altus. I didn't even think about the dead bodies in the Worrell's backyard. Soon I was back in Marshalltown and my mind had no choice but to shift into keepin' the folks there happy and taken care of.

Chapter 17

Extra Work and Somethin' Funny About That Phone

Soon enough, it had turned 1930. Things rocked right along back in Iowa and the Calloway children continued to act better under my considerable influence. I wondered to myself how children can act so terrible. Some children get the idea about what we're tryin' to teach them and others act like they're tryin' to get loose from ever'body and ever'thing. Those Calloway children acted somewhere in between, but they acted like their mama never told them, "No."

I decided I would rectify that. The first thing we dealt with were manners. No hats on in the house, no wipin' your nose with your hand or sleeve, coverin' your cough—that sort of thing. And what I consider the worst offense of all: chewin' with your mouth open. Mick Calloway was especially bad about this, and one day I said, "Mick, have you ever done show and tell day at school?" I asked this question as he was eatin' a peanut butter and jelly sandwich. That sandwich looked terrible as he opened his mouth with every chew and review.

"Sure, Miss Anna." Mouth open.

Fritzy started laughin', "Aruugh." He knew where I was goin' with this conversation.

"Well, was there anythin' you didn't want people to see about you?" Mouth open again.

He thought for a second, "Sure, Miss Anna." Mouth open more.

I got out my mirror and I said, "Now Mick, we're seein' somethin' about you we don't want and that's what's in your mouth. Ever'one open your mouth."

Ever'one dutifully opened their mouths to Mick. He was seriously offenced, and his mouth never opened again while he was chewin', but every once and a while his sister would open her full mouth to him and say, "Show and tell." Jes' to bother him. That was our joke and it really got under his skin. Anytime somebody forgot, they got show and tell.

Fritzy could also do show and tell and he thought that was real fun. He was always there with us and it was good when he could be part of it, too.

Now, in those days, Doc Calloway and Dr. Joe both took in what we call back door clientele. Those were people that had no money, no job and had nothin' to trade with. In a depression, when you don't have nothin' to trade, you're outta luck 'cause you need to have somethin' the good doctors need.

The back door people would come after hours, and they were usually very old or very young. It seems the in-betweens didn't need a doctor or else they had the money or somethin' else to pay with. While Doc Calloway really specialized in the younger people and Doc Worrell was the one that generally saw the older ones, when it came to the back-door folks, whichever doc could get to them first was the one to see them. It really was a kind act on the part of both of the doctors, but ole Doc Calloway got real impatient with the older people. He was accustomed to scarin' the kids he treated into thinkin' they would die if they didn't do exactly what he said. The old people didn't always do exactly as told, and so he would make a fuss about that. This wasn't a problem for Dr. Joe 'cause he was good with ever'body.

Dr. Joe was seein' fewer patients during the day and more at night, 'cause times were gradually gettin' worse. There were people without jobs here in Iowa now, and corn prices had plunged, so even the farmers were havin' trouble. So, after 5 o'clock on many days, right after the Calloway kids went home, I would go over to his clinic and lend a hand. His nurses were tired and had children and families that needed them after 5 p.m.

His nurse, Miss Francis, was so nice to me and helped me learn some of the methods to seein' patients. She showed me how to take the patient's chart and work on it so the patient would have a history. This was very rare that people let a Negro do such things. I think it was 'cause I was cheap labor and also Dr. Joe thought it was a good thing to enable the nurses to go home. I usually had the Calloway kids sent on, and Miss Joyce liked to sit and crochet with Fritzy—jes' the two of them—and that freed me up to work with Dr. Joe. I became his extra hands. I learned a lot about doctorin' and it helped me learn what Fritzy needed, so this was a good thing all around. Miss Francis would review what I had done the next day and leave me notes on how to improve. She was very nice about it and we got on well.

Sometimes he and I wouldn't finish until 7 or 8 o'clock, and even then we had to turn some folks away until the next night. On those nights I got to see what Dr. Joe was really like. He was a good person and did not put himself up above the patients like doctors are sometimes wont to do. He spoke to the patients as equals. But somethin' I noticed and thought odd was how Dr. Joe would sometimes leave the examinin' rooms and go back to his office to use the phone. He'd close the door and be gone, never more than five minutes at a time—but constant, like several times an evenin'. I figured he wanted to talk in private to Miss Joyce, so I didn't pay it any mind.

One night we came in extra late, and Miss Joyce was a bit miffed that Dr. Joe hadn't called to let her know he'd be so late. She had set the table for dinner with the food I had made earlier, and now it was cold as stones on the plates. Dr. Joe was properly apologetic and I warmed the dinner up—but sometimes even Jesus cain't bring somethin' back, and this was one of those times. We listened to Walter Winchell on the radio and then we all went to bed. While Fritzy and I were sayin' our prayers, I realized that Dr. Joe hadn't been callin' Miss Joyce while he was at the office; he was callin' someone else during those times he went back into his office. I racked my brain and figured the only other people he would call could be a bookie, or a girlfriend, or his mama—but his mama was not around and she went to bed at sunset anyway. I hoped it was a bookie. We said an extra amen for the doctor that night.

That night I asked God why he let things like Fritzy, the Depression, and all the sick folks happen. It seems sometimes like God must be on vacation. But I decided these things happen 'cause God is busy and he gets distracted and bad things crop up. Then he has to deal with them after the fact. Kind of like puttin' a kettle on to boil—if somethin' doesn't remind you to watch it, then you forget and all manner of problems can happen. That's why we all gotta keep prayin' and sayin', "Lord, help us." It keeps God pointed at the problems that need fixin,' kind of like that squeaky wheel that gets the attention.

They say God made man like him. And we know that people float in and outta our lives, and jes' 'cause they're out sometimes doesn't mean you should stop thinkin' about them or won't be there for them when they need you. Same thing with the people buried in the backyard. Someone had to be thinkin' about them somewhere, but their kinfolk were probably jes' like the rest of us—busy all the time jes' tryin' to keep their heads above the water. Their lives had to go on in spite of the fact that whoever these people were, they had to be missin' from their lives. I prayed for them and their families who might be lookin' for them.

Chapter 18

School Days

One afternoon when the Calloway kids arrived, Miss Claudia announced she was gonna attend the second grade and learn her cursive letters. She went on and on about school and then looked over and asked me if Fritzy was ever goin' to school. I tried to change the subject by talkin' about how instead of goin' to school I had learned ever'thing from that white girl in the family my parents worked for. I was hopin' by my not goin' to school that might somehow make poor Fritzy feel better about not goin'.

Then I got to thinkin' about what a shame it was that Fritzy was so smart and eager to learn but he couldn't go to school like the rest of the kids jes''cause he was different. Now, I didn't know nothin' about Iowa schools or any schools for that matter. But I went down to the school and convinced them to let Fritzy go to school if I went with him to see after his needs.

Oh, it did take a lot of convincin', but it was finally decided that I could take Fritzy to the bathroom inside the teachers' lounge. The ladies' bathroom happened to have two stalls and they designated one jes' for Fritzy and me to use. That also solved their concerns about a Negro woman usin' the same toilet as the white folks. Why, even the mayor got involved in these discussions. How embarrassin' is that?

So Fritzy and I did, indeed, go to school and enjoyed our time at school even more than the other kids there, 'cause the opportunity to go to school at all was no ordinary thing to either of us. Since he was seven years old and proved to the teachers that he knew as much or more than most of the others, even though he hadn't attended first grade, he started school as a second grader.

Fritzy couldn't jes' pick up his books and walk to school. Miss Joyce would get the car around, and then I would have to carry him out with all his things for school and a diaper bag, like for a little kid. Then, we'd have to have lots of food and water for him 'cause he has to eat a little all day long. We also had to resolve gettin' Fritzy's chair up and down the few concrete steps that the school buildin' had outside. Thankfully, the gym teacher and another male teacher agreed to help us each mornin' and afternoon with that. It was a big deal, but worth it all 'cause I got to sit there with him in school and learn all the things I didn't know or pay attention to before. I always knew that learnin' was the best thing a person could do, and I suddenly got a chance to do it formal-like for the first time in my life.

The kids all crowded in on that first day of school that year. Fritzy and I tried to be quiet, but his chair squeaked a little as we rolled in. I made a mental note to myself to get Dr. Joe to oil it that night. We sat next to the door and Fritzy wiggled a little, and then ever'one got quiet. When the kids were put in little groups they didn't want to be in ours, 'cause we were so different. But I let them touch my face if they wanted to, so they could see if my color really stuck to me. These Iowa people were very curious, 'cause they had very few colored people here in Marshalltown, and their food is even white. I dutifully answered ever'one's questions about why Fritzy was the way he was, and after that we got down to learnin'. It helped havin' the Calloway kids there. They were the closest thing that Fritzy could ever call friends. But, I noticed the kids still stared at him all the time.

Sure, there were kids there that acted like Fritzy had the plague or somethin' and others that tried to make fun of him. Of course, those Bishop boys were always among the troublemakers. But it only took a few evil eye castin's their way on my part to make them scared to cross us too much. And I always made sure Fritzy was clean and cleaned up good after taking him to the bathroom each time, so nobody noticed anythin'. We even slipped in and outta that teachers' lounge inconspicuously during times the kids were outside at recess, so nobody had extra ammunition to tease Fritzy about being different.

It was hard to watch him with that look in his eye. He'd often look over at me and wiggle every answer to questions that the teacher would pose, and he was always right. He would have given anythin' to be able to write. Poor Fritzy couldn't do writin', and he watched the teacher and the other children with real envy, 'cause he knew he would be good at it if he could be like the other kids. But he was already readin' ahead of the other children and he was so smart.

It made me sad to know he was so ahead of the rest in his head. He probably would have been a doctor like his daddy. But, as it was, he would always be a little boy in a wheelchair. But you know, every time we get to feelin' too sorry for ourselves, we have to know that we got a better hand in life than some others out there. I shudder to think of all the smart kids like Fritzy who not only didn't get to go to school, but didn't even have a normal home life neither on account of their parents jes' not knowin' how to take care of them, or not being strong enough to. Many of them were jes' put away in institutions and treated like animals in those days.

One of the things that interested Fritzy was havin' me read the newspaper to him after school. The Calloway kids weren't as interested as Fritzy, but I thought it was good for the whole bunch to learn what was goin' on in the world, so we always did a little readin' of the paper along with readin' their favorite fiction stories. The newspaper had real stories about weddings and funerals, murders, business happenin's, and a whole bunch more. I read it all out loud and Fritzy loved it most. Every once in a while, there'd be a story all about the bodies we had in the backyard, and I would save that story to read later jes' to Fritzy. It was somethin' that I think his mother might have preferred that we skip over, but he liked it and I did, too. It was our little secret.

Those bodies were so interesting 'cause no one could identify them. They were a real mystery. The people who had lived there in the house at the time of the deaths were gone. The newspaper said they moved away to Wisconsin and were interviewed via telephone. They couldn't shed any light on the events. It described them as Dr. and Mrs. Randall Phillips—retired. But somethin' else was fixin' to happen that would pause our thoughts about those bodies for jes' a little while.

Chapter 19

A Bad Thing at the Circus Brings Good Out of the Worst

The most excitin' thing about Marshalltown was the circus. It came from Chicago on its way to Omaha and needed to stop midway, so we always got the big circus and lots of circus people in town. They'd stay about a week during the early fall and take a little R & R. When they'd do their shows, we'd flood right in like bugs to a light bulb.

It was always great fun to see the circus performers in town. They looked like regular people without the bright lights and their showy costumes, but when we saw them on the street, it's as if we were expectin' somethin' else. One time, we saw the contortionist ridin' a bicycle down Main Street. I half expected him to stand on the handlebars—of course he didn't. The tattooed lady showed up ever'where in town, too—at the store, in the pharmacy, at the bank. She would try to be incognito with a hat and long sleeves—even in the beautiful weather. But those tattoos were on her hands and face, too, so she didn't hide it too well.

The beautiful weather was at its best in the fall and always perfect for the midway. The whole town closed down and ever'one took some time off for the circus. Both of the docs closed their offices and let ever'one go for the afternoon, and the Mayor declared a school holiday. Dr. Joe and Miss Joyce and Fritzy and I all walked the midway on that Friday afternoon. Mayor Millichap also made a citywide proclamation that it was Circus Day in Marshalltown. He gave a borin' speech that Donny Doc Calloway helped him write. They were thick as thieves and related somehow.

We weren't movin' very fast 'cause there was so much to see, but we had jes' turned the first curve of the midway. The crowds filled up the whole midway and you could smell the popcorn and hear the calliope music. Dr. Joe and Miss Joyce had already lost money on the nickel toss and they didn't much care that it was rigged. They jes' kept flickin' the coins out there—over and over. No penny or nickel or quarter was gonna stay in those saucers 'cause of the angle they were throwin' from.

"Now, don't waste your money like that. That hawker looks too fat and happy." I pointed to the nitwit runnin' the arcade, but they were mesmerized by the sound somehow. The coins kept makin' this strange sound when they hit the glass saucers.

"Now Anna, sometimes it's not the money or winning that makes it fun, it's the trying." Dr. Joe laughed as he said that, and Miss Joyce and Fritzy sided with him. So I was the odd colored-woman out on that one.

Mayor Millichap came up and hugged Miss Joyce and shook hands with Dr. Joe. I thought he was gonna kiss Fritzy like politicians are wont to do, but he jes' tussled his hair. Fritzy looked relieved.

The Mayor smiled and continued to talk about the wonderful deal he cut with the circus to spend their restin' time there. "Yep, they love us because they get a chance to rest and not be bothered when they are here. Then they give us their most special show while they're here. Why sometimes they even try out new routines for our enjoyment," he bragged.

I was thinkin' to myself, "Yeah, that way if it isn't a good routine they can scrap it before they go to a big city that would give them a bad review in the newspaper. They can test it out on us."

All of a sudden, a huge whoosh sounded through the crowd and then a horrible crash. It sounded like a lot of metal was being dropped from the sky. The ground shuddered.

Mayor Millichap immediately started for the exit without lookin' back. That's what politicians do. They get out when the gettin' is good. That way they can come back later like they weren't a part of whatever the ruckus was.

Dr. Joe knew that sound wasn't good and was immediately on high alert. We walked straight toward the noise. The Ferris wheel was hangin' like a toy on its side. I could hear this creakin' sound, like a large tree before it snaps. It's a fearful sound and one I don't ever want to hear again.

Miss Joyce said she would take Fritzy home so that I could stay with Dr. Joe and lend a hand. I took straight off in the same direction as Dr. Joe, and had no idea what I was walkin' into. I was suddenly aware of wailin' voices and screamin'. Whatever it was, was gonna shake me up—I jes' knew it.

Dr. Joe was already in the middle of it, and he looked up when I came near. "Anna, go to the office and get every bit of supplies you can. Then, call the hospital in Ames and tell them we're going to be bringing about 20 people to them tonight. See if they can send some crews and ambulances out to help for now," he said to me.

I took off like I had been shot from one of those circus cannons. But, I realized I didn't have a car, so I started to look around. The first person I saw was old crusty Bishop, and I knew I would have to contend with the worst if I asked him, but I didn't have a choice. So, I ran over to him and said, "Mr. Bishop, there's a lot of hurt ones and Doc Worrell wants me to get to the office and bring back supplies. Can you drive me there?"

I expected his nasty grin, but what I got was a look of real concern. "Anna, come with me, the car is over here. I was a field medic in WWI, so I can help, too," he said.

The worst part was that I figured I had to ride with all three of his junior hoodlums. They didn't say a word and neither did I. The hoodlums jes' stared back at me like I was a dog. I hoped he wasn't gonna bring them with us, and the answer came quickly.

"OK boys, there's lots of hurt people and you need to learn how to help sooner or later, so you're going to learn to help now." Bishop pointed them in the direction of the Ferris wheel. "Now help carry people to the ambulances that will be coming in the next few minutes."

We drove off in a cloud of dust and made it to Dr. Joe's office in record time. We both jumped outta the car, I found the key under the rock out front, and we ran in. I turned on the lights and we loaded up the car as fast as we could. Bishop knew what to take and yelled what he wanted. I bet it only took about two minutes to load ever'thing up before we were on our way back. I spent thirty seconds of it callin' the hospital in Ames.

The first thing I did was rush over to Dr. Joe to show him the things we brought and tell him about Bishop being a field medic in WWI. Bishop came over, ready to get with it.

A young girl was lyin' on the ground. Bishop and I rushed over to her and Dr. Joe said, "Bishop, dress the wound and tell me if an artery has been cut. If one has, then you need to staunch the bleeding." Bishop dutifully obliged him. As we worked, I heard those Bishop boys gruntin' and pushin' the bent metal off the survivors all around us. I couldn't look up, there jes' wasn't time, but I learned right then that people aren't all bad and that they can change. Those boys did in a matter of minutes. They went from do-nothin's to do-somethin's, but they still had the stupid expressions that some young people always seem to have—only time can take care of that.

Bishop said, "Anna, help me here, I'm going to take off my belt and wrap it around her arm. Then I'm going to help the next person. You stay with her and remove the belt every five minutes or so. Here, hold her good hand."

I dutifully held the good hand and looked over at the other arm and hand. I could tell they were crushed. I said to her, "My name is Anna and I'm gonna help you get through this."

Before I could say anythin' else, she said her name was Paula and she asked me: "Why is my arm so numb? It feels very strange. I feel strange, too."

She looked into my eyes and I saw her fear. I had been wearin' a light jacket, so I took it off and put it over her as best I could. I got her a little more comfortable and held her head in my lap. "Now, Miss Paula, I am not gonna leave you through this. I am gonna make sure that you get some help right now, and that they sew your pretty little arm up and make it good as new," I said. Lord, help me, I'm lyin' again, but this is a good lie and I would tell it again if I was in the same spot once more.

I could tell she was slippin' away, so I called Dr. Joe over. He took over and had a long gaze over her. Then, he shook his head at me and said she had lost a lot of blood and might lose more than her arm. I couldn't let this sweet young girl go that way. Dr. Joe moved away. I glanced over and saw where the first ambulances were rollin' up. This beautiful, young girl had so much more livin' left, and so without thinkin', I grabbed her up and ran like hell over to the first ambulance in the row.

I remember thinkin' she didn't weigh anymore than Fritzy. I guess I was bigger and faster and I got us there first, ahead of the rest of the hurt people. I had Miss Paula in the back of the ambulance faster than the driver could get outta the car and I yelled to him, "Now you get us on outta here, as fast as your ass can take us." He jumped in the cab and the tires threw up dust as we rolled out. I hadn't scared him totally, 'cause he pulled the glass window down and began to tell me what to do as we rode along. "OK, you're going to give her some morphine to help the pain. Break it open and put it in her mouth."

I obeyed.

"Then, you're going to make sure she's not bleeding anywhere else. Then, you're going to open her mouth and make sure there's nothing in it."

I obeyed again.

"Then, you're going to roll her over on her good side so the blood isn't rushing out as fast. Raise her feet." I did it. "Then, you're going to try to put some gauze on the wound. Now press hard and hold it." I did ever'thing he told me.

He told me his name was Marty and promised to get us there in time. I liked his rough attitude, and I especially liked his not being angry about the cussin' I did before.

I had never heard a siren from inside an ambulance before, and it didn't sound as loud as I thought. I figured Marty was deaf from always being around the noise, but discovered he wore earplugs. He turned out to be a real nice guy. When we stopped at the University Medical Center, Miss Paula was barely hangin' on. The staff came runnin' out with a gurney and took her away. I stood there jes' watchin' them take off, frozen in fear for her, but Marty grabbed me and said, "Sit up front—we're going back." I didn't want to go back. This had been hard enough.

"I can't go back, Marty," I said.

"Oh, yes you are. I'm taking us right back. There's some more that need to get here and you're going to help," he said and smiled. "So, get your Negro ass back in that ambulance." He laughed.

The ride out had been fast and scary, but the ride back was like waitin' for honey to set up. It jes' wouldn't end. Marty talked. "This is the most excitement we've had in the past two years, since there was a fire at the furnace plant. It really wasn't all that scary because the men all wear gloves and things; nobody was really hurt. This is different. If that little girl lives, it's because you sprinted her across that field like you were at the Drake Relays."

I had no idea what the Drake Relays were, but thought it must have been a compliment.

The next person we picked up was an older girl with a nasty gash on her forehead. She was lookin' around and actin' a little dazed. Her boyfriend was with her and he was holdin' his leg. I presumed it was a hurt foot, 'cause he seemed OK otherwise. When I held out my very black hand, the girl seemed a little shy about taking it and that's when I realized she had never touched a Negro person before.

I helped them both into the ambulance and we took off. This time Marty didn't hurry quite as fast, but he kept his foot on the gas, nevertheless.

Marty started the minute we got in. "OK, Anna, what I need you to do is make sure that she can see one set of fingers when you hold them up. If she sees two than you got some problems."

"OK, Miss, how many fingers am I holdin' up?" I asked her. The girl started cryin' immediately 'cause she had heard Marty tell me. "I see two sets of fingers instead of one," she whined. "Oh, am I going to die?"

Marty leaned back and yelled, "No, but you're gonna have a hell of a headache tomorrow."

Then I looked at the boy. His foot was so swollen I couldn't get his shoe off and it was apparently broken.

We got to the hospital and I had to get them out—but I also wanted to see if little Miss Paula had made it. We slowly got outta the ambulance, and I could see where the other ambulances had pulled in ahead of us. There were lots of people millin' around now. Some were cryin' and some jes' looked lost. I spied Doc Calloway. He said Dr. Joe was still inside.

Dr. Joe looked tired. I could tell he was ready to go home. But I couldn't stand it any longer. I had to know how Miss Paula was doin'. I told him all about her and her condition and he agreed to go in and ask about her.

Then Marty asked me, "Anna, what were you doing at the circus? Do you work there?"

Ha. Ha. Jes' 'cause I was colored, he thought I was jes' passin' through with the circus! There weren't very many people of color around Marshalltown in those days. I explained to him that I worked for Doc Worrell and took care of his little son who was confined to a wheelchair.

We sat down on a bench and it began to get cold. I remembered my jacket. It had gone with Miss Paula, and now I was cold and I shivered. About that time, Doc Calloway and Dr. Joe walked out together. They looked a sight with blood on their clothes.

Then Dr. Joe smiled and told me that there were some parents who wanted to thank that big colored woman they saw runnin' across the field with their daughter in her arms. "They said they were running to catch up to that woman, but she was faster than the Drake Relays," he said.

There goes mention of the Drake Relays again. What the heck was it, I wondered.

In a flash, an older couple was standin' in front of me. There were tears in the mother's eyes and she grasped my hands in hers. She couldn't say a word. Suddenly, my jacket was put on my shoulders and the man said, "I know that you probably have not had an easy life, but we would not have any life at all—if it weren't for you. You saved us tonight."

I told them I jes' did what I felt—and I felt we could make it. "I knew I could make it to the ambulance before anyone else, 'cause I carry a little boy about her weight around a lot. He's in a wheelchair. I guess you could say I've been practicin' for this particular run for the last couple of years." I didn't mean to run on, but it jes' came pourin' out.

I told them about workin' for Doc Worrell and made them promise to call our office and let us know how she was doin'. I watched them go back into the hospital. It turns out they saved Miss Paula and her arm. It didn't exactly work perfect like it had before, but at least she wasn't permanently maimed. It took a lot of surgeries and years of healin' and therapy, but I had saved a girl and her arm, too.

As we turned to go that evening, I noticed Bishop standin' next to his car. He was gonna be our ride home. I didn't know whether to expect his personality to be the same old one as before or the almost heroic one I had seen earlier that night. Yes, even ole Bishop and his boys had showed some good in their souls that day. I sat in the backseat and fought off numbin' sleep, 'cause that run had taken it outta me.

The circus ended up stayin' in Marshalltown for an extra week. Ever'one was tryin' to heal for a spell and the circus needed time to get the Ferris wheel fixed. The engineer had to send to Chicago to get parts and so the performers, animals, and roughnecks all took a rest right there in Marshalltown. It turns out, most circus people are from other parts of the world, and they usually have their own doctor that travels with the show, and that doctor usually speaks several languages. However, their doctor was down with appendicitis in Chicago, so the circus was on their own. I was glad that Doc Calloway and Dr. Joe were around during the disaster and were able to come in so handy when the circus really needed them, too.

The accident at the circus proved to be somethin' people would talk about for a long time. The Mayor made a proclamation and called it "Circus Renewal Week." We were all asked to help the people any way we could. The news carried pictures and stories and of course it made the front page of the newspaper. On the Sunday edition, there was a picture of Dr. Joe holdin' a little boy in his arms that turned out not to be hurt too bad. It was all we could talk about.

Chapter 20

The Circus Being Here Was More Than Coincidence

During that healin' week, Dr. Joe and I learned somethin' very interesting about circus people. While some of the people in the circus look like you and me, there are some that don't blend in 'cause they look downright scary, like the alligator man. But most circus people are people that would melt into a crowd. You would never know they're different unless you look real close.

Dr. Joe walked in one day and gazed at the clipboard. "Dr. Joe, our next patient is from the circus, too. It's the tattooed lady." I tried to say this with a straight face. She had developed a cough and had to come to see the doc.

"Well, Anna, let's take a look-see." That's what Dr. Joe said when he was givin' some patient the once-over.

In walked a shapely lady that took off her shirt, revealin' an elephant tattooed on her chest. "I have a terrible cough and my throat feels scratchy," she said in a weak-accented tone.

Now, this wasn't your run of the mill elephant, and it wasn't jes' any chest. Dr. Joe's eyes got big and his jaw dropped a little. Afterward, we both concurred we'd never seen anythin' like it.

The elephant trunk ran right down to her navel and the tusks and large ears branched out over her ample bosoms. It was like you were lookin' at an elephant head from the height of the big top.

When Dr. Joe said, "Breathe for me." I could hardly contain myself. He told me later that every time he put the stethoscope up to her front and said, "breathe," the elephant's ears got bigger.

Dr. Joe paused as if composin' himself. Then he asked, "Could you cough for me?" When she coughed, the ears fluttered back and forth like a real elephant trumpetin'. We could hardly breathe out to keep from laughin'.

The lady also had some foreign words across her derrière. But, the thing that I couldn't take my eyes off of was a boa constrictor, tattooed with such detail that it looked real. It wrapped around her neck and down her back. I saw Dr. Joe's eyes follow her backside—he couldn't help himself. And the snake's head came out through those foreign words on her rear. Due to her underwear coverin' the rest of the good parts, we could only imagine what the words said and where the boa went. When she moved or breathed, it looked like the snake was movin' too. We should've paid her for the appointment. It was wonderful! As she got up to leave she smiled. We tried to look sincere, but we jes' couldn't.

Dr. Joe observed later, "It was better than the midway." Then he added in his medicinal tone, "She was very nice and spoke very little English."

In treatin' those circus people that week, we had a few more surprises. For example, that beautiful blonde lady that rides the giant white horse was really a tiny lady with jet-black hair. When she walked in, we expected a blonde, but what limped in was a tiny dark-haired lady without her blonde wig. Turns out, she wore that huge wig of blonde hair piled high on her head to make her look taller. She also made darn sure it stayed on her head during all that jumpin' and ridin'. The reason we knew this was 'cause she came into the office one day with a sprained ankle. She said her name was Andalucía, and she fell off the big white horse during all the commotion that had ensued over the Ferris wheel and had lit on her ankle. Dr. Joe could tell, without even askin' her, what the problem was 'cause it was so swollen.

I expected her to have a strange accent like most of them other circus folk, but she sounded jes' like the folks back home. In talkin' we found out that in fact we shared somethin' in common in being from Georgia. Then, all of a sudden, it hit me. This tiny lady might be Miss Helen's Andrea jes' callin' herself Andalucía 'cause that sounded more of a circus-like name. So I started askin' her some questions while tryin' to act like I was jes' makin' small talk.

"Why, I worked for a lady back in Athens, Georgia, for a little bit, and she told me she had a daughter in the circus that she loved and missed very dearly. Her heart aches so bad 'cause she's mighty lonely these days."

She was interested now and I pretended I wasn't puttin' two-and-two together about who she really was.

"She prays ever'day for her daughter's safety and for the day when she will come back to pay her a visit," I said, and went on. "You know, most mamas still keep being mamas long after their babies are grown up. Sometimes their babies feel so over-mothered they gotta get away for a while. Especially if those babies aren't yet mamas or daddies themselves, they jes' cain't understand why their mamas want to keep babyin' them so. But no matter how big or old they get, they are still babies to their mamas. Why, I bet the alligator man and the tattooed lady have mamas that love them, too. They're out there somewhere worrin' about them, too."

I wondered how the alligator man's mother felt about havin' a baby that people made fun of all the time. I expect she and Miss

Joyce had somethin' in common. I also found myself wonderin' what that tattooed lady's mama would've said about her havin' all those tattoos all over her, 'cause that mama knew her before, when her skin was pink all over before she went and made a freak outta herself. I wonder what made her do that?

I snapped back from my driftin' thoughts when Dr. Joe shook his head from side to side. "It's not broken, just sprained." He wrapped her foot without sayin' another word. Then he went into his office for another one of his famous five-minute phone calls.

As Miss Andalucía sat up, she said, "I expect that lady's daughter will go back and see her pretty soon."

As I got the exam room ready for the next patient, I thought about what a small world it was that I would bump into Miss Helen's daughter. I don't think things like that are a coincidence at all; the Lord plans these kinds of things, you know. I said a real strong prayer that Andalucía was indeed Andrea and that she would do what she said and pay her mama a visit very soon.

The circus people were so grateful, they did another show for us the next Saturday as a thank you. Fritzy said he wanted to see the lions and tigers again. They looked good all locked up in that cage where they couldn't hurt us, but they had the worst snarls. They sounded like the Wicked Witch of the West from *The Wizard of Oz*.

The Mayor took the Calloway kids with him and the rest of us piled into Doc Calloway's Packard and he drove us right up to the tent. The ringmaster came out and opened our car door. "Welcome to the circus! We thank you for all your help and hope you enjoy the show. We have a special show just for you," he said in his ringmaster voice.

He then took Miss Susan's hand and she gave him her best saucy smile as she got out. The strong man picked up Fritzy like he was a feather and put him in his chair. Then, we all climbed out after them. I looked out at the goin's on. It was crazy with people and performers and the midway was back in full activity. Then, the two docs each held a side of Fritzy's chair as we all walked to our front-row seats.

The lions and tigers were on first, 'cause we found out later the cats get restless if they have to wait. Then after they appear, those big cats get dinner and go right to bed, 'cause they're so mean. I could hear them roarin' long before they came out and so could Fritzy. His foot was definitely in the yes position, and he was wavin' his arms in big circles. I knew he loved it. "Fritzy, which is better? Lions or tigers?"

"Tiiiis."

"Why?" I asked, knowin' he would have a specific reason.

"Cooolrrr."

"Yep, better color."

I saw Miss Joyce and Dr. Joe smile at one another, and I knew they liked it, too. I was hopin' Miss saucy Susan would sit at the other end with the kids, which she did. True to form, both of the Calloway boys were tormentin' their little sister and she was yellin', "Don't 'tournament' me. Don't 'tournament' me!" They didn't pay any attention to their manners, and if I had been closer, I would have grabbed each one and given them my eyeball-to-eyeball directive. But I didn't get the opportunity, 'cause I was jes' a little too far away. So, I gave them the evil eye from afar and they quieted down. Fear works pretty good, even from a distance.

The ringmaster entered the ring once again and then came the elephants and horses. Sittin' high atop an elephant was our wonderful little blonde horse trainer. Turns out she was also the elephant rider too. The large elephant lumbered over closer and closer to our seats. When he got close enough to make us nervous, she smiled, grabbed his rather long tusk, and turned her arms toward us as he reared up. She was upside down, parallel to the beast's trunk. She said somethin' authoritative and the animal gently put his feet on the railing. She held long stem roses in both her hands. Andalucía gave us all roses! And then she showered us all with rose petals and glitter. She and I caught each other's eyes for jes' a second; I felt confident that my prayers for Miss Helen were gonna be answered.

Fritzy was movin' every part of his body and yellin' at the top of his lungs. His whole body was shakin' and his foot was in the yes position.

We clapped and waved and petted that elephant's trunk before it went quietly back to the center of the ring.

The Mayor took full credit for the circus being so wonderful. He didn't even make mention of the two people that lost their lives in that tragic accident or the other people that got hurt. A few lost limbs, but the rest were jes' lucky. That's the way politicians are. Ever'thing is wonderful and gettin' wonderfuller where they're concerned.

Chapter 21

Suspicions and Shadows

After the circus folks left town, ever'body was real busy gettin' ready for the Christmas season again that year. One afternoon, Fritzy and I were walkin' home from Bishop's. It was snowy and slow, and we were about midway home, when I looked up and saw Miss Susan's Buick cruise by on its way toward the outskirts of town. It didn't stop and I know she couldn't help but see us. I was perplexed, not only about her ignorin' us, but where she was goin', since it wasn't near to her house or Doc Calloway's office.

When we got in, I dried us off and put the things away. Miss Joyce came in and asked us how our trip to the store was. She knew we probably wouldn't have nothin' good to say about it, 'cause after the experience with the Ferris wheel I thought Bishop would be a bit nicer. But he wasn't. He was back to his old self and acted like that experience never even happened. Miss Joyce told us there would be a new store opening up a mile or so further out, toward the new development west of town.

I put away the groceries and got dinner ready in no time.

Not another word was spoken about the matter, but we were

the first folks through the door of the nice, new A&P that opened up about three weeks later. I only returned once more to Bishop's when I went to offer my condolences—but that's another story for a later time.

Christmas was the best time of the year, and Miss Joyce decorated like a professional with a big, big tree and boughs ever'where and lots of candles and Christmas presents that always hit the mark. I cooked every kind of food I ever knew and lots of it. I understood they were to be home a lot while I was in Georgia. I further guessed that they would be home, bored and hungry without me being there at Christmas, too.

I was gettin' excited about my annual trip home to Athens. I was packin' up some things when I spied out through the front window of my bedroom a car passin' by. You know, sometimes it takes a split second for a person's brain to register what they saw. It was like that with this car. I decided it was Miss Susan's car passin' and then I saw Dr. Joe's car passin' right behind it. It didn't take me any time to know Dr. Joe's car. I was thinkin' to myself, "What is he doin' out and about at 4 p.m.?" That's when it hit me like a mule kick. They're goin' the same way, so they can play—with each other.

I dashed out the front with my pocketbook in my hand and a quick word to Miss Joyce, sayin' I forgot somethin' at the A&P. Then I walked out and down the street a bit, so I could see where both cars were goin', or where they had been. I looked back to see if any pryin' eyes were followin' me. None were noted, and I squinted my eyes in the direction of the cars—my eyes were followin' their two cars as they climbed a hill on Highway 30 that runs outta town toward Ames. They became tiny specks.

I turned and slowly walked back toward the house. I asked myself, "If you saw your husband drivin' his car to a destination near some hotels at the end of town, the same direction that another beautiful woman was also drivin' to, what would you think?" I answered myself, "I would think the worst."

I walked back in sad and dejected. My hands were empty 'cause I didn't go to the store, and I was caught not only empty-handed, but red-handed when Miss Joyce noticed I wasn't carryin' anythin'. Now, I had to make somethin' up, which I was basically opposed to, but in situations such as this, you've gotta fudge a little to consider people's feelin's.

"I realized I didn't need what I thought I needed," I said, knowin' it sounded stupid, but Miss Joyce let it pass without sayin' anythin' and I scurried in.

I went back to Fritzy and fidgeted through our readin' and homework time. As I read to him, I thought about the two of them meetin' and doin' whatever they wanted to do with one another. It was a naughty sight and it made me sick, so I put Fritzy and me to bed early to stop my mind from creatin' the different scenarios and shenanigans.

As I lay there thinkin' about their secrets, I thought to myself that this house had enough secrets as it was. Maybe those people layin' dead in the backyard were dead 'cause of some secret they were part of or that they knew too much about.

I decided it would be best to keep my own counsel on this matter of Doc Worrell and Mrs. Calloway, since I didn't know the particulars yet. I most certainly didn't want to be jumpin' to the wrong conclusions, but my mind was conjurin' up all manner of visions. But somethin' like this requires a person to be very, very sure before they go off half-cooked.

Miss Joyce was a wonderful person, but she had been nipped in the bud over Fritzy. For the last years, she been crochetin' her heart out. Dr. Joe said it helped her cope. I don't think it helped her cope. She jes' made a lot of ugly things that people were forced to enjoy. Why, she even crocheted me a bed jacket that made me look like a shower curtain. About once a week I put it on and paraded around in it to make her feel better—I wanted her feelin' good, 'cause the house was happier when she did.

One thing she did crochet that turned out pretty, were some window shades and valances. She put them all over the house. When the early evenin' shadows appeared and the porch light shined through them into a dark room, it made the valances seem like the curtains on a stage. I used it as a backdrop for my stories. I would begin to tell my story, and sing and hum, and make shadow people with my hands. I told Fritzy about Robin Hood, Super Man and The Shadow while I acted it out usin' my considerable personality. We read comic books, too. Why, I was becomin' so adept at readin' out loud, I think I might have been better at it than that Walter Winchell!

Chapter 22

Secrets Uncovered

Have you ever noticed a person with somethin' botherin' them? They seem a bit subdued and pensive. I had seen that in Hope last Christmas. As I found out when I went back home the next Christmas, it turned out she was coverin' up a whole lot about Gordon. He turned out to be a drinker and a gambler, always up to somethin'. And he was never faithful to her. I guess his relationship with Altus Andrews did have the effect we feared it might. Poor Hope had gotten pregnant by him. When the hardware store found out they let her go. And then Gordon showed his true colors. He, in essence, let her go, too. She no longer served her purpose in makin' money for him to spend. How could a father turn his back on someone he married before God and who was havin' his baby? He had taken up with Maisey Edwards. I seriously considered stayin' in Athens permanent when Hope told me all that. A girl needs her mother, but she had her sisters and her grandmother there, and Fritzy needed me in Iowa, so life went on.

Susan Calloway had noticed somethin' was botherin' Dr.

Joe, too. One evenin', while she and Doc Calloway were eatin' dinner with Miss Joyce and Dr. Joe, Miss Susan took notice that every time she said somethin' funny Dr. Joe laughed and smiled directly at her. Miss Susan came to realize that Dr. Joe thought she was funny, and so she continued sayin' funny things jes' to get a response outta him. And then she caught him gazin' a little too long in her direction before he turned away. But she found herself likin' that a lot.

The truth is, she liked being noticed by him and admired Dr. Joe's quiet strength. He had dealt with Fritzy and also with Miss Joyce's inability to cope with all that had happened to them. Through it all, he never showed the anxiety that we all knew he must have been feelin'. On the other hand, saucy Miss Susan's husband was so duty bound that he woke up before first daylight and worked until long into the night. He was almost like a drill sergeant about his attitude toward ever'thing around him. He demanded that the whole family should fall in behind him and work all the time, too, like they were a little army and he was the general. He expected those Calloway kids to mow and their little girl to clean. The house had to be perfect and the kids had to be that way, too. I expect the reason he was a doctor to the babies and children was 'cause he could better control them and make them do as he instructed. He jes' loved bossin' people around.

I believe that Miss Susan was always tryin' to measure up but couldn't, no matter how hard she tried. She even gave up being a motherly role model for the kids. She was like one of the kids, waitin' all the time to be told off by the king of the household. That's why those kids were never taught any manners. Their daddy flat didn't have any and their mama didn't even consider herself worthy of teachin' anybody anythin'.

So, when Dr. Joe smiled and laughed around her, he made her feel real good about herself. He didn't try to change her or make her feel bad. He jes' enjoyed her. And she began to enjoy him, too. I'm sure she felt some guilt where Miss Joyce was concerned, but decided it was for the better, 'cause Miss Joyce brought Dr. Joe down with her constant depression. Dr. Joe jes' wanted to be happy, and he had so much to be unhappy about that it really was sometimes difficult for him to get through the day. His work was what brought him fulfillment and the rest of his life brought him down. So Miss Susan convinced herself that the man needed a little happiness.

The first time they met was at an out-of-the-way inn about thirty miles from town. Saucy Miss Susan had told Doc Calloway that she was goin' to spend the evenin' with an old college friend in Iowa City, where the university is. But instead, she and Dr. Joe met at the inn near the Amish colonies. The Amish colonies are these Amish settlements where folks go to eat out and shop for textiles and handmade items. Those Amish live like they did hundreds of years ago. They bought a bottle of Amish wine and then one thing led to another till that wine was all gone and so were all their inhibitions. The next mornin' they felt happy and terrible at the same time.

Miss Susan and Doc Calloway had met at the University of Iowa when he had been a pre-med student and she was an undergraduate. They got married and she got pregnant. He got interested in medicine and she raised the kids. Her family was from Marshalltown, so they moved there and he set up his practice. Miss Susan's uncle was the Mayor and ran a great deal of the town. He was also the largest insurance agent in the town. So his powerful base bled off to them, and people were always nice on account of who they were related to. Her other uncle was Randall Phillips, who used to be the town's only doctor before he retired and moved away. Now remember that name—Randall Phillips. He is a big player in my little story. When he moved away it left an openin' for two doctors, since the town had grown bigger at that point and there were more people that needed doctorin'. And so Doc Calloway moved in to fill that comfortable void and convinced his medical school buddy Doc Worrell to come, too.

When things like this happen, you have suspicions that the bad things you suspect are really happenin,' but at that time, you make up your mind to say nothin'. I guess we hold out hope that maybe ever'thing will go away, and what you've been thinkin' is jes' somethin' conjured up in your own mind. But, unfortunately, those suspicions usually prove to be right.

I knew the proof I needed to prove they were havin' an affair would eventually come to me in some way. And then when it did, I wouldn't be able to ignore it. And then I would confront Dr. Joe about it. And sure enough, it did and I did. We were workin' at his clinic in the evenin' and some little kids came in for their vaccinations. Their parents couldn't come during the day 'cause they worked, but they were actually a payin' client. They were from the next county over and the parents owned a bed and breakfast inn nearby.

Dr. Joe seemed a little anxious with the people and tried to hurry them along, but the mother was a talker and she talked about what a wonderful couple the Worrells were and how they had stayed at the inn before. At first, I didn't pay them any mind. People were always tryin' to make a bond with Dr. Joe, thinkin' they would either get a price break or better attention with a personal connection.

I could tell this woman wanted to build that bond, so she started talkin' about havin' had the Worrells stay at her bed and breakfast. Dr. Joe was outta the room gettin' the medical supplies from the pantry, when the woman said to me, "Oh, Dr. Worrell and that beautiful blonde wife of his are just a delight. What's her name, I can't remember?"

I replied with a straight face, sayin' Mrs. Calloway's first name, Susan. The lady nodded her head, yes, and said, "Oh, that's right her name's Susan. Now I remember."

Dr. Joe came back in the exam room and I smiled like nothin' happened, but my heart was hurtin' for Miss Joyce. She had so much hurt in her life and nothin' could undo it. She was never gonna have normal children. So, as much as I might have wished that Dr. Joe had been callin' his bookie, it hadn't been his bookie he was callin'. It was that saucy Miss Susan.

The next day, I had jes' made Dr. Joe's breakfast before he was due to go out on his rounds, but it was still very early. We were alone in the kitchen. I blurted out, "Look, Dr. Joe, who am I to judge you? I should've been a better person with my own family life, but I am on the outside lookin' in, and you are the one who I'm lookin' in at."

I paused to see if he was catchin' my drift. "I see a very sad man that's sad over somethin' he has no control over. You get no joy 'cause you feel terrible about Fritzy and you long for healthy children—and Miss Joyce cain't be whole, 'cause she cain't get past the pain. But worst of all, I think you feel caught in the middle."

"Anna, what are you getting at?" Dr. Joe said this like I didn't know my place—which hurt. I continued as if he hadn't said a thing.

"Then we have Mrs. Calloway, who is too good lookin' for her own good, and her husband is a no-fun kind of guy and is always pickin' on her. I understand it. But, what I don't get is you riskin' what you do have, which is a lovin' wife, and lest' we forget, a bond you made with her before God—for better and for worse. You never mention Fritzy, but he counts, too." That last stab drew some blood outta his face. He looked whiter than white.

Again he repeated himself, "Anna what in Sam Hill are you getting at?"

"I'm gettin' at you and Miss Susan and that bed and breakfast west of here."

Dr. Joe looked shocked. He was caught. He was angry, and there wasn't a darn thing he could do.

After what seemed like a silence that lasted forever, he finally said, "I feel terrible but I can't and won't stop myself. Mrs. Calloway makes me happy, and I know I make her happy, too. Joyce and Fritzy make me so sad. She can't get past the pain, and I can't handle the pain of his not having a full life. This doesn't concern you."

I saw this one comin'—he was gonna want things to continue. There was nothin' I could do. "Well, I cain't judge you and I'm not gonna tell on you right now, neither. But you gotta know that I'm tellin' Miss Joyce the minute Fritzy isn't with us no more. I owe her my truth. Unless, you have a better idea."

"No, I don't have a better idea. I care about Joyce, and you know better than anyone that I live up to my obligations."

"Well, it doesn't sound like you're walkin' on coals to prove your love for Miss Joyce. But for right now, I'll keep my eyes and ears shut, along with my mouth."

Dr. Joe frowned, clearin' his throat and his mind. "We've got a full roster tonight and I really need you to help. I don't want to talk about this again, and I never want you to tell anyone—especially Joyce or Donny Calloway. It would devastate all concerned."

With that announcement he walked out and closed the door behind him. This was one time that that doctor superiority stuff came out, and it stuck in my craw like a bad heartburn. And, of course, he always walked out without sayin' good-bye and that really grated me. I sat still as death for a few minutes. I pretty much had to do what he said, so I made up my mind that I would not say a word to anyone. But, keepin' secrets eats away at a person and bothers them somethin' fierce. After all, the sin of omission is a big sin. I should know—I kept a few myself and this was not gonna be one I wanted to keep any longer than needed.

Somebody out there was sure keepin' a big secret havin' to do with the bodies in the Worrell's backyard, too. Even though it seemed like they did a good job coverin' up that secret, it had to be gratin' on them, too. I supposed this secret wasn't nearly so bad to keep, but it still was a sin.

Time passed and I'd like to say I pushed these things totally from my mind, but they were always in there even if they got pushed to the back to make room for all the rest, includin' lots of worry over Hope. She wrote me a letter and said that she lost the baby and Gordon took her back. Some uneven trade: a baby for that nitwit Gordon. I'm not dumb. I prayed and prayed for my beautiful Hope that God would look around her sin, 'cause losin' that baby was no accident. I knew she was gonna have to do some powerful repentin' to get past that.

I didn't have too much time for worryin' and frettin' in those days, though. There was a Depression on and I needed to work harder than ever before to help Dr. Joe when I wasn't taking care of Fritzy and other things around the Worrell house. We also had to get Fritzy educated. And that was a big undertaking.

Chapter 23

Crime Doesn't Pay

Fritzy was in the third grade that year and jes' turned eight years old. Miss Sonya Eggers walked into the room and controlled our every thought during those days at school. She knew jes' when to praise or prod a kid. She knew jes' when to call on someone that wasn't tuned in. Bam! She got them to sit up and listen. One day after school, when we were gettin' ready to go home, Miss Eggers stood by our desk with a stack of books. "Do you want to take some books home for you and Fritzy, since you're already ahead?"

Fritzy jiggled, yes.

So I asked her to give us some adventure books. Fritzy liked those. So she gave us The Adventures of Hopalong Cassidy.

Fritzy smiled. Sometimes his eyes lit up and he smiled with his mouth and his eyes. He didn't do that very often, but that was one time he did. Readin' enabled Fritzy to transport himself to another world. It was his own imagined world, where I think he imagined himself like ever'one else.

The very afternoon that Miss Eggers gave us that book was a

beautiful fall day. Iowa has big trees that dot the countryside like one of the picture books I read to Fritzy. The trees are ever'where with lots of leaves and when those leaves turn all the colors of fall, there is a beauty that cain't be copied anywhere else. The golds, reds, yellows, and browns made me marvel. It was that kind of day. Perfect.

Fritzy and I decided to go to the bank and then to the A&P. We needed all manner of things since we hadn't done any shoppin' for the last few days. Goin' to school also exposes you to every kind of germ, too. And I had been readin' so many books my throat was feelin' a little scratchy. So I decided I would buy some lemons and make my lemon juice concoction for my throat.

"Fritzy, how about an apple pie?" I felt an apple pie was in order so we could celebrate the season. Plus, we needed makin's for a Friday night sit-down dinner. The grocery list was gonna be long.

But first, we would go to the bank. As we walked along, I told Fritzy that I liked school. He jiggled yes that he did, too. Miss Eggers was a good teacher that really cared what the students learned. And even though we were both real good students, she would have been glad to help us if we needed any help.

When we got to the bank there was quite a crowd of people jes' millin' around. Being Friday afternoon, the bank was a busy place with people puttin' their paychecks in the bank before the weekend, and I was no exception. I needed to deposit my paycheck from the Worrells, so we got in the line that stretched almost to the door. I leaned down and whispered in Fritzy's ear, "Now if you get tired of sittin' in this line, let me know, and we'll get out of it and go to the grocery store." Fritzy gave me the OK sign, which was a side-to-side motion. We continued to wait. I was beginnin' to think I needed to take a load off, but then Fritzy and I began to look at ever'one. I leaned down to his ear and said, "That lady in front of us would like my cookin'." Fritzy laughed, 'cause she was almost as big as I was. "Look at that skinny guy behind us. He needs my cookin'." Fritzy laughed again.

About that time, I noticed some burly lookin' guy that came into the bank, and he had a crazy look on his face. I leaned down to Fritzy again and said, "That guy needs a straight jacket." I laughed and turned away to see a beautiful lady in a stylish suit walk in. She had a beautiful purse and matchin' shoes in beautiful chocolate leather that looked soft as butter. For a second, I envied her with her thin legs and high heels. However, my gaze was disturbed by a sudden noise toward our left. The crazy lookin' guy did, indeed, look crazier than I thought. I got a closer look, and he had a stubble of beard from at least a week, but the craziest thing was the gun he held in his hand. He fidgeted a lot, which made me think he was hopped up on some no-good drug.

"This is a stick-up. Hold still and you won't get hurt. Otherwise I'll blow you away," he told us as he walked from one line to the other, and then suddenly yelled it again. I realized we were in real danger. We were also sittin' ducks, 'cause Fritzy's wheelchair didn't move far or fast. We weren't the only ones in that predicament; there was an old lady up a little ways in front of us, who didn't look like she could do the fifty yard dash any better than Fritzy. We were all in a world of danger with Mr. Burly wavin' his gun around. His buddy was a skinny guy in a brown suit and matchin' fedora he wore pulled down over his eyes. He had a gun, too.

The line of people we were in began to close together around us. I realized that was not good so I whispered to ever'one, "Get back in line, so as to keep the two gunmen separate, where they cain't see one another." I don't know why I said that, 'cause lookin' back it seems odd and maybe jes' a little smart. And sure enough, the gunmen couldn't see one another while they were walkin' up and down the line. I leaned down and whispered in Fritzy's ear,

"We're either gonna get shot or we're gonna trip that no-good son of a gun."

Fritzy motioned, yes.

The man behind us whispered in my ear, "I heard you say that—what can I do?"

"Well, Mister, I don't know, but you're gonna either get shot or wrestle that gun away from him when I sit on him. Do you think you can do that?"

I could tell he was a might embarrassed and also scared.

"Lettin' them get away with our money sounds even scarier to my way of thinkin'," I whispered to him. "Now, when he comes by again, we're gonna trip him with the wheelchair, like we jes' were turnin' around and didn't know any better."

I continued whisperin' to Fritzy, "You know, we do it all the time by accident, but this time it'll be on purpose. You know how I accidentally got Bishop on the shins once?" I rolled my eyes. It hadn't been entirely an accident.

Fritzy jiggled, yes.

So we waited what seemed like forever, and watched the bank robber yell at us like we were cattle. "Get over, I'm coming through." And he pushed us all to the side.

There was a young woman with a little girl in her arms, and I whispered for her to move, "Move up the line toward the teller." I motioned with my hand. "Now ever'body help her." I motioned again at the people to step aside. A man next to her said, "Good idea, move her up the line near the teller window where she's more out of harm's way." We all had our heads down and were tryin' to look like nothin' was up.

I turned to another young man that looked like he could fight. "Now, Mister, I'm askin' you with all my heart to stay behind me. We're gonna trip this guy when he comes by, and then I'm gonna fall on him and hopefully squish him and his gun flat. Then you get in there and help the other young man behind me get the gun. The line will hide us from the other guy." I shook my head side to side and said, "He won't shoot what he cain't see."

We were stuck standin' around while the two robbers were gettin' their money. All we could do was watch. "Put all your money and jewelry in the hat." Burly jes' pushed through the crowd like we were so much undergrowth. "Now take off your jewelry and pocketbooks and billfolds." Then he repeated himself as if we were kids and weren't listenin'. "Now, I want all of you to take off your jewelry and purses, billfolds, and cash and put it in here." He motioned toward his hat for the jewelry, and the bigger stuff was to go in a bag. "And if you don't, I'm going to shoot you between the eyes and take it anyway. So just do it." And for a second I looked over at the beautiful woman with her buttery brown pocketbook, and I was sad to see her dump it into Mr. Burly's bag. But, such is the way material things go. They are here one day and gone the next. So, it doesn't serve any purpose to get too attached to things.

A minute later, the skinny guy was comin' down our row, pushin' and shovin'. Minutes seemed to drag like honey, and as the robber came by with his bag, he looked at me with his beady eyes and said, "You can't get that ring off can you?"

Well, Martin had given me that ring about twenty-four years and a hundred pounds ago, and I never took it off, and an act of God probably wasn't gonna get it off now. I shook my head, "No."

And it was then that I took my chance. As he passed by to go on ahead to the next line, I wheeled Fritzy into him. I did what people used to call cuttin' somebody off at the knees—except these were shins. It put him off his guard, and then I bumped into him like what happened with Martin, and he bumped right over. But, this time I did it on purpose.

"What the he ...?" he said as he went down. He didn't get out the rest of that last cussword either. I pushed hard like I never had before and hoped Fritzy understood. Then I gave him another push. The guy didn't budge much at first, but after that he was down. Then I jes' took my legs from out under me and let Old Man Gravity take me over. As I sat on him I made sure his hand was on the ground. We were scramblin' on the floor, like schoolboys for a few seconds, and the other robber rushed our way, yellin', "Get out of the way and let me through." But, ever'one was so shocked they couldn't move very fast, and they all moved the wrong way and bumped into one another. It gave us jes' enough time for our helpin' hand people that had been behind me in the line. The first guy grabbed the gun and pulled the trigger as he leveled it at the burly robber.

Thank the Lord that he was a good shot or else he would have hit one of us. It took him all of a second to do this. I was still on the floor where my bump had landed me, so I saw the next movements from a very strange angle. Fritzy never blinked even though his wheelchair had toppled over and he was on the floor facin' me. He wasn't even wigglin'; he was watchin' real quiet-like. I remember thinkin' thank goodness he saw the whole thing from the safety of the floor.

Now, if you've never seen someone get shot, it's a crazy thing. The burly robber, who took the bullet, was pushed backward from the force of it. His arms and feet flew out in front of him as he fell back and there was this echo sound that came first. Then, the big noise that comes after, all in a split second, and then the sounds hit us full on. Your first inclination is to run away with your hands over your ears and eyes. But you cain't do it, 'cause it happens so fast. The rattle is somethin' you feel as much as hear. You cain't take your eyes off it and you feel it to your core. Then, there's the sudden mess flyin' through the air. Blood was ever'where and the splatter was like someone flicked red paint all over us, except it wasn't paint. I was still sittin' on the skinny robber and the one that was shot was screamin' bloody murder—for good reason. But, I wasn't movin' one inch—'cause I couldn't. It took two strong men to lift me up, and even then, I wasn't too steady on my feet. I started screamin' for Fritzy, but I could see his face and he was smilin' like I'd never seen. I looked in his eyes and knew that he didn't fear death or the unknown. That's a powerful thing when you possess it.

The cops came and helped me walk and stand upright. Then they upright-ed Fritzy and got him settled back in his chair and took skinny robber away. He deserved to get smushed. He would have shot Fritzy and me if he'd had the chance.

The young man who pulled the trigger asked me, "Are youalright, Ma'am?"

No one had ever called me Ma'am before that day, but ever'one in the bank was so nice. They made my deposit while I sat down in a chair and cried. Then the newspaper came and took our young hero's picture and we all relaxed a little. But I couldn't stop cryin'. That's what happens when you live through somethin' that should've killed you. You jes' sit around for an hour or two afterward and dribble tears like a nitwit.

I was very proud of Fritzy. He was brave. Now I was thinkin' that I didn't need to tell the Worrells the whole story, but it would get back to them if I didn't, so Fritzy and I decided to tell them tonight after we got back from the store. Oh yeah, we were still plannin' on the store.

But I couldn't really move. My knees got weak and Fritzy and I started shakin' like leaves. "Hey, Fritzy, we need to go home and rest. We've been through a lot. We'll have to make do with leftovers tonight. I don't think I can make it."

A nice policeman named Sammy offered to take us home, and we accepted his kind offer. We sat in the back of his black-and-white patrol car as the late afternoon sun shone through on Fritzy and me. We were very much alive and I was real glad. The policeman knew what Fritzy and I had done at the bank, but didn't mention it as we rode along. There was somethin' else he wanted to talk about.

"Don't you live in Dr. Phillips's old house?" he asked. "It was really a shame about the doctor's son and his wife. Dr. Phillip's son and daughter-in-law, Cameron and Michelle, were my age and we went all through school together. He was a nice guy. It's a shame they never found their bodies."

I suddenly forgot about the bank robbery.

"They searched and finally called it off," he went on. "The authorities thought they would continue the hunt when the spring came and before the animals got hungry to try to find the bodies, but they never had any success. Dr. and Mrs. Phillips finally moved up there to live near where they disappeared. I heard the police continued the search, but they never found them."

"Who do you think are the bodies buried in the Phillips' backyard? Do you think Dr. Phillips had anythin' to do with it?" I asked him. I had jumped right to the best question. Maybe I would get a decent answer.

The policeman said there was no way that the Phillips were involved, sayin' they were too nice and honest and that Dr. Phillips had even delivered him into the world.

"Well, somebody had to bury those people in the backyard. They didn't crawl in that hole on their own and slush dirt down on themselves." Fritzy laughed when I said that. The policeman didn't.

He continued talkin', though, recountin' one time Dr. Phillips and his wife were arguin' in the office when he went in with a sore throat. She was raisin' a ruckus and he was ignorin' her and writin' up some paperwork. She finally stormed off and slammed the door. 'Cause they didn't get along so well, he said he was surprised they had retired to be together alone on some lake.

As we arrived home, Miss Joyce was rightfully startled about why the police were droppin' us off. I told her the story of all we had been through that day. I said it fast, so as to get it out, and I hoped Miss Joyce didn't get it all. Now, I didn't mention who did the sittin', 'cause I didn't think it made me look good. I decided not to mention it. There goes that sin of omission again. I told Fritzy, "Now Fritzy, I don't want you alludin' to that either. It's our secret." I had said that earlier, but repeated it for good measure.

Fritzy did a no with his foot. I knew that he wanted me to tell his parents the whole story, but I wasn't about to, for fear they'd send me back to Georgia in a New York minute.

Miss Joyce held him in her arms and Fritzy didn't calm down for an hour. He shook and made noises all during our dinner of leftovers. I was so tired I couldn't go to the grocery, and I certainly couldn't create and cook a dinner. The letdown from the darn adrenalin rush had jes' drained me like a broken pipe. I was as tired as a cotton picker at dusk, and Fritzy was as frisky as a colt.

When Fritzy and I settled down for our prayers, we had a lot to be thankful for. "Now Fritzy, let's say a prayer for the bad guys. Let's pray that they see the error of their ways and start livin' a repentafull life and find true love that keeps them on the straight and narrow, 'cause it doesn't look like anythin's been done for them this far."

Fritzy moved his foot no and looked real angry and serious.

"Look, if we cain't forgive and introduce goodness on somebody, how're they gonna get better? But you don't think they can change?"

"Nooo. Thh don't," Fritzy managed to say with great effort.

So I changed the subject and promised we would follow the stories in the newspaper about those bad robbers and see what happened to them. I was also thinkin' if they somehow managed to get outta jail, we'd have some inklin' of where they were. I hadn't thought about them possibly wantin' to come after us at all while the robbery was goin' on, and while we were being so brave. But I sure thought about it now, 'cause ever'body in town knew where we lived. We were sittin' ducks if they didn't go long term in the clink. And we would sure be on their dance card if, and when, they got out.

The next mornin' we got up and read the Times-Republican. The front page showed the skinny, smushed bank robber being escorted outta the bank lobby by the police. Underneath the picture it said, "Robbers Apprehended by Police at the First State Bank Yesterday; No Money Lost."

Why, it was like we had never been there. I wondered about not being mentioned but was glad we weren't, 'cause that hid us even better from the robbers. I wondered if I would ever see that fella that pulled the trigger again, or if I had seen him somewhere before. He didn't look familiar, but then this is a small town, and there was always the possibility we could see him again. If we did cross paths, maybe he could tell us more about the robbery and why the cops didn't want to talk to us about it—or even interview us. I let the matter drop then, but I was still uneasy about the robbers. And I also began to think that night that Sammy the policeman that had brought us home might be able to shed some light on the dead bodies in the Worrells' backyard—if I ever was able to talk to him again.

Chapter 24

Money Isn't All It's Cracked Up to Be

I tried to work hard and low after that. I didn't want the Worrells thinkin' I would knowingly take Fritzy into danger. People didn't talk about it in the doc's office, so I was glad that Dr. Joe didn't get the full story. I didn't think the full story would make them happy and confident in me. But, I had done what Fritzy wanted, and I had done what I wanted, and that was the most important thing.

About two weeks later, somethin' happened that made me realize that money isn't the "end all" in life and that we gotta be doin' better things than jes' sockin' our money away and countin' it. Now, with that said, it seems like every problem I ever had was linked to money. Altus and Martin were after some money from me when Martin had his ill-fated experience. We were in the bank robbery 'cause some bad guys wanted money, and this other experience I'm about to tell you about is also all about gettin' money.

Fritzy and I started our normal rounds that day. That included a trip to the bank. While we were always lookin' over our shoulders after the previous experience we had that day in the bank, goin' to the bank had to be done, so we had no choice but to get accustomed to makin' our rounds to the bank again. We usually walked, even when the weather was bad, 'cause I didn't want Miss Joyce to drive. She drove like she cooked, so you can imagine how I felt about that. After we went to the bank, we walked to the A&P. But since it was a lot farther, we sometimes had to ride with Miss Joyce when the weather was real bad. I didn't like that 'cause of the obvious. But that day the weather wasn't too bad, so we started out walkin' toward the bank. There were two banks in Marshalltown and both were across the street from one another, so you had a fifty-fifty chance of doin' business with one or the other—or you could use your mattress for keepin' your money like some folks do.

I remember promisin' Fritzy that we would get some hot chocolate after we got our money at the bank that day. There was a chill in the air and I didn't want either one of us gettin' a cold. We turned the corner as I was talkin' about that hot chocolate, but Fritzy didn't answer. He was lookin' ahead at the commotion goin' on in front of our bank. There was a crowd of people beatin' on the door and a lot of angry noise. I hurried us up as close as I could get to the crowd. There were so many people crowded around that I couldn't read the paper on the front door, but the bank was locked up tighter than one of its vaults. "The bank ain't doin' business today and probably won't reopen," said a guy fatter than me, who was up in front. "The Depression has finally hit us, too," piped in a woman to my left. You could feel the despair. You could feel the helplessness. I felt it all.

I realized that Fritzy couldn't see anythin' 'cause he was down low. So I leaned down and whispered in his ear, "Fritzy, we've got problems. The bank is closed. We gotta get up front of this crowd and see what that sign says. Then, we gotta go to your daddy and tell him what's goin' on. He stands to lose a lot more than I do." So I gently made my way to the front of the group.

The sign read:

> *To whom it may concern:*
> *This banking establishment has been closed by the state of Iowa due to insolvency. It will reopen if and when deposits reach the assigned level set forth by the state of Iowa. See banking code 125.*

Well, if that don't deflate your soufflé, nothin' will. I decided that we needed to rush over to Dr. Joe's, so I took us off in a considerable hurry. What raced through my mind was that I had every penny in that bank, which amounted to $412—about a year's worth of hard-earned pay. I had judiciously put every check in that bank, and now I was very upset, 'cause the darn bank across the street was doin' jes' fine—business as usual.

We rounded the corner by Dr. Joe's office and raced in the front door. He was standin' in the waitin' room talkin' to saucy Miss Susan, which stopped me in my tracks. What an awkward moment. That saucy Miss Susan looked down at the ground, avoidin' my eyes, before runnin' off like a scalded dog. But Dr. Joe looked me straight on.

When I told him what had happened at the bank, he gave me a smug smile and told me he had learned about the bank closin' the day before and had already taken all of his money out. My jaw dropped down to my considerable bosom. Then he turned around and walked back into an exam room and closed the door. I was what one would call chagrinned—shocked and displeased all at the same time.

None of this was lost on Fritzy. He wiggled like a worm on a hook and said, "Baaaad."

Fritzy was the only friend I had in the world at that moment. I vented to him, sayin' that Dr. Joe and I had some differences of opinion on a few things, and he had jes' reminded me of our differences. He had done it in a lot of different ways and on a lot of different levels over the years. But he did it all at once this time. Fritzy knew that it hurt me more than Dr. Joe would ever know.

So we turned around and slowly walked toward home. The wind was pickin' up and my spirits were fallin' low. Fritzy's little wheelchair was squeakin', but somehow it was comfortin' to hear it as we wheeled along. It kept me thinkin' about other things besides Dr. Joe.

I told Fritzy I was gonna retire early that night. So he would be listenin' to awful Walter Winchell with his mama and daddy alone.

We walked up the ramp on the front porch, and I paused at the door. I was thinkin' to myself, "Do I want to continue with this little lie?" After all, I believed Dr. Joe did this to me to remind me that he doesn't want me to tell Miss Joyce about saucy Miss Susan. Or worse yet, to get rid of me 'cause I knew about their sin. Or, maybe he didn't tell me about the bank closin' 'cause I don't count for nothin' in his world, and he plumb didn't care. Whichever way he was leanin' didn't bode well for me. Lastly, could it have been 'cause I am colored? The last thought was the cruelest 'cause there was nothin' I could do about it. After all, it's like this, we're all born to be whatever we are, and we cain't change it. After all, a sruffy dog didn't ask to be born a sruffy dog. However, I think God grades us on how well we deal with what we are born to. Take Fritzy, he was always happy. He could have been sad about his condition, but he jes' woke up and tried his hardest every day.

It didn't matter that Dr. Joe and I were at odds right about then. I decided that I would not let it split Fritzy and me up. Fritzy deserved better from both of us—and besides the money was too good up here at Worrells' house. There goes what I said about money. It always gets down to money. Money is the root of ever'thing—good or bad. Either way, I was destined to be out the money I lost at the bank.

I walked us by the bank every day after school for a month hopin' there would be some miracle, but of course there wasn't. And I tried to read every story the Marshalltown paper wrote on it, but there was nothin' gonna happen. My money was gone like a bad dream—the shock hits you and it goes away, but the memory lingers forever. My nightmare wasn't as big as some other folks the newspaper wrote about. Why, they even said one rich farmer lost upward of $60,000. His family had been bankin' with that bank since the 1800s, and they had ever'thing in that bank. I heard the old fella took to his bed when he found out. They say he didn't get up again, he was so old and depressed. We were all wishin' we hadn't used that bank. A good mattress would've served us better.

The pisser-thing was that the bank could still sell the notes and loans that people owed to it, so if you had a loan at the darn, defunct bank you were notified immediately that you owed your money to a new bank. The darndest thing was, that if you lost your money in the bank they wouldn't let you have your money back, 'cause they were what they called "insolvent," but you were still on the hook to them for your loans. The bank was still sellin' off its notes and taking in money, they jes' weren't givin' any out. No wonder we into a Depression, with bread lines and orphanages ever'where—and bankers smokin' cigars in their book-lined studies. The darn bank laws didn't suit the people—jes' the bankers.

The darn government was to blame 'cause they let ever'body buy stock on what they called "margin." That meant you didn't have to buy the stock in a company with a hundred percent real money. You jes' put down a little old payment of a whole lot less, like about twenty-five percent. Ever'thing rolled along real fine until the stock prices went down. Then you had to ante up the difference to the stockbroker. Folks ran from that and didn't pay, or went clean outta their savin's from the banks. All this was taking the lifeblood of money outta the bank. No wonder the banks went belly-up. Why, even our mailman bought stocks on the margin. Ever'body was doin' it, but that didn't make it OK.

That night when Dr. Joe got home, I jes' turned tail and went into my room. I did not go help him that evenin'. I took Fritzy with me and we played card games and listened to Amos 'n' Andy, which is a darn-sight better than that Winchell man. I had taught Fritzy how to play cards. He had a card holder and he would lift his leg toward the card he wanted. He would point to the right card with his toe. Then I would grab it. He was pretty good at the game.

After a while, I asked Fritzy what he thought about the bank thing. Fritzy frowned and said, "No."

I promised him I wouldn't mention it again after that night but that I was gonna tell Dr. Joe what I thought and then move on from it and forget about it.

Fritzy frowned some more and said, "No."

"No? What kind of Christians are we if we don't forgive 'n' forget? I ask you that? Besides, I think showin' someone the error of their ways is what should always happen. Not jes' punishin' somebody. We got the wrong idea about punishment. The idea should be enlightenment."

I started in on my soapbox, preachin' to Fritzy about the sin that was committed here. It was the one that some people call the eleventh sin—the sin of omission. When someone doesn't tell you somethin' they know is important to you, that's the sin of omission. For instance, you're sittin' there, jes' goin' through life and then you get a chance to take advantage of somethin', but then you find out it's gonna hurt some poor nitwit, but that doesn't stop you. You jes' move along smooth as ice on a lake, do your deed and never look back. But it never fails, the fickle finger of fate points you out for some little detail you messed up on, and then it all comes tumblin' down. Or maybe you don't get caught up in your sin, and then you jes' let it sit inside you and it eats a little away at a time. Or maybe, you don't feel bad or sinful at all. That's the worst one.

Why, that sin of omission gets more people in trouble than any other one I've ever wanted to think about. I fidgeted around 'cause I started thinkin' about Dr. Joe and Miss Susan and my particular sin of omission havin' to do with that matter. I didn't mention that thought to Fritzy, though.

Fritzy was still wigglin' somethin' awful, but I continued talkin' to him about the sin of omission.

Oh, now that's the one you're gonna have to explain when you're facin' down St. Peter at the gate. Why, I can jes' imagine that nasty gangster Al Capone spendin' hours tryin' to talk his way through that gate. Not to mention whoever it was that had somethin' to do with killin' those people they dug up out in our backyard, they're also gonna have plenty of explainin' to do when the get to those gates. All I can say is, I hope I'm not behind either one of them in line. Hell will be frozen over by the time I get to my turn."

Fritzy laughed hard, 'cause he could see Dr. Joe standin' in the doorway watchin' me. I guess he heard ever'thing I said. I was a little embarrassed, but not sorry for what I said. Upon closer inspection, I also saw a sadness and a tiredness in Dr. Joe's eyes. That's when I knew some of the things I had said hit home.

He told me not to worry about a thing, jes' like he was talkin' about the weather. He said he missed me at the clinic that night and that the patients were askin' about me. He said I would never know how much I was loved around there. Why, Dr. Joe kind of broke up when he said that.

I was tryin' to be my gracious self for Fritzy. With that, Dr. Joe turned and walked away. I hadn't noticed Miss Joyce behind him, standin' there lookin' little and meek. I guess she heard ever'thing, too. She said she was sorry about the money I lost and that she and Dr. Joe were gonna try to give me a raise and maybe I could find a better bank.

But I resolved to buy a better mattress. I'd had enough of white man's ways when it came to money.

Miss Joyce looked embarrassed when I said that. As if she could speak for all white people—which she couldn't.

The bank was closed and that was that. After a while, they boarded up the windows and vagrants began to make it their temporary home. I noticed that when I walked by and saw them sneakin' in through a broken board. I heard a long time later the bank folks, who owned our insolvent bank here in Marshalltown, moved to Chicago and started another bank. So I have to ask, "Who was the worst bank robber? The guy that stole with a gun, or the owners and the government that forced the bank into insolvency and then sold the notes off?" The answer here is all three.

Chapter 25

God's Gradin' Us

We tried to forget about bank robbers and the Depression jes' like we worked at puttin' the dead bodies outta our minds and began to concentrate on livin' day to day. I was proud of Miss Joyce when she started writin' again for the Times-Republican. She had studied journalism at the University of Iowa and wrote for the university paper and then at the Times-Republican when she and Dr. Joe moved to Marshalltown. She quit after she got pregnant with Fritzy. It turned out she was still pretty good at writin', and when she would get a story published, she'd read it to us. Fritzy always loved havin' the newsapaper read to him, and he especially like to hear her read—so did I. I think it was the only time I saw her truly happy. She would smirk that funny, pretty smile she had, and then settle in to read us her story.

Miss Joyce had a way with words, and she used it for worthy causes. She'd interview anybody in town, with somethin' entertainin' to say, and then she'd write it up better than it sounded in the first place. She interviewed the people who lost money when the bank failed, and she even interviewed the people that owned the bank. I didn't like those people, but she got to the meat of the story ever' time. I always thought it was strange that the bank people had the robbery and the bank failin' within a precious few weeks of one another. Yes, that was very odd. Miss Joyce tried her hardest to make the link but couldn't.

I was glad Miss Joyce didn't want to pursue workin' for Dr. Joe, 'cause a lot of doctor's wives do. The main reason for me feelin' this way was I didn't want them to be together anymore than they absolutely needed to be. They never really healed much after Fritzy was born, and the wounds were still there, even if they weren't the original cause of them. This valley between them was deep and gettin' deeper, and there was nothin' anybody could do to help it. Besides, it was better for Fritzy with me helpin' Dr. Joe at the office in the evenin's, and his mama workin' at the Times-Republican during the day. That way, Fritzy had someone with him at all times. He and I spent our good time together during the day, and I knew he liked it better that way. While I helped Dr. Joe, Fritzy spent time alone with his mother. I'm not so sure he liked that 'cause she was pretty helpless where he was concerned, but they made the best of being together, and I know they truly loved one another.

The freedom we felt during the days let us roam the town and find out the answers to things we couldn't have known otherwise—like the dead bodies. I helped Dr. Joe several evenin's a week, taking care of his back-door clientele that couldn't pay. They came in the evenin's, after his staff went home, and I was glad to make the extra money. Dr. Joe was a good man when it came to things like that. He was always helpin' people. That's what docs are supposed to do.

One of the causes Dr. Joe took on was for the homeless and the poor. I mentioned, earlier, about those vagrants jes' wanderin' around the town square. They needed taking care of, now more than ever, 'cause all the monies from the government were to get businesses goin' again and the government figured the businesses would make jobs and hire people and then there wouldn't be any poor after that. But in the meantime, while they were waitin' for that day, ever'body was poor. I was very aware of these people, 'cause I'd push Fritzy's wheelchair around the park every day. We'd stop and openly stare at the people, and I'd explain to him that ever'body had somethin' goin' on in their lives. Nobody's got a smooth life. That is the nature of livin'.

I wanted Fritzy to know that he didn't have the worst life by a long shot. I told Fritzy all the time that it's how you deal with your troubles that's important. Jes''cause he was in a wheelchair, it didn't mean that he was off the hook in tryin' to be the best person that he could be. Fritzy shook his leg from side to side, which made me realize he didn't entirely agree. But I always reminded him that God is gradin' us, and that included him.

He understood. Sure enough, most people have mountains of problems and a story to tell and of course these poor people did, too. Fritzy pointed to a homeless woman with a little girl standin' beside her as she sat on the park bench. He pointed with his leg. "Arrugh. Shooon't bbbe," he would say.

One night, a hobo man came to see Dr. Joe. I started thinkin' that we had a bunch of things needin' to be worked on in the Worrells' backyard, and a group of wood-workin' projects he could help with in the coming weeks. Nasty Ruff had chewed ever'thing he could get his nasty mouth around and, as a result, the bushes and plants needed some extra lovin' in that Ruffian-abused backyard. Why, even the back door looked a little chewed. I figured that this man, who was named Scottie, could fix some stuff. The next Christmas was coming round again, and I was sure he could help me do some Christmas decoratin' for Miss Joyce, as well as some yard work.

We would help him some and the church would help him some, too. The next day Scottie showed up over at the Worrells' house and was ready to work. However, Ruff wouldn't leave him alone and thought this was a grand new game. Scottie would start cleanin' up the leaves and then the dog would jump in the middle of the pile. It was funny once, but a second time—not at all. So, I took Ruff inside and had to deal with him in the house. When Ruff had abused me enough, with his counter-perusin' nose and his dog smell, I let him outside. Scottie had burned all the leaves, and I didn't think Ruff could get into any trouble now.

Ruff started to run around in big circles like he always did. At first, we tried to ignore his shenanigans and continued on with our work, but he was such a pest. So, I threw a stick to make him run away from us a little. He was always a sucker for that. However, I was the sucker this time.

Scottie had propped his hoe up against the fence and was standin' there wipin' his brow. The stick fell somewhere in their direction and Ruff took off. Scottie ignored the dog. I considered it a good sign that Scottie was beginnin' to care more about food I served him than the Old Crow he swigged from his jacket flask. This made me feel a bit pious—and you know what the Lord says about that: "Pride cometh before a fall."

And while we had our guard down and were feelin' prideful, Ruff grabbed the hoe and started runnin' off toward the open gate. Scottie started yellin', "Stop, you fool dog." Of course, he didn't move very fast, 'cause he was tired and old and Ruff was way ahead.

That bad dog Ruff had grabbed the hoe like it was a giant bone. It stretched five feet wide and the gate was only about four. However, Ruff, with his pea-sized brain, didn't know that. He had no idea what was about to happen to his stupid self. Ruff hit that gate in a flat-out run. He hit it with such force, as to knock him dead forever. He laid on the ground like a Raggedy Andy doll. I went runnin' to him and bent over the poor carcass. "Oh, Ruff, I let you kill yourself; they're gonna surely fire me now." I looked up toward the heavens, but there were only gray, Iowa-colored clouds—jes' like the darn food.

I heaved real tears and couldn't believe I was so upset. As naughty as he was, Fritzy adored him and I had even gotten to where I liked his silly dog personality. After all, a dog didn't ask to be born a dog.

We decided to bury him over near the fence. He always liked to sit and bark his fool head off by the fence. He might as well be there eternally. I didn't know what I was gonna tell the Worrells. They would probably think I knocked him off.

Scottie went and got some burlap rags from the shed, and we wrapped Ruff's poor body in them. Then, we said some words over him and I cried some more. He really wasn't so bad a dog. He jes' ate the icin' off my cake one time. Oh yeah, and then he ate saucy Miss Susan's muffler. I thought I'd better stop there. It's not nice to speak ill of the dead.

Scottie picked up the shovel and set to gruntin' and diggin'.

Then Miss Joyce came up behind me and took my hand. "I take it Ruff met a bad end?" I swear she was almost smilin'. I nodded my head up and down and my chin was settin' to quiverin'. I still didn't notice Miss Joyce lookin' any too sad.

"Yep, Mrs. Worrell, it was fast. He ran himself into the gate. Took him right out," Scottie said and stretched his arm out for emphasis and rammed his fist into his hand.

Then Miss Joyce suggested we do the honors right then before Fritzy got back. He was out with his daddy in the car. It was one of the few times they went somewhere, together, and then this had to happen.

Miss Joyce very seriously began an impromptu sermon

forgivin' him for his tawdry past and wishin' him Godspeed to dog heaven. We all cried like paid mourners.

I was also busy thankin' the Almighty for not puttin' any more dead bodies in our diggin' path.

Miss Joyce concluded, "And dear Lord, please help us to understand your ways and to adapt to them as best we can."

Jes' as Scottie gently placed poor Ruff in the hole and started the dirt coverin' process, Ruff jumped up outta there like he'd been shot from a cannon. It wouldn't have been so funny if he hadn't been wearin' his naughty, Ruffian grin. He ran around the yard, with the burlap rags in his mouth, as if to say, "Stupid people, you fell for my trick—again."

Scottie took off after him and Miss Joyce and I fell to the ground laughin' our fool heads off. Why, that darn dog had nine lives!

I squinted my eyes at Ruff and said, "Nasty Ruff! I'll get you yet." We laughed so hard, we fell down, and we cried. And that was the second time in my life I laughed myself into cryin'.

Then we all walked toward the house. We stopped on the back porch to say good-bye and pay Scottie for his work. That's when Scottie said, "Say, I wanted to ask you about the man who's been standing on the street curb watching me work almost all of the day? Is he connected to you somehow?"

I looked over to the spot, but there wasn't anyone there. A chill ran up and down my spine like a neon zipper sign. I walked to the front yard to see the fella, but he was already gone.

The thought bothered me, but there was nothin' I could do. So, I ignored it. Besides, we had jes' been through an emotional experience, and I couldn't make my mind jump that fast.

When Fritzy and Dr. Joe got home, we tried to look innocent, but we couldn't stop laughin'.

Scottie came every day for several weeks after that, until one day he jes' didn't show. That's the way those folks did things. Earn a little money and then they were off on a train somewhere. I guessed he went down South where it was a little warmer. I understood; I liked warm myself.

By then the yard was clean and nice and all the little things that needed fixin' were done, so Scottie's timin' was right.

Chapter 26

An Uninvited Guest

We were fixin' Thanksgiving dinner and puttin' corn in ever'thing 'cause it was that time of the year, again. That farmer had been to the doctor once more and given us even more corn. I was makin' cookies and good things to eat, and Fritzy and I were goin' all over town lookin' for all the things to make a good meal and a happy holiday. We went into Mr. Bishop's 'cause we were in a hurry and he was surprisingly pleasant, maybe on account of the fact that he had competition in town now.

There was a line behind us so we hurriedly took our groceries and bustled out into the snow. The weather was terrible. There was a side wind that took the grainy snow sideways into our faces, and the snow hit Fritzy's metal chair and bounced off like little itty bitty pellets. We hurried home with the bag of groceries in Fritzy's lap and drew big happy breaths of warm air when we bounded through the door. I noticed that Fritzy's face was redder than usual and his nose was runnin' like a spring. I asked him, "Fritzy, you feelin' OK?" His foot didn't move very fast as if he was thinkin' about what to say. It went to maybe.

I thought he was lookin' a little peaked, so I said we'd better take his temperature and get him somethin' warm to drink when we got home. I got up close to his face and I noticed he looked a little glassy-eyed too, like when you have a fever. I was always especially worried any time that Fritzy got sick, 'cause Dr. Joe warned me that in his condition it might not take much to do him in.

Dr. Joe was goin' to show up before the next patient, and he was goin' to bring some wintergreen poultice that we could put on Fritzy's chest. It would help keep the cold in his head and not let it go into his chest. Sometimes it worked; sometimes it didn't.

Dr. Joe came home before his next patient. He walked in without even a hello and told me to rub some wintergreen poultice on Fritzy's chest and then put him under the covers. All I could do then was to keep him warm and give him a lot to drink.

We did not celebrate Thanksgiving. We worried about Fritzy and the Worrells ate a quiet dinner by the radio. I solemnly ate my beautiful dinner in the kitchen.

I rocked Fritzy in the same chair that I rocked him in when he was a little guy, never guessin' that he would make it this far, and I listened to his gentle breathin' fearin' that the end was goin' to come sooner than later. I hoped he could get well this time, but worried he might not. One day he got worse and we thought it was gonna be curtains, but the next day he got better and we breathed a sigh of relief.

Fritzy got well, but jes' barely. It was a good thing, too, 'cause Dr. Joe and Miss Joyce were gonna leave the next week to go to Chicago for a couple of days. The doctors were gatherin' for a convention and it was gonna be in Chicago, which it hadn't been in a long time. So they were pleased to get the chance to go when it was this close. It was also a chance for the Worrells to get away from all the daily things that wore them down. They had never taken time off from Fritzy, except the trip to Atlanta.

I knew we would do fine without them. The Calloway children were gonna spend one night at our house, 'cause starchy Donny and saucy Miss Susan were goin' to the convention, too. I wondered if Miss Susan and Dr. Joe would behave themselves or find a way to sneak off together for a moment, but, thankfully, my thoughts got back quickly to the task at hand. Friday night I was gonna cook my surefire spaghetti with tomatoes hidden in it so none of them would realize they were eatin' somethin' good for their little selves.

All the kids were in the house runnin' around with that nasty Ruff chasin' close behind. He was nippin' at the little girl, Claudia, 'cause she ran the slowest, except for Fritzy, who didn't run at all. Ruff jes' gave Fritzy his usual lip kiss and I shuddered, but Fritzy loved it. While they were runnin' about, I was standin' at the kitchen sink and lookin' out the window not thinkin' anythin', when I spied a man standin' across the street lookin' at the house. He had a fedora pulled down across his eyes, and he was jes' quietly lookin' our way. I felt a sense of evil and instinctively stepped away from the sink. A chill ran up my spine, and I looked to see where the kids were, jes' to make sure I had ever'body accounted for. Ruff even stopped to listen. He might have been smarter than he looked. But I somehow doubted it.

When I looked back the man was gone and it was almost dark. I had this uneasy feelin', so I fed ever'body as fast as I could. The kids didn't notice my uneasiness and were teasin' one another, but it was mostly Miss Claudia that was gettin' teased. I looked around at their happy faces and forgot all about the stranger, 'cause the kids started laughin' and makin' fun of my rolls. They were very hard on account of me being distracted over the stranger. The rolls were overcooked and felt like rocks, so the children were throwin' them across the table.

"Don't you do that again or I'll give you the Anna ear pinch," I told them.

Mick picked one up and threw it at Ruff, who caught it midair and started chewin' it like a bone it was so hard. I couldn't help but laugh, even the greatest cooks have a failure every once and a while—and this was my once. But they forgot about the rolls and were off to the next bit of naughtiness, which was throwin' spaghetti cheese at Miss Claudia and it got in her hair. Whew, she was gonna smell like fine aged cheese for a while.

The boys smirked as they held their noses to make fun, and I shooed them off like summer flies. They went into the rumpus room with Fritzy and settled down. I concentrated on doin' dishes and lookin' back out into the dark, dark night. I was tryin' to see the man again. Miss Claudia sat at the table and pretended to read her story, but she jes' looked at pictures. We were all settlin' in.

Then the boys started screamin' loud and ran into the kitchen, leavin' Fritzy in the rumpus room yellin' at the top of his lungs and shakin' all over. "Anna, Anna, there's a man staring in the window at us!" the boys stopped and then yelled. "Oh, we left Fritzy! Anna, help us. We can't go back in there."

I took off toward the back of the house, but when I got in the rumpus room, there was no bad guy to be seen. I grabbed Fritzy, but he said, "Yes." I knew he wouldn't lie. I leaned down and whispered in Fritzy's ear and asked him if it was the man from the bank robbery.

I had saved the article from the bank robbery, and I showed the article to Fritzy again, 'cause I wanted him to be on the lookout for the bad bank robber guy, too. The paper had the robber's picture real clear on the front page. I did this 'cause I wasn't sure if Fritzy got as good a look at the robber as I did while ever'thing was goin' down. This way, at least he would know what the bad guy looked like from the photograph.

Fritzy looked scared. He wiggled, yes.

My worst fears were confirmed. We both knew. The bank robber was back. I told Fritzy not to let anyone else know about who the man was.

Fritzy wiggled, yes.

I walked around the house makin' sure ever'thing was locked up tight. I rattled the doors and checked the locks and ever'thing seemed good. I was feelin' tired from all of the day's shenanigans, but pushed myself to finish up.

Then I announced bedtime, assurin' the children that no boogey man could find them in the dark, so we weren't leavin' any lights on. I forced ever'one to brush their teeth and put on their pajamas. None of them were very talkative and they climbed in, under the covers, with only their little heads peekin' out. They jes' wanted to be safe. I turned out the lights.

There's a certain margin of safety in the dark that kids don't understand. It's easier to be safe in the dark 'cause you're harder to find, plus the odds of steppin' on a toy go way up in the dark. That way it's also hard for bad guys to see where we are, too. Maybe the bad guys would fall over that nasty dog—serve them right. I knew the bad guys only wanted me and Fritzy. So, I made the decision to get the Calloway kids back over to their house as soon as I could the next mornin'.

Their Grandmother was gonna watch them the next night. The sooner I got the Calloway kids outta harm's way, the better. But, until then, we would jes' have to be harder to see in the dark. I went to the front of the house and turned off the porch light. Then I crept into my room and kept ever'thing dark. I got undressed in the dark and found my nightgown, then I crept into bed real stealth-like and tried not to make any noise. I listened to the darkness and tried to imagine how a bad guy would get in. I couldn't.

Jes' as I was about to fall asleep, I heard the noise. A person hears noises all the time when they sleep. Most of the time you get used to the ones that happen through the night and you jes' learn to ignore those sounds, but when you hear a noise that doesn't jive with the others, it sets you on edge. This one set me on edge. I could hear the hardwood floors creak, but it wasn't quite like footsteps, it sounded like somethin' else. I knew naughty Ruff was in with the kids, and I had closed the door to their room, so I didn't think it could be him. I laid there in my full-listen mode and tried to decide what I was hearin'. Then I jumped about a mile high. Somethin' wet touched my hand.

Darn Ruffian had done it again. He was always playin' tricks on me. His toothy grin was shinin' back at me in the dark reflections, and I could hear his tail waggin' as it hit the side of the bed. Thud. Thud. Thud.

I rolled over away from him. He had a dog breath on him like you wouldn't believe. Must be all those table scraps he had got the kids to give him at dinner, not to mention my hard-as-a-rock rolls.

He jes' wagged and smiled. That's when I realized that ole Ruff would be nervous if someone was around, but this dog was cool as could be. I decided we were safe, for right now, so I rolled over and went to sleep. The mornin' was gonna come early with this crew of wild ones, and I would have to make sure they got a good breakfast before I dumped them with Grandma Calloway.

We got up early, and after I got ever'body fed, we all went outside to play. I took that opportunity to check for footprints around the windows. It had rained a few days before and the ground was still soft, so any footprints would show. Sure enough, there were some footprints right where the boys had said there would be. My fears were confirmed. Someone had been here and stood around for a while. I saw cigarette butts on the ground around the window, too. Why, he could have jes' set this big, white clapboard house, with its beautiful green shutters, up like a tinder box if he had thought about it. I was glad he wasn't that smart. What all this proved was that our bad guy must be outta the hoosegow. I would have to call the newspaper to see if they knew anythin' about his release or escape as soon as it opened up for business on Monday.

Chapter 27

Not Time for Dyin' Yet

The answer came earlier than I expected when I raced out to pick up the paper from the front lawn. There on page two was the story about Mallo Smith, being the skinny guy I sat on during the robbery, havin' escaped from the pen two days before. The story emphasized that he was armed and dangerous. Of course, the reporter didn't have to tell me that tasty bit of news—I already knew that without a doubt. What's more, the timin' had matched up perfectly, 'cause that was when Scottie said he saw the stranger across the street. So, the bad guy was back and he would be seekin' revenge, with a little Mallo malice mixed in. And I figured both parts would be aimed at me and Fritzy.

I showed the article to Fritzy and told him we were gonna have to be ready when that guy came. I knew he couldn't call the cops, but he could alert me without the robbers knowin' it. Fritzy and I were scary calm. That's how you get when you have to win and you don't have the winnin' hand. I'd get that way with Miss Edwina sometimes, when I jes' knew my hand was darn atrocious. I'd stop and think: I can do this. I can win anyway.

We had to be able to communicate with each other somehow. So we decided our signal would be Fritzy makin' a sound that repeated itself three times if he needed to warn me of somethin'. It was a guttural noise, but if you didn't know Fritzy, it jes' sounded like any retarded kid. However, it was not a sound he made frequently. We also decided on another signal so he could leave somethin' to let me know if there was somethin' wrong. I would make sure he always had a ball in his lap. If he jes' knocked it outta his lap and let it roll onto the floor, Ruff would leave it alone. Ruff only went after balls if they were thrown. So Fritzy could drop the ball and its thud when it hit the floor could be another signal.

I hated to leave Fritzy alone, but it would only take a few minutes to run the Calloways over to their house and into their grandma's open and very critical arms. Grandma Calloway was one of those people that Miss Edwina calls a matron of class. She said some women like that care more what's on their tombstone and what they wear, than about the details of their life and love. She cared how the kids were dressed more than if they were fed. Miss Edwina named her right.

That day she was waitin' with outstretched arms for the Calloway kids. But when I asked her what she had planned for lunch for them, she said she supposed they would jes' have somethin' from the kitchen and then listen to the radio.

I jes' knew the kids would love that, and I was thinkin' to myself, "How did she raise a doctor?" The answer is she didn't. The kid raised himself, and that's why he was such a no-fun fella.

Grandma Calloway invited me to come in and stay awhile. But I wasn't fallin' for that one. She was hopin' that I would end up puttin' lunch together for them, but I was needed elsewhere.

The wind was blowin', but otherwise it was a clear, cool day with leaves whirlin' ever'where like little cyclones. My worries about Mallo Smith settled back down on my shoulders as I ran toward the house.

The day was still young, so I figured Fritzy and I had time to get ready and put some angles together to thwart our enemy if and when he showed. I threw open the door and rushed in. I stopped in my tracks. There was the ball standin' all alone on the spot where I left him and Ruff. Neither one were where I left them. I began to run through the house. I didn't yell though, I tried to be quiet, but all 300 pounds of me couldn't do that. So I hurried as best I could, holdin' my breath all the way. I got to the rumpus room and there was Fritzy with Mallo pointin' a gun at his head. It seemed pretty silly to me at the time, I figured Fritzy had never been able to run from anythin' in his life, so why point at gun at him? As scared as I was, that thought ran across my mind.

"Let him go. He can't hurt you," I said.

"Yeah, and he can point to my mug shot with that good toe of his. You're crazy if you think he can't. He just called me a son of a bitch with that slurred out face of his," Mallo said.

Fritzy looked insulted. He always hated people talkin' about him like he wasn't there. I continued, "He cain't hurt you and neither can I. We promise not to testify. Besides, the cops never interviewed us. It's like we never existed."

That insulted me to say it, but it was the truth. We wouldn't be credible witnesses Dr. Joe said. If he and I were white and able, we would've been talkin' ourselves silly down at the station. But we were Negro and infirmed, so we weren't credible witnesses. I bet they interviewed Miss Butter Leather 'til she was blue in the face. She was credible enough, plus she looked like Eleanor Powell with legs jes' that good.

So, now Mallo was standin', free, in the rumpus room with a big, fat revolver aimed at Fritzy. Then, it dawned on me. Where was that rascal Ruff? He was not usually prone to being quiet around strangers. I looked at Fritzy and held my hand out in a pettin' motion. Mallo look over at me like I was nuts. I could tell by the look in his eye, he thought I should be crazy, 'cause I was a big colored woman.

Then Mallo said, "Now, Anna, I'm going to put you and Fritzy in the pantry where you can't get away. I'll do the honors there. It's something like shooting fish in a barrel. Ever heard of that?"

Of course I heard of that, but I didn't reply.

"That should contain the noise, so the neighbors won't come running. We wouldn't want that." Mallo smiled as he took the safety off his gun and then motioned us to get goin' toward the pantry.

I looked over at Fritzy and he fidgeted more than usual. He was makin' a motion that he did when he was playin' with Ruff. He kept makin' the motion. I couldn't figure it out. We filed into the pantry and Mallo made me go first 'cause I was so big, then he pushed Fritzy in backward in front of me. We were wedged in there good.

I started thinkin' about my own mama, and how I hadn't visited her enough or told her I loved her enough, and that I would never see my grandchildren. Then I was angry that I would never know what would become of Altus and that nasty son-in-law of mine, on account of I would be dead. Then I thought of how much I loved my girls and that they would be orphans after this. The tears began to roll down my round cheeks and they tasted salty. Fritzy look angry and he wasn't cryin', 'cause he was madder than a hornet, but he kept makin' his Ruff motions. Fritzy showed again this time that he didn't fear dyin', 'cause he'd always been so close to it, I guess. But, I feared dyin' when I thought about my family.

Mallo was taking aim and Fritzy was wigglin' more than ever

and yellin' that sound he said he would make three times. Suddenly, Ruff came through the air like a pony-sized bird. I could hear his nasty growl and smell his dirty fur in the small pantry. Ruff pushed Mallo forward with such force they crashed into us, and the cans, flour, and boxes started goin' ever'where and fallin'. They fell down on us like a heavy-ass rain. Then the gun went off and shot right into the tomato soup above my head. We looked red-orange with all the soup ever'where, and sticky, too. Ruff looked better to me than he ever had with that bristly fur and his horrible dog breath. He had old Mallo by the neck and, once again, I jumped down on Mallo. But this time I had a dilemma to deal with. 'Cause, when I sat on him now, there wasn't anybody around to help me up and watch the bad guy or phone the cops. Plus, the phone was in the other room. I panicked and felt a surge of fearful juices race through my body.

Ruff was growlin' with one long wail underneath. It was like he was mad but hurtin' at the same time. There were drops of dark red mixed around the soup, too. Somebody was hit. I couldn't tell if Ruff was hit by the bullet or jes' expressin' himself—but I knew one of them was hit. Then, Lord help me, I took a giant can of navy beans and whacked Mallo on the head. If I couldn't move then he wasn't goin' to either. It made an awful gash and he started cussin' up a storm, so I hit him again. I heard a definite crunchin' sound the second time, and he quieted down. Then, I leaned down in his ear where Fritzy couldn't hear and I said, "You move again and I'll make a place in your head the size of my fist." He didn't move. I looked around and I couldn't see where the gun fell to, so I jes' had to decide not to worry about it that minute. I made a fake gun with my hand and looked over at Fritzy. Fritzy figured out what I meant and motioned to his left—jes' outta my vision range.

Then I scooched over toward the phone and outta the pantry,

enough to let Fritzy through. Fritzy looked at me with his most serious face and tried to move his wheelchair forward in a movin' motion. He did this with his one good leg, and I tried my best to push his wheelchair on the other side, with my foot, so he wouldn't be goin' in circles. He was near the phone now, and I hoped he could pull the phone off the cradle and onto the floor near where I was. Fritzy looked scared but kept tryin'. First, he tried 'til he got the phone down, then he kicked it with his good foot.

Suddenly, Mallo came to and started to move around again. I could tell I hurt him pretty bad, 'cause he still looked kinda drunk in the head, but I could still see the hate in his eyes. He was a bad sort no matter how you sliced it, and—Lord help me—I hit him again. This time, I jes' knew I crushed his skull. He didn't move any more, and his mouth opened and no sound came out. I was not too far a distance from his face, and I looked at him with real malice. I wanted him dead. He stood for all the wrong things in the world and I wanted him gone.

Fritzy did so good, he knocked the whole phone thing down, which was more than I thought he could do. Now, that it was on the floor, maybe I could stretch and reach it. Fritzy stayed by the phone and knew how to punch it down for the operator. We might be able to make this work, if I could jes' talk into the thing.

I could tell he wanted me to say somethin', but I was so far away. "Taaaak." I finally figured out he was sayin' 'talk.' Then I yelled, "Help! We're at Doc Worrell's house. We need an ambulance and the cops. Hurry!" I couldn't hear anythin' back, but Fritzy shook his foot, yes.

That's when I looked at Mallo again. His eyes were open, but it didn't look like anybody was home in his head. I decided he was dead or very close to it. There was a puddle of blood around his head like a halo, and he was lookin' real pale, even for a white man.

As Fritzy and I looked at one another we heard the first sounds of sirens coming nearer. I suddenly felt weak and very tired. I saw tears runnin' down Mallo's cheeks, but his face was still—stoic-like. His eyes were open wide, and I knew he was feelin' somethin'. I jes' wasn't sure what it was. I suddenly felt very guilty for what I had done.

I looked at Fritzy and we knew, once again, we had come very close to meetin' an early end.

As I lay on the floor, I could hear the cops coming up the wooden ramp. Ever'one always took the ramp instead of the steps to the wooden porch—it was easier. It was then that I realized the doors were all locked, and they would have to break in to get to us. I saw the white uniforms of the ambulance drivers and the dark cop uniforms through the front windows, all waitin' to get in. They were yellin' for us to open up. But we were in no condition to respond. So, Fritzy and I started yellin' at the tops of our lungs. I thought it took forever, but they finally figured out they would have to break in. They broke the windowpane beside the front door. I could see a long uniformed arm unlockin' the door, and I started breathin' right again, 'cause I sure hadn't been doin' that before now.

The same cop, Sammy, from the bank robbery was there. He couldn't believe what had happened. He started talkin' about us being the people from the bank robbery and that this was the bank robber.

Then the ambulance driver sure enough turned out to be Marty. We sat mesmerized, watchin' Marty work on Mallo. He looked real dead to me.

In small towns, your chances of bumpin' into people more than once are much higher, and I guess that's why they say people from small towns are nicer—they have to be! I hugged Sammy and Marty and sat down on the divan, cryin' into my hanky once more. I realized that Marshalltown had sure been full of adventure. You could say it was the adventure of my life.

The cops had put the phone back and taken out the cans that were shot up. Nothin' was left but Mallo's puddle of blood and a lot of tomato soup over all of us, the pantry, and other places it jes' sort of oozed and splattered onto. I knew it would take copious amounts of bleach and water to get that mess up. I noticed there was a hard outline beginnin' to form around the puddles where the blood was beginnin' to dry. I was thinkin' to myself that I needed to get to it before it all dried up and got crusty.

Sammy was standin' beside me when he started talkin' about being there at the Worrells before as part of the investigation when they found the bodies in the backyard.

I heard him tell one of the other officers, "I'm not part of the ongoing investigation, so I am not up to date on their findings. All I know is that they said they were both women. That's all I know."

In spite of all that was goin' on, I perked up and managed to think fast enough to ask if he knew how old the dead women were.

"No, those bodies were a mess. They were almost down to the bone in decomposition. Couldn't tell a thing. Just a lot of bushy, dirty gray hair on one and a lot of bushy, dirty blond hair on the other," he said.

Sometimes people give information when they don't even know it. He continued, "The one body was someone older and the second body was someone younger and blonde. That's all I know."

The conversation ended abruptly when it was time to transport Mallo. Marty hurried him out on a stretcher and the cops helped him put his bag of emergency things into the ambulance. They threw the doors closed with a final thud. Then Marty took off at his usual speed. He was closin' his side door as the engine roared to life and the ambulance took off down the road. I could hear the tires screechin', and as the siren got further and further away, it became quieter and quieter.

Chapter 28

Even Ruff Plays a Role in Fate

While the cops came back in to finish their reports, I jes' sat there kind of paralyzed. I had no idea if I wanted Mallo to live. I didn't know anythin' about him. Sometimes knowin' how someone is the way he is makes a whole lot of difference as to how you think about him. I was sure there was a sad story connected to that horrible little man. I was sittin' there ponderin' about Mallo. Then it hit me. Ruff! Where the heck was that dog? He had saved us and now he wasn't around anywhere. I surmised that he must have drifted outside with the cops coming and goin' and leavin' the door open. We jes' needed to see him.

I decided that I would never speak ill of Ruffian again. So, I got up off the divan and pushed Fritzy around the house lookin' for somethin' to show us where he was. First we looked outside 'cause he was always runnin' in and out. Then we went from room to room. By then, it had been a good half hour since Mallo left. That's when we saw him in the rumpus room. He was layin' on his side and not movin'. Fritzy and I cried out together, "Ruff!" and the cops came a runnin'. One of them said, "It's just a dog," and turned around and went back to his report. That's when I started yellin'. He saved us from Mallo. There was no way we were gonna let him jes' die there. It had happened so fast, we jes' didn't realize he had been shot. I felt guilt for not missin' him any sooner after he saved us. And worst of all, we weren't there for him like he had been for us.

So, the cops came and helped us pick Ruff up. He was still and his eyes were closed. I was beginnin' to feel pretty helpless jes' about the time Marty walked back in from deliverin' Mallo to the hospital.

He looked tired but sprang into action. He put Ruff in the ambulance and told us to follow him to the vet. One of the cops walked over to the phone and called a large animal vet that took care of the horses, pigs, and cows, 'cause that was the closest vet. That way, the vet had a heads-up on what was coming. We all piled in the cop car. I made them take Fritzy with us. The two- or three-minute trip to the vet was very sad. I felt Ruff had the bullet somewhere inside him and that wouldn't bode well for him. Fritzy and I locked eyes. I was certain Ruff had to be a goner, but I didn't mention that to Fritzy. We sat quietly and looked out the windows as the cop car hurried us along our familiar streets to the vet's. When we got there, the vet was already operatin' on Ruff. Marty was standin' there lookin' forlorn, but he smiled at Fritzy. It was one of those smiles that have a little pity mixed in.

Marty jes' shook his head and said the same kind of leg shot had taken a prize huntin' dog out a few weeks ago. He lost too much blood. He said he thought this would go the same way. Marty didn't coat his condition with sugar, he jes' let us know the odds. I guessed Fritzy should hear it straight away like that, even though it was hard.

I felt guilty thinkin' about Ruff and not thinkin' about Mallo. But Marty said somethin' that made me feel better. He said,

"Anna, I see a lot of living and dying in my line of business. And I can tell you that dying is not the end. There is something about it that's proud and endearing, even for something like a dog." He said if Ruff didn't make it we shouldn't cry. He had led a great dog life.

We sat there for what seemed like an hour, but it was only about twenty minutes. Finally, the vet came in and introduced himself as Dr. Heinrichs. He paused and glanced at the wall like he really didn't want to look us in the eye. "Your dog is barely hanging on. And it is my opinion that he won't make it. But, I've been surprised before," he said.

Doc Heinrichs looked sad. He had been lookin' at Ruff's innards and probably had a pretty good idea of what was goin' on with him. So I didn't doubt his opinion, but I really wanted him to be wrong.

Fritzy had been so strong through the whole thing, but now he jes' whimpered. There was nothin' I could do. We all sat quietly for another forty-five minutes. I noticed Fritzy had his leg in the yes position the whole time.

Then, a lot later, Doc Heinrichs came out and smiled. He said we had our prayers answered.

"Ruff's going to make it. But, you're going to have to change his name," he said.

He told us he had to take one of Ruff's legs off. He had tried to save it a couple of different ways, but had to give up on that. The bone was jes' too shattered. The vet squinched up his chin fun-like, and told us not to worry that he would walk jes' fine. He said that dogs are one of the few animals that can lose a leg and still be OK. Doc chuckled and said, "You may want to rename him Tri-pod."

The doc was busy laughin' at his own joke. Then he paused and asked me if we lived in Dr. Phillips's old house.

"Yes, we do. I work for the Worrells and this is their son, Fritzy," I said.

When he started talkin' about what a shame it was about their son, I first thought he was talkin' about Fritzy. But he wasn't. He started goin' on about how the Phillipses shouldn't have gone out that day to ski.

I was hopin' he would keep talkin'.

"You know the son had moved up there near Madison to start a new business and his business was beginning to fail. He just couldn't make it work."

"Yes, his parents were up there visiting from Marshalltown, and they had rented a house on the lake. I think they ended up buying it and moving up there full time to look for their son and his wife." Doc Heinrichs looked tired retellin' the story.

I continued to say, "Oh."

"The parents had come up to give them some money to keep it afloat. Mrs. Phillips wanted the doctor to do that, but the doctor was not convinced. Then the son and wife died. I heard they sold his company and made a nice profit from all the machinery even though it wasn't making any money. Then they pocketed a big insurance policy on the kids. Plus, the old doctor had done very well in his practice so he really was set," Doc Heinrichs went on to say.

This was one of those cases when people would sometimes tell me private things 'cause I looked like a person that wouldn't tell a soul. Even if I wanted to spill the beans, who would believe a very large Negro woman? Not many.

Now here we go with the fickle finger of fate again. If Ruff hadn't been hurt, I might never have met Doc Heinrichs. And if I hadn't met him, I wouldn't have heard this part of the story. And if I hadn't heard that part of the story, I wouldn't have been able to put it all together.

Fritzy began to get restless. We had come to see the dog. But Doc Heinrichs said Ruff was asleep right then and suggested we come back to see him the next day.

So Marty said, "Come on, I'll give you a ride." He helped me place Fritzy in the ambulance and he sped us home without the siren. It was kind of a letdown after all the excitement.

Then, as if ever'thing was fallin' into place and the answers were there in front of me all the time, Marty started talkin' about how he drove the meat wagon for those bodies some three years ago when the bodies were discovered in the Worrell's backyard.

He said that he remembered thinkin' that those bodies somehow were related. Not relative-like, but holdin' hands. They were holdin' hands. He said the police thought it was very strange, and the coroner said he'd never seen anythin' like it. He said the case had jes' sort of closed itself 'cause no one had been missin' in Marshalltown, and there weren't any leads.

We arrived home, walked in, and looked around. The house seemed cold and tired and empty. Marty looked sympathetic and asked if we wanted him to stay on the couch that night. He explained that his wife had died and the kids were grown, so nobody would miss him until tomorrow, and the ambulance didn't go back into service until tomorrow mornin' at eight.

I was a little embarrassed, 'cause a white man spendin' the night at the house he didn't normally belong in and where there's colored help wasn't so good. But, I was more scared than embarrassed. I didn't know where Mallo's partner was, so I said that would be very good.

I looked over in the pantry's direction, thinkin' I had a powerful big mess to clean up the next day.

It wasn't even nighttime, but we were so tired and our minds were full of the day's action. I felt a whole lot better knowin' that Marty was on the couch. He had been in the fray of it all in WWI, so I knew he could handle himself if one of Mallo's buddies came back. I hurried to settle down Fritzy and get our prayers in order. We had a lot to be thankful for and a lot to worry about. We needed some powerful prayers. But before I could get the prayers said, I looked over and Fritzy was already fast asleep. I fell asleep immediately, too. The Lord had to kite us that night. No prayers got said.

Chapter 29

We're All Good with a Little Bad Mixed In

The next mornin' started with the phone ringin' off the wall. Grandma Calloway called to say that Ruff made the front page of the paper. I hadn't yet called the Worrells to tell them about what transpired the day before. They were gonna hear about it sure enough. But I now had better get on the horn to them first. But first, I ran out to the front step and grabbed the newspaper. I was tryin' to figure out what to tell them and what to omit. That old sin of omission was propped up on my shoulder as I ran back into the house with that offendin' paper.

The hardest phone call I've ever made was that phone call. I held the paper in my hand as I looked at the headline and Ruff's picture in the paper. It showed Marty carryin' Ruff's limp body out to the ambulance. I handed the paper to Marty, who jes' smiled.

I held the phone close to my ear. One ring, two ring, then he answered. There was this awkward pause, while I drew in a deep breath and started talkin'.

"Hello, Dr. Joe, this is Anna. We had a skirmish here last night. A bad guy broke in the house, but Ruff thwarted the man, but the bad guy shot him," I spurted out. I explained that we were all fine, the house was OK, and they didn't steal anythin', but that Ruff was injured and they would have to take one of his legs off. Dr. Joe said that they were gonna come home early that day anyway, so they would leave immediately.

"Oh, and Ruff made the front page of the newspaper. They called him Rin Tin Ruff. Isn't that a hoot?" I tried to lighten the conversation. Dr. Joe didn't laugh and the phone went dead. He was already on his way. There was still the distinct possibility I could be in hot water.

I decided the best thing to do was make waffles. Now my waffles are crunchy on the outside but soft on the inside, kinda like Marty. His Chicago accent grated on me a little like that Walter Winchell, but they were worlds apart. Marty was a feast of greatness and that Walter Winchell was jes' grated blue cheese. Stinky, but OK in small doses.

I whipped the waffles up in no time and served them hot with butter and warm maple syrup. Fritzy and Marty ate 'til they were as full as ticks. I did too. Then we cleared the table. The big job was staring me in the face.

I put the rinsed dishes in the sink and set forth on the pantry. When you've got a big mess like that, you start at the top and work down. Then you have no need to have to cleanse somethin' twice. Never start out workin' on the floor. Do the floors last, 'cause dust and stuff settles on them.

I took and eyeballed all the cans for punctures. What I found was real interesting. Several bullets were lodged in the cans. One was lodged in the green beans and looked to have been the bullet that almost sent Ruff to dog heaven. It came from the bottom of the can—up, which is why I thought it was Ruff's bullet. The good thing was that it hadn't stayed in the dog like I thought.

I dumped it all in the trash and kept workin'. I had to race the clock to get things cleaned up by the time the Worrells got back. Fritzy pointed out a few spots I had missed, and we were done by lunch. Exhausted, but done. I had only about twenty minutes left to spare before the Worrells walked in.

Miss Joyce raced over to Fritzy, then they looked over at me.

Then would have been a good time to remember the sin of omission I've been tellin' you about. Well, that sin was sittin' right beside me—rearin' its ugly head, 'cause I had never told the Worrells the full story about our part in apprehendin' the bank robbers in the first place, but I needed to tell it all now and fess up.

"Dr. Joe, Miss Joyce," I paused, "you remember I told you that Fritzy and I were in the bank the day it was robbed."

They looked at me like I had three eyes, 'cause they had no idea what was coming next. I continued, "Well, Fritzy tripped the bank robber and I sat on the little vermin. He swore revenge on us, 'cause we were helpin' send him to the pen. Somehow he got out and found us here and there you have it."

Dr. Joe gave me his judgmental look and demanded more information about how Ruff got shot, how Fritzy and I managed not to get shot, and what happened to the bank robber.

So I went on to explain how we hid in the pantry and Ruff jumped Mallo from behind, but somehow the bullet went through Ruff's leg and now he jes' had three legs left, emphasizin' that he saved our lives 'cause Mallo was fixin' to pull the trigger with a little better aim before Ruff jumped him.

I further explained how I sat on him and whacked him on the head with a can of beans to keep him still while Fritzy wheeled his chair over and managed to knock the phone off the hook and talk to the operator.

Dr. Joe had already walked off toward the pantry and muttered that it looked OK and that we jes' needed to call a carpenter to fix it up. We all agreed. Miss Joyce rolled her eyes and insisted that we go to see how Ruff was doin'. So we locked up tight and went across town to good old Ruff's bedside.

We all stood around the silent Ruff. "Ruff, can you hear me?" Miss Joyce whispered. Fritzy made his familiar noise and Ruff looked over at him. His eyes were barely open. Ruff lifted his head and then put it back down again—real fast, like it hurt.

Fritzy pointed to the bandage on his stumpy leg. I jes' nodded my head, yes.

Fritzy had tears wellin' up in his eyes, and Miss Joyce looked like she also was fixin' to well up too. Dr. Joe looked stoic, 'cause he'd seen so much death and sadness in his job. We were all there, not only to support Ruff but to thank him, as if he really knew what we were sayin'.

I was havin' severe guilty feelin's about all the things I blamed on Ruff. That's when it hit me. None of us is all good. We're good with a little bad mixed in. Some have more bad mixed in, but sometimes the good swoops in and outweighs the bad—like it did this time with Ruff.

The problem with Ruff was that when he was good, he was real, real good, and when he was bad it was real, real bad, but his good won out that time. That helped me understand somethin' important, and that somethin' was that God tests us all the time to see how we're doin'. He looks at us to see if there's improvement. No improvement found, you get tested again. When you're finally over the trials and you pass your tests, then you get called back to heaven. Or, if you're too bad to deal with—you can get called back to heaven anyway. Either way, you end up at the pearly gates. Those of us that are still tryin' to improve get to continue tryin', and that's why we're still here. Tryin' and failin' and then succeedin' or failin' again. That's life's little circle I was tellin' you about earlier.

Ruff had passed his test with flyin' colors, but he was still on earth; I guess 'cause God had some more things for him to do. He was still there with his three legs and his awful hair, and I was still there feedin' and yellin' at him for his considerable daily naughtiness.

Dr. Heinrichs was very nice. He had no way of knowin' that he saved the bane of my existence.

We left and went back home. It was cold and Marty came back later to the house and reported on Mallo. Turns out he was gonna make it, too, but they said the gash on his head would make him walk with a limp for the rest of his life, since it did somethin' to his get-a-long.

I immediately felt guilt, but the guilt was on a count of I hadn't insisted the cops listen to our description of the bank robbery in the beginnin'. Maybe they would have kept the two bad guys in a better grade of jail if they had known all the details. But, I hadn't insisted on talkin' to the authorities, 'cause I'm not white and I didn't think they would listen to me. Also, I wish I told the Worrells earlier about the part we took in stoppin' ever'thing at the bank. It's that old sin of omission again, and it never seems to go away.

Chapter 30

More Fate Brings Doc Phillips to Town

Ruff couldn't even entertain us with his silly way of being. He finally gave up and started lyin' next to Fritzy's chair. Animals are funny like that. They understand their people and when they're disrupted, and we were all disrupted. It took us weeks to get back to normal after the shootin'. And wouldn't you know it, jes' as we were gettin' back on track, the Mayor died.

It was sudden-like. He was yellin' at his dog to get off the divan when he keeled right over like a tree in a strong wind. Slow at first and then: boom. That's the way a tree goes and the way he went, too. His secretary, who was quite good lookin', jes' happened to be there and witnessed the whole thing. As her story went that he was yellin' and had the attack, but Marty said he looked like somebody other than himself dressed him. Marty also said he looked real disheveled and the bed wasn't made in his bedroom. Now, he was a widow-man, so it didn't matter what he did in his off hours, and this was during lunch, so we all jes' shook our heads and moved on.

We left Ruff in his backyard when we left to attend the

funeral. Dr. Joe had to throw a ball out into the yard to get Ruff away from the back door. Ruff always fell for the ball trick. He still stared real forlorn at us when we closed the door and went off for the wake. The Mayor was a big deal in the town and kept gettin' re-elected 'cause ever'one said he was a top-drawer fella. The whole town was in genuine mournin' and needed a pretty big place to have ever'one visit.

It was decided that the wake would be held at saucy Miss Susan's house, since it was nice and in the center of town. It had a long driveway that could handle the cars, and people could park next door where there was plenty of room in Doc Calloway's office parkin' lot if need be. The Mayor was widowed and saucy Miss Susan was his niece on her father's side, so a lot of the plannin' fell to her. Her father's sister had been the Mayor's wife. When we got there to the house, she was workin' on her makeup and hair. She looked her sexy, saucy self.

Word traveled fast about the Mayor and the whole town showed up with some kind of white Iowa food. I had come early over to the Calloway's house to help out. They had mountains of food in the kitchen that nobody was goin' to eat if I didn't keep bringin' it out to the table and the sideboard. I knew the Calloway kids wouldn't eat it—they were finicky. Only the adult Iowa folk would eat it, 'cause they didn't know any better. So, I rushed it out to the dining room and people gobbled it up like turkeys eatin' grain. I was puttin' it out as fast as people were bringin' it in. The leftovers would go to Ruff. He'd eat anythin', and he needed his strength those days. After the onslaught finished comin', I planned to give Miss Joyce, Fritzy and the Calloways some real Southern comfort food when we started the healin'. That's a long process and it takes a lot of food to do it right. I was already thinkin' about my comfort chicken fried steak with gravy and the sides I would put with it. I had already decided on a rhubarb pie to chase it with.

I was puttin' out a tray of what looked like white sugar cookies—which didn't taste too bad—when an older gentleman spoke to me. "Anna," he said, "you have been a godsend to the Worrells and the Calloways."

I had absolutely no idea who in the heck this white fella was. He wore tweeds and had a white mustache and head of hair that would make a bald, thirty-year-old envious. He looked very distinguished, but he didn't ring any bells with my infallible memory. He had one of those comfortin', calmin' voices that make people stop and listen. He had my attention.

"Oh, I should introduce myself. I am Dr. Randall Phillips. I was the doctor here in Marshalltown before Dr. Worrell and Dr. Calloway. After I retired, my wife and I bought a house on a lake in Wisconsin," he told me.

He had my interest, and thankfully he kept talkin'.

"We haven't been back to Marshalltown since I retired, but I wanted to come when I heard about the Mayor. It's a shame. He was my brother-in-law, you know. We were married to sisters."

All the bells began to go off in my head. This guy was gonna know a lot. In fact, he was gonna know a lot about the backyard for sure. He had me thinkin' he might be a murderer.

I absently said, "Has the town changed much since you left?" I figured I'd be vague and then get down to business.

"The town hasn't changed too much, but the house you live in has changed a whole lot. When I sold the office to Dr. Worrell, I sold him the house, too. It was a package deal."

"Oh, who did you buy the house from? Or did you build it?" I asked, tryin' not to look as interested as I truly was.

He said he bought it from an older couple who had no children; he thought they ended up movin' to Des Moines with a relative. Then he started reminiscin' about how they used to sit out on the back porch and drink coffee in the mornin's when the weather was nice and that he thought it a shame that the Worrells had enclosed it. Doc Phillips said when they moved to Wisconsin, he insisted on a place with a great back porch like that one.

I was thinkin' to myself, "Why don't I like this guy?" He had the bedside manner a doctor needs, but there was somethin' smarmy about him. I decided to jump into the conversation with a real scene-stealer. "You know they found some dead bodies in the backyard when they dug the pool for Doc Worrell's son. Got any ideas about that?"

The doc looked a little taken aback when I said that. I could tell he was givin' me the uppity look that white people do when a Negro woman says somethin' out of line. His eyebrows went up and his eyes squinted. I knew the look.

"Those two bodies were probably Indian burials," he said. "You know this was an Indian settlement a hundred years ago."

With that, he turned and walked away—jes' like Dr. Joe used to do when things didn't go his way and he didn't want to talk about a subject anymore.

I walked back into the kitchen to fetch some more white food. I needed to concentrate on how to get the Calloway family through this week of complications.

Fritzy wasn't with me when I was talkin' to Doc Phillips, so I stopped by to update him as best I could. "That man doesn't bode right with me, and I don't know why. I know he's hidin' somethin'," I said.

It was then that Fritzy let me in on his secret.

"EEE saaay diiff," Fritzy said in his special language.

"What are you sayin'? That he's lyin'?"

Foot in the yes position.

"How do you know?"

That's when Fritzy touched his lips.

All I could think was kissin'. "You mean he's kissin' somebody? I jes' saw him hug someone over there. Is that what you mean?"

"Nooo."

Fritzy did what he did when he wanted me to move him; he scooched forward in his chair. So I forgot about what I should be doin' and pushed him over near Doc Phillips. Fritzy squinted his eyes, and I could tell he was concentratin' real hard. I couldn't tell what he was gettin' out of it, 'cause we were outta earshot. Then Fritzy signaled to me that I should move him to another part of the room—which I did.

Then Fritzy said, "Dooc told liii."

"He told a lie?"

Leg shot up, yes.

That's when, darn it, he touched his lips again.

About that time Miss Joyce came over and asked me to get some more white food from the kitchen. And she whisked Fritzy away with her to sit with saucy Miss Susan's brothers, who came in from Chicago.

I noticed that Fritzy didn't take his gaze off Doc Phillips for the next two hours. I hadn't understood what he meant, but there was definitely somethin' goin' on with the lip touchin'.

Doc Calloway came into the kitchen and looked his serious self. No smiles there, even when he was with the kids. But I always tried to be nice to him. He buttered parts of my bread, too.

He proceeded to tell me that Mrs. Calloway and he were very sorry this happened to the Mayor—and the void that his loss caused. He said that he and Mrs. Calloway would be doin' more things down at city hall and that he might even like to run for Mayor himself, eventually. He paused as if I needed a pause to take it all in, and then went on about how Mrs. Calloway would probably need more help, 'cause she would be needed by his side for most of the city affairs.

Ah, that key word, affair, caught my ear. Little did starchy Donny Calloway know that his wife was havin' an affair with his best friend, Dr. Joe. Boy, would that take the starch right outta him!

The doc went on sayin' he had talked to Mrs. Calloway and she wanted him to tell me there was always a job for me with them if things ever had to change in the future with my employment with the Worrells.

That was white-speak for if the Worrells couldn't pay me anymore, due to the Depression, then I could come to the Calloway's full time. White people poached each other's maids and cooks all the time. It was an accepted happenin'. That way, the maid went over to the new people for more money and then she went back to the old people for more money still. That's how she got a raise, 'cause the white folk weren't big on raises for their household people. After all, nobody wants to pay more for somethin' they paid less for last week, unless they jes' have to.

I didn't tell Doc Calloway this but there was no way I was goin' to the Calloway's. Between the awful Grandma Calloway and saucy Miss Susan, I'd be a mess—not to mention the hellion brothers.

In my kindest, whitest voice I said, "Oh, why thank you. That's very nice of you to offer. I'm not sure what the future holds right now. But, it's good to know."

I also laughed 'cause the word, poach, jumped into my head. They were tryin' to poach me, while Dr. Joe was poachin' saucy Miss Susan. We were all poachers of one kind or another and it didn't matter the color.

I looked over at Fritzy, who was outta earshot, but I could tell he heard. He had a pretty horrified look on his face, all the way from the dining room. That's when it hit me: He could read lips.

Lookin' back, it made sense. He was stuck in a wheelchair

mostly watchin' other people from a far away distance doin' what they do best—talk. He taught himself. Fritzy was like that. He was smart beyond his years in some ways, but jes' a little wheelchair kid in some others.

I sashayed over to him and said, "You understood what Doc Calloway said, didn't you?"

"Arruugh, yeeesss," he said, and I whispered, "Well, who do you think is responsible? And more importantly, who do you want to eavesdrop on this next week?" I laughed and so did Fritzy.

It took forever to get ever'thing cleaned up after the crowd left. Fritzy was forced to sit in the kitchen and watch me run around pickin' up dishes and used linen napkins. He fell asleep. Miss Susan was already in bed with the door closed. She was wrung out. Jes' like I would be after I got ever'thing done.

Chapter 31

Rings 'n Things

The next mornin' I asked Fritzy what he wanted to do.

"Boooook," he said.

Now, when he said book he could mean a book to read or the library. After the day before, I was bettin' it was the library. We got dressed and went there straight away. We walked in and Fritzy pointed the way with his foot straight out. I dutifully pushed.

We had stopped in the newspaper section where all the old newspapers were kept. I filled in Fritzy's thoughts and said, "You want to know about the disappearances? So, when do you think they happened?"

"Houuse selllll."

"When the house sold?"

"Aruugh," he confirmed.

Fritzy and I stood before the librarian in charge of archived newspapers. Her nameplate on the desk said Miss Smith. No first name.

I'm sure we looked a sight to her, but we were past carin'. After all, you don't see a little boy in a wheelchair and a huge black woman all the time in the middle of white-plate Iowa.

I told her we would like the newspapers for around the time Dr. Randall Phillips retired. She paused and looked at us with rather steely eyes. I couldn't tell what she was thinkin'.

Then she said Dr. Phillips was her favorite and that she and her husband went to him for years. She went on about how nice he and his wife were. I remember thinkin' it was odd that this woman had no smile.

"Oh, you knew his wife?" Fritzy squirmed and tried to kick me about that time. I ignored it.

"Yes, she was a lovely woman up until the accident. Then, after that, she couldn't do much and they moved away," she said, disclosin' to us that their son and his wife were killed in a skiing accident in Wisconsin.

The older woman thumbed through the archives and brought us both articles from the retirement notice and the accident, along with the obituary for the young couple. The events had all taken place within a month of one another. Then she left and went back to her desk. She still didn't smile.

I whispered, "Look Fritzy, it says here that they ended the search in Wisconsin. Does that mean they found them?" I pointed to that part of the paper. "I am willin' to bet their bodies are in the backyard and they aren't in any Wisconsin."

Fritzy shook his foot, yes.

But I wondered why Sammy told us both of the bodies were women.

Then I opened up the story on the young couple. The son looked like his father without a mustache, but with that same huge head of hair, only dark. He was smilin' in the picture and looked quite handsome for a white man. She was small and looked a little mousy to my way of thinkin' and was the definite lesser good lookin' of the two. However, they made a nice couple in their mid-thirties. There was another picture of them standin' together in happier times. The article was glowin' and positive. It went on to say that the couple was doin' some cross-country skiing when they got caught in a snowstorm and lost their way. The article never actually said they found the bodies. It jes' said they disappeared. The gist of the story was that they froze to death.

I caught myself wonderin' what had really happened to the young couple. About that time, I noticed Fritzy was intently focused on the librarian. She was on the phone at the main desk. Fritzy looked nervous and was movin' all around—couldn't sit still. I figured he would tell me what she was sayin' later, now that I had discovered his newfound talent.

The newspaper article went on to say that the doctor had decided to retire 'cause of the death of family members and that he had moved to Bone Lake, Wisconsin, and built a house. It sounded good, but Fritzy and I knew better. We were sure there was a reason that Doc Phillips needed to get outta town.

We rushed back home to see Miss Joyce and ask some questions. I wasn't sure how or what I would ask, since I really didn't have the feel for where this whole thing was goin'. So I jes' asked Miss Joyce when they bought the house from Doc Phillips.

She said it had been nine years since he sold them the house and the office buildin' and all the patients if they chose to stay.

Fritzy said, "Pooool." So I asked her to tell us as much as she could remember about diggin' the pool and findin' the bodies. She recalled clearly that it was on a Saturday in early November and how she noticed what looked like a woman's ring in the dirt—it was shiny, and she had reached down to pick it up.

"It was a diamond ring, but there was a hand connected to it. I was so upset when I saw it," Miss Joyce said. "Joe was used to dead bodies, so he took a much closer look and ascertained there were two bodies, and then we called the police immediately. The cops came and dug the hole bigger, so we got the pool expanded bigger than we originally planned, for free." She smiled at the end 'cause of the bigger pool. I wasn't smilin'. I clean the darn thing.

"What did you do with the ring?" I asked.

"I gave it to the police, and as far as I know, they still have it."

I looked over at Fritzy. I could tell he was very interested in that.

Then I asked, "What do you think about the bodies? Was there anythin' that either you or Dr. Joe noticed?"

"Actually, one of the bodies was dressed nicely or what I thought to be in nice clothes. The other body was in kind of a nightgown. I thought that was odd," she said.

"A nightgown?" I whispered, "So, what do you think, Fritzy?"

"Gooo baaac."

"What do you mean? Go back to the library?" I was perplexed but agreed we would go next mornin', first thing. Miss Joyce must've thought we were real intellectuals, goin' to the library two days in a row.

We went to bed right after that, so we could talk amongst ourselves and try to figure out who the dead bodies were. Fritzy asked where the young wife was from, if she was a Marshalltown girl or from somewhere else. It took forever for him to spit that out, but finally I understood what he was gettin' at. We went to bed before I had time to contemplate his reasonin' for askin' that.

The next day at the library Fritzy kept sayin', "Ask Shuuuuzz."

I finally figured out he did not want me to ask the same librarian we had talked to the day before. He must have figured out what she said on the telephone—and it wasn't good. There was somethin' about her that upset and disturbed Fritzy.

I had to wander around the library for what seemed like an hour until I found Miss Schultz. She was our regular helper when we'd come to check out books for Fritzy. She liked to talk and we were already friendly with her. She started to take us over to the newspaper section, but Fritzy would have none of it, insistin' that she bring the papers to us in the children's section.

He kept sayin', "Briiiing heeeere."

Even Miss Schultz understood that.

So then I told her we were lookin' for any stories about the people that Fritzy's family bought the house from.

"You work for the Worrells, right?" she asked me.

I said, "Yes, I never knew the Phillips family 'cause they were before my time, but I am curious about them." I looked a little wistful, hopin' she would tell us some more about them. It worked.

"Well, people are curious about you. So, I guess it goes both ways." Miss Schultz gave us a sweet smile. I had always figured as much, 'cause I was one of the few Negro people in the town and people met me at the office, grocery store, school and places, so they knew me jes' enough to be curious. I could tell she thought I was OK, though. I usually can figure out if someone is gonna like me in the first few seconds. She was sure a chatterbox for being a librarian, but we were glad about that.

"Their son's death was quite a blow to them. He was their only son," she told us, addin' that Mrs. Phillips had always been a bit odd somehow. "She over-mothered the son. Never let him out of her sight. I always considered it a miracle he found someone and got married. She had a pinched-up face." Miss Schultz mimicked the pinched-up face. "I heard she didn't like her daughter-in-law much, either.

"It was an odd contrast, because the doctor was so wonderful and compassionate, but she ran that office like a Hessian general. She turned people out if they couldn't pay, and she turned patients away if someone was more than ten minutes late to an appointment. Nobody liked her," Miss Schultz added, sayin' also that she heard he came back into town for the Mayor's funeral, but that Mrs. Phillips didn't come.

"Did you know the daughter-in-law?" I asked her next.

"Yes, I did. She was a real sweet, quiet girl. Went to Marshalltown High School. They were high school sweethearts."

I hoped the answer to the whole mystery was sittin' right there in front of Fritzy and me, but nothin's ever that easy.

"Do you remember what her rings looked like?" I kept on with the questionin'.

Miss Joyce had told me about taking the rings into the kitchen and then washin' them off, so I had an idea of what they looked like from her description. And now I was hopin' Miss Schultz would describe the same rings again to me. Then we would get an idea if the body was that of the daughter-in-law, or not.

"I do remember," she said. The engagement ring was small as I remember, with a small diamond in the middle and a couple of smaller diamonds on either side. But, it was the wedding ring part that was different. It was a line of intermittent rubies and diamonds. Not big, but very nice. I bet there were six or seven of each color—all in a row."

I couldn't hide my disappointment. That wasn't the ring Miss Joyce described. I looked over at Fritzy. He was disappointed, too. We got up to leave. I pushed Fritzy back to the house real slow. He and I were thinkin' every bit of the way. We had no answers when we got home, and I decided we needed some first-rate food to help us think. I cooked up a meal of fried chicken, mashed potatoes, green beans with onions, tomato aspic salad, and fudge brownies for dessert.

What were we missin'? Then, one more question jes' popped into my head: What did old Mrs. Phillips' wedding ring look like?

That night we discussed it. "If the wife was not a nice person, maybe Doc Phillips knocked her off. It's cheaper than a divorce, and you never have to talk to them again. He could've done it easy with some doctor medicines he had," I said.

Fritzy shook his foot. "Nooo. Heee taaakkk wiffffe on phooone."

I couldn't figure out what he meant. So we went to bed and the next mornin' we went back to the library to ask what the ring looked like. This gettin' to the library ever'day was gettin' to be a hassle.

"Oh, Mrs. Phillips's ring was nondescript. I always wondered why she didn't have a better one. After all, Dr. Phillips made a good living and they could have had a much better ring. But they didn't. It was small, with a couple of smaller diamonds on either side. I think sometimes, even though a husband makes good money, they keep the original ring from when they were young and money was sparse and maybe it symbolizes the real love."

"Gold or silver?"

"Gold," she said.

Fritzy and I looked at one another. That was the ring Miss Joyce had described. Unfortunately, it could be about anybody's ring. So about all that description of the ring could do was rule out somebody that had a totally different ring. Mrs. Phillips havin' a similar ring might've meant it was her, but maybe not.

Now, I was thinkin' to myself, if one of the bodies found in the hole was Mrs. Phillips—and we still weren't too sure about that, then who could be the other? The problem was, I didn't think of that question while I was there at the library. I thought of it at home. So, we needed to go back to the library in the mornin', again. Before we went back I asked Fritzy, "Why don't you like the other librarian?" This time he answered.

"She's a baaaak maiiiil."

"You mean blackmailer?"

Foot in the yes position.

That's why he wanted us to ask Miss Schultz all our questions. I was determined to ask her ever'thing we could possibly think of so we wouldn't have to go back for a while.

"Miss Schultz. Can you show us the wedding announcement for the son? What was his name again?"

Turns out, his name was Cameron. Cameron Phillips. Miss Schultz said she thought he was an engineer by education. Went to school in Ames. She also said he was a nice lookin' man like his father.

"How old would he be now?" I pressed her.

"Oh, about forty-five or fifty. His dad is seventy or a little more, now. Both Mrs. Phillips were about the same age as their husbands. So, if the couple died twelve years ago, they were in their late thirties when it happened," she said after some hemmin' and hawin' doin' the math.

I was plumb stumped. They had said the second body was that of a woman. I could smell that fickle finger of fate once more as I sat there tryin' to figure out who the second body was. Sammy said it was another woman, but not much else. I didn't even know how old either person was—and that's somethin' that people weren't gonna volunteer to a 300-pound Negro woman—so I was fallin' into a melancholy state over not being able to do ever'thing, jes''cause of my color.

I was tryin' to stay positive and not think about me, and my being hobbled. Who could it be? That thought lingered in my mind like a bad dream. I couldn't answer it.

Chapter 32

A Flower Wilts

Well, our mystery solvin' was put on hold again, 'cause the next day we got a call from Dr. Troy. He was upset. Miss Edwina was very ill and she asked for us to come. We learned that she had cancer. Turns out she had found out about it when she went to the doctor to find out why she wasn't able to conceive babies. She jes' never told nobody, and it took a while before that cancer started winnin' its battle over her.

While I was packin' us up for the trip I remembered how I thought she looked a little tired when I was visitin' last. I knew right away it must be somethin' bad or she wouldn't have been askin' for Miss Joyce like that.

Over the years they had become telephone friends, even though it cost a lot of money to talk long distance like that. They did it anyway. Lookin' back, it was worth the money 'cause neither one had any real close female-type friends. They talked about things they couldn't tell anyone else.

Fritzy, Miss Joyce, and I all boarded the train and endured a sad trip with low spirits all the way into Georgia. The only thing that made it a little brighter for me was that I would get to see all my kinfolk again. But I couldn't help but think about Miss Edwina and how much fun we had on that first train trip. It seemed so long ago. I kept seein' things that would remind me of it—like the metal toilet I held her over. I'd never forget that.

We finally got there and made our way to the Parker mansion. It looked jes' as perfect as a mansion could look, even though sad things were taking place inside.

Izzy and Camellia met us at the door with very sad faces. No piano-key smile for us now. Even my beloved sister looked tired. Izzy took our things at the door and motioned for Miss Joyce to go on to see Miss Edwina.

Now, when you love somebody you don't want them to see how sad you are for them. I could hear Miss Joyce greet her before she closed the door to Miss Edwina's bedroom. She was downright cheery and sweet. She didn't want Miss Edwina to know jes' how sad and scared she was for her.

Camellia said she knew Miss Edwina was real sick when she quit her liquor. That told her the end was comin' near. Camellia's voice broke when she said that. She frowned and told me it was the kind of bad you want to end as soon as it can. She said Miss Edwina was jes' driftin' in and out. Dr. Troy was so down. He could hardly walk.

We decided we'd better cook up a storm, 'cause half of Atlanta was gonna be there on the doorstep when the inevitable happened. I followed Camellia into the kitchen and listened to my sweet sister sing Abide With Me. We cried as we sang it together—sisters in arms.

Abide with me; fast falls the eventide; The darkness deepens; Lord, with me abide; When other helpers fail and comforts flee, Help of the helpless, oh, abide with me.

About that time, Miss Joyce came in and sat at the table.

Camellia plied her with a piece of pecan pie to try to get her to settle down and stop weepin'. She ate the pie between tears.

She pursed her lips and said, "Edwina wants to say goodbye and tell you something. She mentioned it was something special. She fell asleep right before I left, but when she wakes up you can go on in there."

I steeled myself up to see Miss Edwina. The room was dark, even though it was daylight outside, 'cause the drapes were drawn tight. Miss Edwina lay motionless in the bed, and I wondered if I should go back to the kitchen until she could wake up enough to open her eyes and talk. Jes' as I turned to go she said, "Wait."

"Oh, Miss Edwina, what you gone and done now?" That was all I could think of to say. She caught on and laughed a little. Then she mimicked me like when she was drunk on the train. "I gone and got drunk is what I gone and done."

By then I had come close and was holdin' her hand. "You're still beautiful."

Miss Edwina smiled. "Thank you. You are too, Anna. You are too." She shook my hand a little. "Lemme talk." I dutifully obliged.

"I want you to take care of Fritzy until the end. Tell me you will?"

"You got my word on that," I promised.

"I want you and Camellia to help with the bazaar every year from now on. I already hired someone to run my benevolence fund after I'm gone, so it can continue. But you all get your colored people to keep being a part of it. OK? You're what makes it interesting."

I gave her my word on that, too.

"I want Camellia to stay with Troy as long as he needs her."

"She'll stay. She loves you," I said with a sureness I felt.

"One last thing. See that Troy marries my cousin. She's younger and almost as good lookin'."

I laughed. "Why, Miss Edwina, I will give that my best effort. I never thought of myself as a 300-pound colored cupid before." Miss Edwina laughed a little.

"I already talked to Camellia about that. Help make it happen for me. I'd feel a lot better about things. Troy is innocent in some ways and needs someone that is as good a person as he is. And she is." She grew silent for a few seconds.

"I gotta sleep now. One last thing. Life was a great adventure for me, albeit short."

I left the room with a lot of questions. Miss Edwina was plottin' to make ever'one better even at the end. I'd have to see this cousin of hers. She must be somethin'.

That night, with Dr. Troy holdin' her hand and her brothers standin' nearby, Miss Edwina took her last breath. There wasn't a dry eye in Atlanta. We started cookin' as fast as we could before the undertaker even got there. People would be bringin' things, but would expect a full layout of food as they drifted through the black and white marble entrance.

The undertaker came and took our precious, beautiful Miss Edwina away. It was even sadder to my way of thinkin' 'cause that hearse did not hold a candle to the seven-passenger Hudson.

The next day people gathered at the mansion.

Camellia and I were standin' around searchin' for the cousin. Then, as if on cue, in walked through the door a most beautiful woman of about thirty years old. Miss Edwina said she was good lookin' and she was. She had that same beautiful skin, hair, and height, but she was ten years younger. She walked over and hugged Dr. Troy—which we considered a good sign. Maybe we wouldn't have to do much to help it along.

Then Camellia started laughin'. Then we both laughed. She'd already told Dr. Troy what she wanted him to do. We were standin' there when it hit us both. We looked at each other and laughed. "Anna, she told us about it not so we could do the match-makin'. Dr. Troy. He can do that hisself. But, by tellin' us, we would be of a like mind when somebody new came to live at the mansion. We would welcome the cousin, 'cause Miss Edwina told us to. That sly Miss Edwina. Always plannin' even after she gone. I bet that cousin knew, too, by the way she was smilin' at Dr. Troy."

Ever'thing was gonna be OK. In fact, we were all gonna be OK. We left to go get ready. It was time for the funeral, and ever'one began to trickle out so as to get a good seat at the Presbyterian Church. It was big and nice and the little children that Miss Edwina loved and helped were gonna sing her off real beautiful-like.

Dr. Troy drove us over in the Hudson. When we got there we were all seated on the back pew—but it was OK, 'cause we cried the loudest for her and preferred for people not to notice, anyway. Don't get me wrong, there was a lot of laughter, too. Ever'one told Miss Edwina stories and there were quite a bunch as you can well imagine. Then the mostly black children sang *Jesus Loves Me* in their little high voices, and we wept tears of joy for what she'd done for us all. Then we went back to the house, cried some more, and ate plate after plate of some of Atlanta's finest food. Hardly anythin' white on those plates!

The next day the place looked like a wreck. Plates ever'where. We had a row of Negro people washin' and dryin' for hours. Wash, rinse, dry, and then we set things out on a table to get ever'thing real dry before we put it away. Then we counted the sterling silverware. You always lose a couple when you have a big crowd like that. Miss Edwina always said it was OK though. "If someone needs it to pawn, then so be it," she would say. It got where the pawn man jes' called her periodically and she'd run down and buy it back after ninety days. But mostly, she'd jes' run down to Rike's, Atlanta's fancy department store, and replace the pattern—Francis I. Beautiful stuff. It was real intricate and it set a beautiful table.

Now that ever'thing was done, Miss Joyce got on the train back to Marshalltown, and I caught a train to Athens. Camellia and the others took Fritzy for the week. It would be a pleasant change for him and there were lot's of colored kids to entertain him while the rest of us took a rest.

When I got to Athens I saw my mama was lookin' real old. I noticed that when she and Hope met me at the train. In fact, she was lookin' old and Hope was lookin' sad. I was sure enough answered in my prayin' that Hope would soon sweep Gordon out the back door like so much floor dust. Gordon would leave and then come back botherin' her every time he got drunk, jes' like Martin used to do to me. Jobs were very scarce back in Atlanta and Athens, and Hope was havin' a hard time findin' a new job.

I was selfishly thrilled when Hope asked about goin' back to Iowa with me. It would be nice havin' my daughter there, even though I knew it wasn't an ideal life for her. She deserved a second chance at findin' a good husband and havin' babies, and Marshalltown wasn't too likely a place for that to happen. But I had to trust that God knew what he was doin' in dealin' her this hand, and it didn't have to be a permanent move for her.

So I convinced Miss Susan to hire Hope to tend to the kids. Hope was way overqualified for that job, but the Calloway kids sure benefitted 'cause she was so smart and could help them much better than I could with their homework. And Miss Susan could be goin' on her politicin' runs with Doc Calloway. During the summer and sometimes even on school day afternoons, Hope would still bring the Calloway kids over and we would all sit and read together. During the warm months they would come by to take a swim in the pool. It was there in the pool that Fritzy was able to play right along with the other kids. I enjoyed watchin' that, and was grateful to have Hope's assistance in helpin' to get Fritzy in and outta it.

Ruff always insisted on goin' in it with us, which made a real mess. But Fritzy loved it, so I let Ruff swim, too. The Worrells decided to heat the pool, even in the winter, but sometimes I drew the line on gettin' in during that time. A body can jes' take so much. Ruff went in every day whether we did or not—he had Fuller brush fur that kept him warm and it was always dirty besides.

Chapter 33

Gettin' Closer to the Truth

It was during that summer after we got back to Marshalltown and Hope was there that Fritzy was ready to work again on our ongoin' mystery. It had been percolatin' in the back of my mind the whole time I was in Georgia. Since I still hadn't said nothin' about it to anyone back home, I was glad to be able to talk about it again with Fritzy when I got back. So Fritzy and I got up early and prepared to go once more to the library. When we were almost ready to take off, we saw Miss Joyce chewin' real thoughtful on a piece of toast.

I don't know if Miss Joyce heard us talkin' about our mystery solvin' plans or whether she jes' had ESP, 'cause as we were gettin' ready to leave that day, she said, "I've been thinking about what you asked me about the bodies—you know, before we went to Georgia. I've told you all I know, but the fellow that sits next to me at the paper covered the story when it happened. He might know things we wouldn't even know to ask. His name is Bill. Bill Brimmer."

It was decided that Miss Joyce would first talk to him and

then come back and tell us what he said. She insisted that after all, she was the reporter. So, the next day Miss Joyce came home brimmin' with news. "Oh, did I get an earful. That guy has always been curious about the bodies and wanted to ask me all about it, but the case was officially closed by way of the Mayor's office. Now that the Mayor is gone, it can be reopened," she said.

She had no idea why the Mayor had done that, and we all assumed that he must be protectin' his brother-in-law, Dr. Phillips.

"Oh, yeah, I've been meanin' to ask you, how is the Mayor related to Miss Susan?" I asked her.

Turns out the Mayor and Dr. Phillips married Miss Susan's father's two sisters. They were her uncles by marriage. That's why they had different last names. Miss Susan's mother and father, Mr. and Mrs. Henry Hill, were deceased. They died in a terrible car wreck out on I-70. They hit one of those ice patches that forms the next day after a thaw and then a hard freeze. Miss Susan had jes' married Doc Calloway, but they hadn't had any of the children yet. Her parents were on their way to Davenport to see a political candidate. The people in the other car were also killed.

"Susan was still grieving when I met her. I guess you don't ever get over something like that. I think it has affected her in a bunch of ways," Miss Joyce went on. "For one, she's trying to live for every minute because she saw her parents lose out on so many years."

I was thinkin' to myself, "Oh, Miss Joyce, if you only knew. If you only knew."

That's when it dawned on me why she was havin' her way with Dr. Joe. Understandin' the reason and motivation, why a person does what they do, is enlightenin'. It doesn't make it OK, but at least you understand the why.

When Miss Joyce got up and went to work one mornin' that same week, Fritzy and I decided to spend extra time in the backyard. After all, that's where ever'thing ended up. I pushed him around the back sidewalks. The pool people had put in sidewalks in a sort of scrolling design around the yard that made a beautiful flower bed on the outside and a sidewalk for me to push Fritzy on. That amounted to a lot of diggin' on the pool people's part, but they'd only hit pay dirt once with bodies, so-to-speak. We carefully and slowly made our way through the yard. He and I were quiet except for the squeak I never got oiled. I kept forgettin' to get Dr. Joe to take care of that.

That's when it hit me. "The person in the nightgown might have been sick or somethin'. The person with the nice clothes was probably someone who was carin' for her. Could it be a mother and child? They would hold hands. Sisters would hold hands. Lovers would hold hands. Those were all the people I could think of that would hold hands.

So we were in the yard and Fritzy was lookin' around. He motioned that I should push him some more on the sidewalks. He was still shakin'. About that time Miss Joyce came walkin' up. She always came home for lunch. I couldn't tell if my cookin' was so good she would come home for that, or if she jes' wanted to see Fritzy. I think maybe it was a combination. "Anna, what do you have for lunch? Do you have enough for one more?" she asked.

Of course, I had nothin' but good stuff and enough for a Boy Scout Troop. So we went inside to find a nice young man of about thirty-five standin' in the rumpus room. Miss Joyce introduced him as Bill and explained that he had some real farfetched ideas about the bodies

He struck me as a serious type, and we all sat down at the table so he could spread some photographs before us. He was not put off by Fritzy's condition, but we were all a little rightfully concerned about whether it was OK for a nine-year-old boy to see such photos.

I didn't say nothin', but I covered his eyes. "I'll tell him what I saw. No sense in creatin' nightmares where we don't have to." People can be nitwits where children are concerned.

The pictures were horrible. First they showed these two bodies in the dirt and then they showed them laid out on the ground by the hole. It brought it all back to me. I was suddenly weak when I saw the pictures. Their mouths were open like they were moanin'. Nobody would ever kill anyone if they could see what their dirty work did to a person's body.

Bill said, "The strange thing about this is the bodies are holding hands. Of course, they could have been holding hands when they died or had the hands placed together after death. We have no way of knowing."

I said, "Can you tell me who was found missin' during that time? Maybe we can figure who they are by process of elimination?"

Reporter Bill agreed. "Actually, I had the same idea, so I brought the information. There were several people who died or left town during that time. Here's the list. Plus, the grocer's wife ran off with a lover at that time. No one has mentioned her since. No one has mentioned who the lover was either. There's nothing in the paper about it, but I thought I would mention it anyway. I've heard that the grocer is a real jerk. Luckily, my wife does all the grocery shopping."

"Did she have good legs? Was she blond?" I blurted out. For a minute I thought ever'body was thinkin' I was talkin' about Bill's wife. Ever'one looked at me at once. I didn't back down. "Besides, it would stand to reason that old Bishop would do somethin' like that. Have a good-lookin' wife and then knock her off." There, I'd gone and said the unspeakable. I felt it though. But, that didn't explain why she ended up in a shallow grave holdin' another older woman's hand. But it was still fittin' to contemplate.

The next person Bill mentioned was the Mayor's wife.

Fontaine was her name and the picture showed a woman that looked like a professional dancer. I bet she had great legs. She had died of natural causes and the obituary in the newspaper said she was buried in the Marshalltown cemetery. I felt a visit to the cemetery coming on when Bill said, "We can go there tomorrow and take a look."

"I'm puttin' my money on Dr. Phillips. He doesn't ring jes' right for me," I said.

Ever'one looked shocked. Miss Joyce said, "What do you mean?"

"I'm jes' sayin' that he had the opportunity. It's his backyard and all. In fact, he probably buried the bodies there, never dreamin' that someone would build a swimmin' pool. After all, how many people in Iowa would ever build a pool?"

That old fickle finger of fate was showin' itself again.

Ever'one nodded their heads, yes. We were finally gettin' somewhere.

Bill said, "Now, do you think he knocked them off or just buried them for convenience? After all, doctors are always burying their mistakes—not literally mind you, but figuratively. Ah, this could be literally though."

Again, ever'one nodded their heads, yes. Then Miss Joyce said, "I bet somebody died and he didn't want them to get noticed, maybe? Could it be a patient who didn't pay?" She looked over at Reporter Bill. They smiled. "Then would he just bury them in the backyard?"

"Yeah, but I think we may be on to something with the who part," said Bill as he pulled out some more papers from the stack of stuff he had brought with him.

The next person or persons that left Marshalltown were Dr. Phillips's son and his wife. They disappeared during that time. The son couldn't be one of the bodies for obvious reasons. But the wife could be. The last person was a Miss Edith Andressen. The obituary picture showed a very beautiful girl. She was twenty-one and had been a senior at the University of Iowa. She died in a car wreck somewhere on I-70 near Iowa City, but she was from Marshalltown. Somehow, she seemed the least likely victim we all thought.

I looked over at Fritzy and he was frownin' as he did when he was in deep thought.

Then Bill said, "I will leave all this stuff with you to look at some more, but I have to take those pictures back to the paper. If you have any thoughts, let Joyce know and maybe we can get some kind of break. It would be good if we broke the story in the Times. It would make us look good."

He got up to go, and I noticed a nice smile exchanged between the two of them. I felt like my imagination needed a well-deserved rest, so I ignored their smiles. We had enough problems with dead bodies in the backyard.

After he left, Miss Joyce and I sat down and talked through the women and who might be the candidates for the dead bodies in the hole. We were workin' from the premise that one of them was the older Mrs. Phillips. The rings matched, but the reasonin' jes' didn't match up.

It stood to reason if his wife died, he'd have a funeral and mourn her passin' like most normal people. If she was real sour like they say she was, maybe he had enough and knocked her in the head one day. Or, I thought to myself, maybe it could have been an accident, as I well know that kind of thing can happen in the heat of an argument; but I wasn't bringin' that up. None of it explained why there was someone else in the hole—and why they were holdin' hands.

Dr. Joe came in from work and we had dinner. Fritzy and I ate in the kitchen and the Worrells ate in the dining room. I made meatloaf with macaroni and cheese. It was divine. I also had yeasty rolls, butter beans, and a tossed salad with lemon dressing and sesame seeds. The dessert was a Brown Betty. Life is good when you eat right.

I took a long bath and went right to bed. The mystery hung over me like a puffy cloud, and I felt like I could almost make out the answer, but it was jes' beyond my reach. That night, I dreamed that I was at the circus and was walkin' down the midway. There was a crowd of people ahead and a murderer jes' outta reach. I couldn't see the face, and they disappeared into the crowd before I could make them out—couldn't tell if it was a man or woman even. Then I started runnin' to catch them, and strangers stood in my way 'cause they wanted to protect the murderer. After that, I woke up and it was still the middle of the night. I knew there was some of the Brown Betty left, so I lumbered into the kitchen. I was still half asleep when I saw Dr. Joe standin' in front of the refrigerator. He looked hungry, too. I guess we had the same idea.

I put the dessert out, but he wanted a meatloaf sandwich. Also a good choice.

We sat at the kitchen table, and I quizzed him about any other ideas about who might be in the hole.

"Well, I have absolutely no idea," he said. "I think the ring matches the one Mrs. Phillips wore. So, I think it's Mrs. Phillip's ring. But the big question is, who is up in Wisconsin being Mrs. Phillips—if the original Mrs. Phillips is still here?" Dr. Joe looked thoughtful. "If the coroner had given me a chance to look at those bodies, I might have noticed something important. As it is, I have absolutely no idea about the bodies. They whisked them away pretty fast."

"Dr. Joe, have you ever been to Wisconsin—maybe near Bone Lake?" I paused to see if he figured where I was goin' with this conversation.

"Do you have any idea how many lakes there are in Wisconsin?" he asked.

"No. But let's visit the one where Dr. Phillips moved to." I smiled as I said that. "You know you need a family vacation. Take Fritzy to the lake. Maybe visitin' the good Dr. Phillips would be in order."

He caught on then. "You know, Anna, we might really enjoy it. We could drive up and spend a few days."

"Yes, Sir." I agreed, but advised him to tell ever'one we were goin' to Michigan, though. We didn't want to arouse any suspicions.

We both went back to bed after that, but I didn't go to sleep. I was too excited. All I could think about was the chance to go on a vacation and solve a mystery.

Chapter 34

An Out-Of-Place Visitor at the Library

The next mornin' I made ever'one waffles and listened to Miss Joyce and Dr. Joe plan the trip. They would have to find a nice bed and breakfast and get a room for Fritzy and me, too. We were to leave on Thursday and stay through Sunday. They were gonna fish with a guide, and I was gonna work my magic with cornmeal and my special spices if they caught anythin'. That would surely give us enough time to figure out where Dr. Phillips was livin' and who with. They would be taking Fritzy out in a boat, and I could tell he was gettin' excited.

My most important trick was to find the tartar sauce recipe. It was special and secret, and I had it hidden somewhere. I made it with my own homemade pickles. Yum.

After the Worrells left for work, we went back again to the library that day. On the way, I asked Fritzy what he wanted to know at the library. He had somethin' on his mind. So we went to the library. This time he wanted to sit near the first librarian, Miss Smith, but he didn't want to sit where she could see him. I think he wanted to see her lips.

I kept askin' him what he wanted me to do. He had motioned me to move him several places, but the final spot was behind the stacks. It was within seein' distance, but jes' to the left of Miss Smith's desk and about twenty feet away. We could see her very clearly from the side, but she could not see us through the row of books in the stacks we were behind. Fritzy sat there and watched her for a solid hour. He never twitched. His eyes never left her face. It was kinda maddenin' to me 'cause he didn't tell me a thing. There was definitely somethin' he wanted her to talk about, and he was playin' the waitin' game until she did.

Then, the most interesting thing happened. This kid came in and she took somethin' outta her desk. It could have been a coincidence. But I knew this kid, and he didn't strike me as a future Rhodes Scholar hangin' out at the library. He seemed like a future road worker hangin' out at the town pool hall. The librarian gave him the nicest smile as she took the envelope and held it in her hand, and the young man accepted it and hugged her. The young man went on without stoppin' to imbibe in any books. Then I recognized him. That young man was Bishop's oldest boy. What was he doin' huggin' the librarian?

Fritzy looked over at me and smiled. Then he motioned that we should wait. So we waited another hour. Then she got up and went to the bathroom.

We rushed over and I pretended to drop somethin' near the desk, and Fritzy made his wigglin' noises, which people are used to. I opened the drawer and grabbed a similar lookin' envelope, and we made off to the stacks once again. What was in it? I carefully opened it and there was a check made out to a Margaret Smith in the amount of $30. It was her payroll check for the month. Fritzy nodded his head in understandin', and I ran as fast as I could, without makin' a commotion, back to the desk and stuck the check back in the drawer.

We left in a hurry and didn't stop until we got home. Besides, nothin' made sense. We had no idea who that was. We didn't even know the name of the librarian, other than the fact she was a Miss Margaret Smith.

The next day was Wednesday and we were leavin' for Michigan (really Wisconsin) on Thursday. So, we had a lot of things to do. We were havin' a picnic on the way, and I was busy fryin' chicken and bakin' sugar cookies, heatin' tea to pour over ice and makin' cole slaw. It was gonna be good. The biscuits had already come outta the oven and the cookies were next. Fritzy started shakin' and that's when he said, "Wooooman is Biiish's wife."

"The librarian?"

"Noooo."

"The body?"

"Nooo."

"With Dr. Phillips?"

"Yeees."

We would know for sure in two days.

Chapter 35

Bone Lake: A Fittin' Place to Find Out About Some Bones

Dr. Joe asked both Miss Joyce and me if we had ever'thing we needed as we piled into the Chevrolet.

We were more than ready.

We stopped at one of Wisconsin's beautiful lakes and then we all got out and had ourselves the perfect picnic lunch. I even had a red checkered cloth to spread for the spread. We ate with reckless hunger, and when we were through I asked Dr. Joe, "What if Dr. Phillips really did kill the people from the backyard? What will we do?"

"We will report him to the authorities in Iowa and let them extradite him back to Marshalltown. What do you think I'm going to do, pull a gun on him or something?" Dr. Joe said smugly.

"Well, no, I was thinkin' maybe you could extract a confession from him. Knowin' what really happened is more important than puttin' him in jail if he's guilty. After all, we don't know his reasonin' for committin' the crime if he did."

"Anna, you've got it all wrong. Justice is the most important thing here. If he murdered somebody, he should be punished," Dr. Joe insisted.

Miss Joyce said, "I think we're jumping ahead. Let's find out as much as we can right now and then we can make decisions. We're not a judge and jury and we're not the police."

We all nodded our heads in agreement, but I noticed Fritzy didn't.

Two hours later we were in Wisconsin weavin' around Bone Lake. It was early afternoon when we pulled in and got settled into Bone Lake Bed and Breakfast. It was technically in Luck, but named for the lake. It was quaint and well appointed all at the same time. I could tell right off that I was gonna like this place. The biggest thing goin' on around there were the fishin' boats that took people out to the middle of the lake to fish. Dr. Joe was gonna do that with Fritzy in the late afternoon, even though Fritzy was only capable of watching him do the fishing—but first he was taking Miss Joyce with him and Fritzy and they were gonna sit out by the lake. Since they were taking Fritzy with them, that was gonna free me up for a little scoutin' on my own. I had planned to go near where the old doctor's house was, and I knew jes' where it was, 'cause I had looked it up in the Luck phone book.

I started out walkin' toward Dr. Phillip's house and kept a steady pace. I knew it wasn't far. I decided I should wear a hat 'cause I really didn't want him to recognize me if he was out and about when I walked by. I was dependin' on the old adage that all Negroes look alike and that he wouldn't figure out who I was or even notice me.

As I approached the house, I noticed someone bent over plantin' some kind of flower in one of the beds, and I have to say she was beautiful from the back. She had a Mae West rear end and when she stood up I slowed down. I had to time my walk-by where I could get the maximum view at her, whoever she was. She was gorgeous. She was wearin' shorts and had a lot of beautiful blond hair.

Then she turned around.

My first thought went way back to my childhood when the little white girl taught me about superlatives. Now a superlative is the highest of the high when it comes to describin' somethin'. And the first thought that jumped into my mind was that this was a superlative woman. My guess was she was forty-five or maybe a little younger, but the years had been very kind. Ever'thing about her was superlative. She had a superlative rear-end. She had a superlative face; she had superlative blond hair. But most of all, she had a superlative smile with movie-star teeth. She was God's gift to any man with a pulse.

She smiled and turned back around to work on her flowers. I walked back to the Bone Lake Bed and Breakfast. My head was full of thoughts. Again, I have to say she was gorgeous all around, and I started thinkin' maybe the old doctor traded in his old naggin' wife for this one; some beautiful women are willin' to go for an older man, particularly if they can provide them with comfort like a doctor could certainly do.

But I still couldn't get a feel for who the other body was if the first one was old Mrs. Phillips. Who could of needed disposin' of to make way for the new wife? The better question was, who would hold hands with old Mrs. Phillips?

I slowly walked up to the Worrells as they were sittin' and waitin' for the boat man to pick up Dr. Joe and Fritzy for fishin.' They were on a bench and I sat down beside them. Fritzy looked happy and his parents looked content—a rare thing. Fritzy had been quiet, but as the small fisherman's boat with two men in it drew closer, he began to get more animated.

The boat kept gettin' closer and closer and then Fritzy finally said, "The guiddde."

Miss Joyce said, "I think that looks like Dr. Phillips. But, who is with him?"

"Well, whoever is with him must be somebody kin to him," said Dr. Joe as he squinted some more. "Look at all that hair. Just like his."

Sure enough, as the boat drifted closer we saw a very handsome man of about forty-five with white streaks of grey hair beginnin' to take over his dark mane. He looked jes' like the newspaper picture of Cameron Phillips. He sure wasn't dead.

The old doctor walked up to us with a solemn look on his face. He knew the jig was up. He couldn't run and he couldn't hide. He had to give them a ride 'cause he was the fishin' guide. I was stuck on the shore 'cause I had to face the fact that I could sink the ship.

What an awkward moment. I couldn't imagine what they were gonna do next.

"I have dreaded this day. But I knew it would come," said Dr. Phillips. I was glad he wasn't talkin' about me gettin' in the boat.

Dr. Joe said, "Just tell us the whole story, and we'll try to help as much as we can. We're not here to take you away to jail or anything." So much for his lofty justice conversation earlier.

It was decided that Miss Joyce and I would walk back to the bed and breakfast, so we could get the car and drive to the Phillips's lake house and bring Fritzy's chair with us. Fritzy and his father boarded the boat and were gonna float over to the house. We were jes' dyin' to hear what was gonna be said.

We arrived first and parked the car. Miss Joyce and I sat there waitin' for the men to make it ashore. I found myself gettin' nervous, 'cause two men against one man and a little boy that cain't move is no challenge. But I reckoned they surely wouldn't have let us go off without killin' us too, if that was the plan.

"Miss Joyce, let's walk around where we can see the water. OK?" I said.

So we got out and scurried around to the sloping grassy edge.

I could see the boat and the men. They looked OK. I breathed a sigh of relief.

We sat down on a bench and waited and watched. They finally made it safely ashore. I wondered what they talked about as they came around to our place. Dr. Joe picked Fritzy up and put him in his chair. He motioned us into the back of the house to a sittin' room and there was old Mrs. Phillips! She looked mean and surly except when she smiled and then her whole face changed. It was amazin'. Some people are like that. They always look mean and then they smile and you get this wallop of a smile. Figure that. I couldn't figure anythin' 'cause I was still in shock about seein' her change so fast, as well as seein' her alive in the first place.

Dr. Phillips introduced us all around.

"Randall, you need to tell us what's been going on up here at the lake and if it has anything to do with who was buried in the backyard," said Dr. Joe.

We all sat down and then all eyes settled on the old doctor. But it was old Mrs. Phillips who spoke. "I feel like we really don't owe you an explanation, since we didn't do anything really wrong." I knew she must be hell to be around. What a bearish woman. She must've put the good doctor under a spell to snag him all those years ago, and she must've been able to keep the spell up and turned him into a murderer or somethin'.

"Now, don't go off on them," the old doctor replied, like he was talkin' to a child. "They came all the way to ask us that very fair question."

Cameron agreed with his father and tried to contain his mother. It was then I noticed a wedding ring on his finger.

About that time the beautiful woman I had seen in the yard before came out to greet us. "Hello, I'm Cindy Bishop Johnson."

Then it occurred to me that Miss Cindy was Bishop's missin' wife. Those nitwit kids of hers had the same hair and skin. I was deep in thought when it dawned on me that I couldn't blame her for leavin' Bishop. He was a real horse's ass and those boys were horrible. I wondered if Bishop beat her. But I also remembered the shred of humanity he and those boys had shown and wondered if they were the way they were before, or after, she ran off.

Beautiful Miss Cindy had a large diamond on her left hand and a beautiful sundress that jes' covered the important parts of the rest of her. She smiled and we all smiled back—we couldn't help it. Even Fritzy. We were mes-mer-eyed once again.

She sat down. The young Mr. Phillips answered ever'one's unasked question by volunteerin', "I changed my name to Johnson, and we're legally married as Cameron and Cindy Johnson." Then he sat down.

Dr. Joe said, "OK, now, if she's Mrs. Cameron Johnson, a.k.a. Phillips, what became of the first Mrs. Cameron Phillips?"

I could tell he was tryin' to handle this as delicately as he possibly could.

"She left me," he said, "and moved to Milwaukee and got married and has a couple of children." I noticed the word divorce was not in that sentence.

"So, she's not dead?" Dr. Joe asked him.

"Hardly. It sure would have simplified things." Cameron shrugged as he said that.

"May I ask why she left you?" Miss Joyce was pretty bold askin' that, but she was a reporter and they're always good at askin' questions.

Cameron said she left 'cause he couldn't have children and she wanted them. She got remarried a fellow that worked on cars, he said.

Things were beginnin' to play out here. Logic always wins out over passion or excitement and this was no exception. The first Mrs. Phillips wanted children, and the second Mrs. Phillips/

Johnson obviously did not have that on her mind—after the no-count ones she had with Old Crusty.

"So, why didn't you continue living your life back in Marshalltown? You could have gotten divorced and moved up here?" Again, Miss Joyce was pretty direct.

The answer turned out to be pretty simple: Insurance. "There was no need to divorce. It just sort of happened. Michelle and I almost died out there on that cross-country ski trail. We were lost for three days. Finally, some hunters happened to see us in an inlet by a cliff. We had slid off the trail in the snowstorm and would have been dead soon. We were clinging to a ledge on the side of a cliff." He paused. You could tell it was kind of emotional for him.

"The man and his brother had done some illegal deer hunting, it was before the season opened, when they spied us. He didn't want to call the authorities for obvious reasons and so they rescued us themselves. We would have been dead if they hadn't come along. They had ropes and helped us down. It took hours."

He glanced over at Miss Perfection and continued, "While we were stuck in that situation, I realized I was a very unhappy person. My business was going to pot and I was facing the fact I didn't love my wife anymore. We had just found out I couldn't have children and she was devastated. Being lost like that forced us to re-examine our lives. I knew that Cindy was very unhappy, too. She had been my first high school sweetheart before Michelle. We had always loved one another, even while she was married to Bishop."

The room was quiet except for Fritzy's squirmin'.

Seemed that Cameron and Michelle realized their life insurance money would pay the creditors and the people to whom they owed money. Michelle could move away and start over. It would be simple to create new identities. Starting over also gave Cindy a chance to do the same. She moved to Milwaukee immediately. None one of them ever went back to Marshalltown. The doc could retire and he and Mrs. Phillips could move up there. Cameron could be with Cindy. It worked out for ever'body.

Fritzy squirmed some more. I leaned down and asked him why. "Mizzz Smiiiii."

"What about Miss Smith?" I asked for him, not knowin' why.

"Oh, Miss Smith, the librarian. She's Cindy's half sister."

We were all dumbstruck. Miss Cindy sure got the better half of that deal, 'cause Miss Smith was as plain as any white woman I ever saw.

Cameron was doin' all the talkin', while Miss Perfection was quiet as a china doll. He explained that they had worked a deal to send money to Miss Cindy's kids through her sister, Margaret Smith.

Then it dawned on me. A woman that looks like that probably doesn't have much of a brain and the boys were better off with the sister that did possess one. Maybe sis got the gray matter, while china doll was truly the Kewpie doll. I looked over at Miss Joyce. I could tell she was thinkin' somethin' similar. How could a mama go off and jes' leave her kids like that?

Dr. Joe asked the question again, "So, what happened in the backyard of our house?"

Then Dr. Phillips took over. He took a sip of his drink, which was somethin' stronger than iced tea. "A doctor sees all kind of people in a practice, as you well know." He motioned at Dr. Joe. "And you make life and death decisions daily. You always try to do the best for all concerned. Sometimes you make life-changing decisions in an instant."

You could tell this was painful for him. There was sadness in his eyes, and they glistened a bit, but he continued.

"Most people are good and then they do something one time

that isn't. You have to ask yourself, should they be punished for being good all their lives and then be judged for doing something that wasn't good just that once? Then they're thrown out for whatever reason. Even ostracized for what they did. They pay a heavy price for their actions."

I was figurin' the doctor had made a powerful mistake with his doctorin'—but I was wrong. He had been a good doctor to the end.

"I knew everyone in town, because eventually everyone would come to me for whatever ailment they had. Even the healthiest people came by. I could never turn anyone away. I was the only doctor in the town and it was my philosophy to help them all." He looked over at old Mrs. Phillips who visibly squirmed when he said that.

"One day I got a call from a lady who had been a patient of mine before she grew up and moved off to Iowa City. She was distraught. Her daughter had gone to someone that performed a pregnancy termination on her. It had been late in the pregnancy and the butcher should never have tried to perform the procedure. The girl was in a terrible condition and the fetus had still not aborted. She was bleeding to death. The mother and the girl's boyfriend were on their way to Marshalltown, bringing her from Iowa City. It was a terrible situation. They should have gone immediately to the hospital in Iowa City, but they didn't because of the obvious shame they would endure, and the young woman didn't want anyone finding out. So, they were on their way to me. I got in my car and met them half way. If I could staunch the bleeding she would be OK. I knew her life was in jeopardy, so I drove faster than I ever had. The roads were icy though. They were driving fast, too. I got midway but they weren't there at our appointed meeting place. I kept going down I-70 and then I came on the car wreck. I got closer and knew one of the cars immediately. It belonged to Mr. and Mrs. Hill."

That was Susan Calloway's mother and father he was talkin' about!

Dr. Phillips nodded and continued, "One of the cars had obviously hit some black ice and skidded out of control and run into the other. Sure enough, it contained the people on their way to see me. The young man was driving. He was rattled, but OK. The mother, though, had gone through the windshield. She was dead. The daughter was still barely alive and was beginning to deliver the baby. I got there just in time. The girl died in her young man's arms, but the baby was born alive."

We all gasped as he continued, "He was in remarkably good shape for his size. Tom, the young man, took my car, found a phone, and called for help. When he returned, I took the baby with me to Marshalltown without waiting for the ambulance. I felt bad leaving Tom at the accident, but he needed to be there to explain things. He chose to omit the part about the baby being born and my appearing at the scene of the accident."

There wasn't a dry eye around us. We were all so sad. This young girl died 'cause she couldn't stand the stigma of not being married. Hell, in my world and in my time we jes' got married and went on with our lives as best we could. I could tell what Miss Joyce was thinkin': It was so unfair. She tried so hard and had Fritzy and in spite of ever'thing that girl put her baby through before it was born, it was a normal baby.

The doctor took another drink of strength and continued. "The mother and daughter died there on the highway and were taken to a hospital and last rites were administered to them at the hospital by a Catholic priest. The girl and her mother were devout Catholics, but had obviously sinned and therefore were not eligible to be buried in consecrated ground. Even the mother was held accountable as a sinner for helping her daughter abort a baby. No amount of talking could change their minds. I know I tried. They had no relatives to see to their service or pay for their burial. The father had died when she was a small child."

Turns out Tom contacted Doc Phillips to tell him about this dilemma and to inquire about how the baby was doin'. It was decided that the doc would take custody of the remains and ever'one thought he would donate them to science and send the bodies back to Iowa City to the medical school. But instead, he did somethin' that, lookin' back, could be considered a little odd. While the girl lay dyin' in Tom's arms she had asked that she and her mother be laid to rest together. So the doc buried them together in the backyard holdin' hands, thinkin' no one would be the wiser.

That's the way things happen. You don't know a person's motivation or their reasonin' or their circumstances. Take the old doctor, he was jes' tryin' to save someone's life, and he found himself in a God-awful mess.

The good doctor paused and went on to tell us, "Mrs. Phillips and I took care of the baby for a solid month. He lived. He thrived." The doctor smiled. "He's here with us now." He smiled again.

He pointed outside, and there on the lawn stood a handsome teenage boy. He waved at us. We all dumbly smiled back. The young boy they called Frankie came in and sat by Miss Cindy on the arm of the divan. She hugged him. Then he got up and went back out to his dog that was whinin' at the door.

"You see our Cameron also wanted a child. He was devastated when he found out he couldn't have children. He and Cindy got married and adopted Frankie," Dr. Phillips explained.

"And the young man—Tom?" Miss Joyce asked.

Doc Phillips said that he was a pharmacist in Des Moines. He got married and had five kids.

"Does he know what became of his baby?" Miss Joyce asked him in her very direct manner.

The doctor didn't answer the question right away. His momentary silence was deafenin'. "Yes, he and I talked about it at length. He was a nineteen-year-old student with very little money and no future if he didn't graduate. I made sure he graduated. There was no option for him to take the baby, so it was decided that we should raise him as our own." He said Frankie was a blessin' and very happy, as they were also.

Once he had told us ever'thing, he said we could report him if we thought we should. As he no longer practiced medicine, there wouldn't be anybody that could take his practice away or yank his license.

We all stood and looked out at the young man playin' with a yellow Labrador Retriever. I could tell Dr. Joe was mullin' over what to do. He silently put Fritzy in the car, and we curved back around to the Bone Lake Bed and Breakfast. We got Fritzy outta the car and stood there lookin' at the beautiful lake.

"There's nothing to say really," Dr. Joe said as he looked out across the lake. Miss Joyce put her arm across his shoulder and they went for a walk near the lake. I knew they were gonna let things stay as they were.

There was that devil sin of omission again. Sometimes, but not often, it's for the better. I'm glad there weren't any murders after all. Murders are always so murderous with a lot of evil swirlin' around. Now, we really could put the mystery to rest.

I started thinkin' that we all have somethin' to overcome. As I told Fritzy, Ruff was gonna do OK with his three legs. He was doin' OK in his condition. And I was doin' OK considerin' havin' to work 'til the end of my days. And I thought his parents were gonna do OK with dealin' with him, too. I gave him a hug and said, "Even ole saucy Miss Susan is gonna do OK with that borin' husband and those nitwit kids. We all have somethin' to deal with and the good Lord is out there gradin' us on our dealins'."

So with that we got somethin' to eat and got ready to go back to Marshalltown. We still had some loose ends to bow tie once we were back.

I asked Fritzy: "Do you suppose that awful Mallo and Margaret Smith are related somehow?"

"Naaaa," he said.

"Do you suppose the bank robbery and the bank closin' are related somehow?"

"Naaa," he said once more.

"You're tryin' to get outta another trip to the library, I suspect." To which he replied, "Yaaa."

Chapter 36

The Nicest Place on Earth

"And, you, young Miss Reporter. What made you choose me for your story?" *We were suddenly back from our journey to the 1930s.*

I was flattered again that Anna called me "young," but I ignored her question, and asked, "What ever happened to the bodies?"

"Well now, Marshalltown is one of those places where people are better than in other cities," *Anna said.* "There's not many places as happy to my recollection, however, I am sure there are places that are as good. I am jes' not aware of them. I felt it every day when Fritzy and I walked around. The Chinese laundry man was very kind, the librarian was very kind, and the school was very kind. Ever'body cared. Ever'body, that is, except old crusty Bishop. He was mean as a bear with a gall bladder attack most days, but even he cared in a time of emergency.

"Miss Joyce and Mr. Bill got credited for solving the mystery; no one even had any idea that Fritzy and I were the true sleuths. Even Mr. Bill never knew about how Miss Joyce was really able to put two and two together about the identity of the bodies. She omitted a lot of what we discovered on our trip up to Wisconsin and chaulked it up to her research of the newspaper archives that led her to the police report about the car crash on the highway. She did have to reveal that the woman and her mother were in the sort of trouble that made them both guilty in the eyes of their church. Too bad the secret that was so important to the girl and her mother did have to get told after all. The article in the paper simply concluded that Dr. Phillips had sympathy for victims of a car crash who were forbidden a proper burial due to their differences with the Catholic Church and allowed their burial on this property since there were no other identifiable relatives to tend to them.

"I don't know why I was surprised when the whole town turned out later to respond to the fact that the Catholic Diocese would not approve the mother and her daughter to be buried in consecrated ground in Marshalltown. I guess all sinners are welcomed eventually. Who are we to pass judgment? I suppose all the good citizens of Marshalltown knew ever'one who ever lived in that town was guilty of some sort of sin of some sort, and judgment is up to God. So is punishment.

"The Worrells weren't Catholic, so they really weren't part of the ruckus, but the Calloways were and they were powerful upset and started a group of people at the church keepin' vigil. But they did respond in a way I'd never seen before. Many folks came together for a candlelight vigil and sang songs. It was beautiful and sad at the same time. Pretty soon the hearse pulled up with the young girl's and her mama's remains. It eased on into the cemetery real slow-like, in case the priests were gonna put a stop to it. But the monsignor nodded his head. He didn't look any too happy, but he let it pass. They gotta go somewhere and the Catholic cemetery is as good a place as I can think. They mow it ever Thursday you know.

"So the mystery was solved, and the young girl and her mother had found a final restin' place in Marshalltown, one of the nicest places on earth with some of the nicest people on earth. I knew it was different 'cause people seemed to be nicer to me—a person of color. It's jes' the kind of place that responds to the needs of others. When somebody's hurt or outta work, they get help.

"I think ole Bishop was embarrassed at my seein' his good side that one time he lent a hand to help the hurt people, 'cause he had made up his mind to go through life being mean. People sometimes have funny ways of dealin' with the dealins' that they are dealt. You know, old Bishop's life was a lot sadder than Fritzy's in a way, even though the hand he was dealt wasn't nearly as bad. Maybe he really loved that Miss Cindy and she jes' didn't love him back. He sure must've at least loved lookin' at her beauty. I don't know if he knew where she was, or if he knew about her sendin' money to the boys or not. I don't even know if the boys knew that money came from their mama or if they jes' thought it came from their aunt, Miss Smith.

"Even when the bank robbery happened, there was help from total strangers. Which brings me around to Mallo. He stayed in jail for fifteen years and got his GED. When he got out he moved to California and ran a snow cone stand. He married and has little Mallos. He was too old to have kids in my estimation. But it's OK, 'cause he was reformed. He found God. We still write to one another. He's sorry for what he did to us. He also came to terms with his awful parents and how they raised him. He's determined not to make those mistakes his parents made on him, and he decided not to make the same with his kids. My choice was to forgive him.

The bankers that left Marshalltown moved to Chicago and ran more banks. They made a lot of money doin' what they do. The interesting thing was that Mallo confessed to me about ten years ago that the bankers paid them to rob the bank 'cause it was insolvent. That way their insurance would pay for the robbery with new money to cover the fake money in the first place, and no one would be the wiser. It probably would have saved the bank, if we hadn't stepped in to foil the robbery. There goes that fickle finger again. The bankers got outta that tight spot, but I'm sure they're being watched by God himself. God keeps score, and I bet those bankers are zero for zero in the top of the ninth. But that's between them and God. I never said nothin' about what Mallo told me. It would've been too long ago for the law to do anythin' about it anyways.

"After my mama died, Faith and Newman decided they wanted to be closer to us. They moved to Chicago for better jobs. Amelia and Ceril moved to Cedar Rapids and Hope eventually moved there, too, and found a husband. I had six grandchildren, so on a count of me, my whole family ended up here, way up north."

I could see Anna's eyelids getting heavy, so I interrupted. "What about Fritzy?"

"Well, I knew you might want to know how that ended. I haven't told you a lot of the ends 'cause there's jes' too much more to tell. Why, if I was writtin' a book I'd have to start another to tell you how the War howled on, and how we all got through it and did our best to cope with death ever'where. It would take at least a whole nasty chapter in the next book to tell you how Altus ended up. But this is enough for now. I'm tired of talkin' and I need to rest."

Anna paused and looked more intently at me sitting in front of her.

"By the way, who did you say you were again?"

I shuffled in my chair. "Why, Miss Anna, I haven't been entirely honest with you. I'm one of those kids you used to read to after school. I'm Claudia Jean Calloway, but I go by my nickname 'C.J.' now, and my married name is Renfro. I had to come back and tell you how important you were to us and hear you describe what I couldn't understand as a kid. My mom and dad would never tell me all of it. As a grown-up and a reporter I had this urge to get to the bottom of the story. And I also want to thank you for saving me from those brothers of mine so many times."

"Oh, little Miss Claudia, it's so nice to see you grown up into such a pretty and businesslike woman." *Anna smiled so big I thought her cheeks might burst, and then a more serious look came across her face and she said,* "Now, I hope you understand that the story I told you is not about me, or your mama and daddy, or any of the other people we've talked about, is it? It's about women havin' children or not havin' children. It's about life and the givin' of life and how God and fate have a hand in it. It's about the choices we make, and how we ultimately benefit or don't benefit from our actions."

"Well, you aren't entirely there yet with the end of your own story are you?" *Anna laughed. Then she looked thoughtful.* "You're a reporter like Miss Joyce was. I wonder if she didn't influence you somehow?"

She did indeed influence me. And no, my story's not over.

I hugged Anna as I left and watched her make her way to the dining room for her dinner before I left. But I knew I'd be back.

Excerpted from the feature article, "A Mother's Day Tribute"

Des Moines Register, Sunday, May 13, 1973

By C.J. Renfro

Anna's story is a different kind of story. It's not really about solving mysteries or dealing with bank robbers or any of the specific incidents that peppered her life. It's about what happens to us because of the choices we make. Most of us do try to be good people and do the right thing. We always try to make the best choice with the information we have to work with. We're just women destined to follow our inner guide, although it seems we are always trying to take a different path somehow from what was intended. Sometimes, we don't even realize why we are put in a particular situation and that what we do and say can immediately change our lives and someone else's without even realizing it.

I started off intending to write a story about the Great Depression and a woman who helped a disabled child in a wheelchair. But, it turned out that the whole story is really about women, and what choices we make about having babies, dealing with the men in our lives, and whom we chose to love. This is a story that could just as well happen today in much the same way it did in Anna's time. The cast of characters from her story are just like people we know or could meet any day on our own Main Street in our own town or city.

For instance, there was Miss Joyce, who had a baby. But her son, Fritzy, didn't turn out the way he was expected. She had to live with her choice to be a mother—a choice she first thought was an unlucky choice, but later proved her wrong. And poor Sidney. If it's true that his mother was an alcoholic while she was pregnant with him, then he paid the price every day of his life for her habit and the choices she made. Miss Edwina didn't have a choice. She couldn't be a mother. But she made the best of it with her benevolence fund. Sadly, she was a beautiful flower, but she wilted the soonest. No one expected that. Of course, everyone expected Fritzy to wilt first, but he didn't. He had an inner strength not visible on his crooked surface that saw him through both difficult and adventurous times.

My mother, Susan Calloway, had healthy, happy children, but she wanted something more. While I don't approve of her lack of faithfulness to my father or to her friend, Joyce, I learned from Anna that it's not up to us to judge. People sometimes find themselves in circumstances that cause them to act in a way that none of us can understand. I don't believe my father ever knew of the betrayal. But, odd as it seems, I don't think it would have changed his relationship with my mother, or even with his friend Joe. My father was married to his career and blind to anything else at the time. It's hard to understand that sometimes a man and a woman decide to stay together in a marriage even when they no longer share anything in common but the same roof over their heads. Perhaps it is sometimes easier and more dignified to simply ignore or turn one's cheek to suspicions, or perhaps you're just too busy and turn your back to the obvious. Maybe you just grow to love that person you once loved as a mate in a different way, and you don't want to lose them as a roommate no matter what truth you may suspect.

I did some investigating to confirm that Andalucía (a.k.a. Andrea the elephant rider) did return to Athens. At first, sweet Miss Helen in Athens thought she could never fully recover from her broken heart. That broken heart also broke her spirit. She loved a man who didn't love her, and had a baby she didn't necessarily want. Luckily, another man loved her and her baby unconditionally along the way, but her guilt would not allow her to fully receive his love. However, Miss Helen eventually realized that there are many different kinds of love to be experienced in life, and that loving her daughter was more important than any love she felt in the past. Anna played a role in influencing that daughter to forgive and understand her mother. It was like Miss Helen's life came full circle when her daughter returned home; it would complete Miss Helen's reason for being.

Anna played another important role in helping save a young girl from the Ferris wheel accident. Her family would have been devastated if she died; she was their world. Looking back, if Anna hadn't been right there on that day to save her, more folks would be dead today, because that girl grew up to be a doctor, specializing in helping the poor and indigent. The Lord decided it wasn't that girl's time to go that day and she had a special role to play in the future, and he put Anna in her path to save her. She became a surgeon in spite of the fact that one of her arms was basically useless.

Old Mrs. Phillips and her son's first wife covered up lies to get what they wanted, but that made it possible to go on and do some good things, too. Three happy families exist today where there had been a family of unhappiness.

The woman, who goes by Mrs. Johnson now, got pregnant

and did "the right thing" in marrying a man she never loved and even had another baby with him. But then she found her true love and turned her back on her own flesh and blood only to turn around and adopt someone else's baby as her own. As it turns out, she did a better job of being a mother the second time around. Some would call her actions selfish, but those actions actually gave someone else a purpose in life. Mrs. Johnson's sister, the librarian Miss Smith, made a choice to play a part in raising her sister's boys. She never found a husband, so her choices for having kids of her own were improbable. Mrs. Johnson secretly helped her sister by sending money—the thing that many parents substitute when they find themselves incapable of expressing love. But incidentally, those Bishop boys turned out all right thanks, in great part, to Miss Smith. Maybe they made fun of Fritzy just to help them feel better about themselves. While she only got a chance now and then to be a mother to those boys, she is now a full-time grandmother and babysitter to the Bishop boys' own children. They are both happily married and lead seemingly normal lives. Perhaps growing up with an example of "what not to do" is part of what makes some marriages a success.

And the poor girl that lost her life on the highway coming to Marshalltown wasn't really the one that made the final choice about having or not having a baby. The girl was so young and couldn't think ahead thirty years to the time she would have cherished having grown children. None of us really can. And the girl's mother, who did what any good mother would do in accepting her daughter's mistakes, was just trying to help. The "fickle finger of fate," as Anna calls it, swooped down and caused that wreck, but it must have been God's plan for that baby to live. We can't know why he took the mother and daughter then and there, but we have to trust that it was part of a greater plan. Now they are at peace, buried in the Catholic cemetery thanks to the loving people of Marshalltown.

And Anna? She has healthy, smart, beautiful girls and some grandbabies now, too. To Fritzy, she was not only a surrogate mother, but also a best friend. She doesn't consider herself a saint for taking care of a severely handicapped child in a wheelchair for fourteen years; she says Fritzy was her muse. In the ancient world, a muse was a source of inspiration. Anna says he helped her see that her life has been as lucky as a four-leaf clover.

About the Authors

Catherine Team has enjoyed several careers, but none more than becoming an author. She owned an advertising agency for almost twenty years, spearheading the company through her artistic vision up until its sale. After that, she taught advertising and communications at the college level while pursuing the ongoing challenge of managing her father's real estate interests. "But *Anna* trumped everything else!" said Team. Commas and periods were applied with the help of her dear friend Beverly and the sum of the two worked to bring *Anna* to life.

Beverly Smirnis has enjoyed a long career as a publicist and journalist, mainly as a publisher of private specialty magazines. She has long aspired to apply her writing skills to something with a "longer shelf life" and thus was thrilled when her friend Catherine Team asked her to collaborate on *Anna from Atlanta*. "I laughed and cried in helping define Anna and the other characters in this book and the unique challenges they faced in their time period," Smirnis said.

Like *Anna from Atlanta*, the authors' own stories are about the will of strong women. The two authors from Fort Worth, Texas, met and became friends while working together on their children's high school senior prom. Both shared anxieties, but also dreams, about what was next in their lives as they faced becoming empty nesters. The economy had taken a turn for the worse, leaving both ladies anxious about how they would support their children in the college years, and yet the business slowdown left them with some time to work on "that book idea" they had discussed.

And so, in 2012, Team wrote a story based on her 90-year-old father's reflections of his youth. Though historical fiction, it is based on the real story of a severely handicapped boy whose life was enriched when "one of the first black women the town had ever seen" arrived through a remarkable stroke of fate to live with his family in rural Iowa. *Anna from Atlanta* came alive on those pages. Smirnis put her skills in editing and publishing to the task by tying *Anna* together into a manuscript and fine-tuning the story narrative.

In the process of writing the book and before it was published, both authors saw their children graduate college, both families saw children married, and both undertook new work projects. With the economy back in Texas and the "slower days" well past, *Anna* got shoved to the back burner many times. But Anna, as you will discover, is very strong-willed. Her story would be told!

In the end, Team and Smirnis realized that what they had created was not just a story about the main characters, but a story about women—women of different races, backgrounds, and ages, and the paths they choose and, oftentimes, the divine path that is chosen for them, though they may not realize that until later. The same has been true for the authors of *Anna from Atlanta*!

Acknowledgments

In Anna's own words, it was "the fickle finger of fate" that played a hand in bringing together all who were involved in the making of this special book.

Anna would call it a "sin of omission" not to thank Daniel Bechtel. It was his excellent storytelling— passed down straight from the real Anna he knew as a boy—that sparked his daughter Catherine Team's imagination and respect for African-American people. Mr. Bechtel was, in fact, one of those errant little boys that Anna made come over and read to Fritzy.

It's long been said, "We don't meet people by accident. They are meant to cross our path for a reason!" A high school prom committee meeting brought the authors of this book together. A trip to Acapulco brought together co-author Beverly Smirnis and her husband, Steve.

Growing up in Toronto with opportunities to appear as an "extra" in a number of movies gave Steve Smirnis expertise in continuity and timeline, providing him with a unique insight for interjecting ideas and checking historical accuracy of certain scenes in the book. He was a willing listener as his wife read aloud the manuscript to test his reactions to it and seek his input. Over the course of months turned to years, it was refined and reread numerous times.

At just the right time, a business networking event that Beverly and Steve Smirnis were attending led them to meet Bennett Litwin, an accomplished author and scriptwriter who would become an integral part of the advisory team to finally get *Anna* to print.

As with anything important, it took the will of one person to recognize a true story and add imagination to bring it to life, and another to help ignite the process and lead the assembly of all the talent needed to make sure that *Anna* achieves all that we hope it may. Once merged, the ideas became one.

The authors extend special thanks to Daniel Bechtel, Steve Smirnis, and Bennett Litwin for their integral roles in bringing *Anna* to life in these pages. The authors would also like to thank the people of Marshalltown, Iowa. It was, and still is, a special place that made this story possible.

Letters From Hope, the squel to *Anna From Atlanta*
Coming Fall 2017

I haven't told you a lot of the ends 'cause there's jes' too much more to tell. There's so much more to tell you how the war howled on, and how we got through it and did our best to cope with death ever'where. I knew the time was comin' for my Mama to leave this Earth but I had no idea so many others would soon follow, nor that my daughter Hope would be doing duties overseas. Through our letters back and forth, she kept me informed about the battlefield, and I reported news back on the home front. Nobody escaped the suffering of war. People's lives were like a deck of cards that God shuffled around; he took some and spared others. Some were sent home forever changed physically and mentally.

It was hard trustin' that God had a plan and was in control, but we jes' had to. And a' course you want to know about what he had in store for Fritzy. I'll just say his life was still too short, but he lived longer than most of us would have predicted and the war also played a part in how he would meet his maker, too. — Anna

LIKE *AnnaFromAtlantaBookMovie* on Facebook for announcements about the second book *Letters From Hope* coming soon, other news and updates, Anna's recipes and more.

CPSIA information can be obtained
at www.ICGtesting.com
Printed in the USA
LVHW041447161218
600666LV00018B/568/P